AS SICK AS OUR SECRETS

An Allison Parker Mystery

To Bonnie
— enjoy —
Adair Sanders

Adair Sanders

ISBN: 1500683639
ISBN 13: 9781500683634
Library of Congress Control Number: 2014913738
CreateSpace Independent Publishing Platform
North Charleston, South Carolina

CHAPTER ONE

The four year old's legs pummeled the soft ground of the apple orchard as she fled in terror, desperate for a place to hide. The afternoon sun beat harshly on her body, fueled by adrenaline, birthed from painful memory of previous beatings. She had asked the man if she could pet his dog. Wasn't that what she was supposed to do?

As she burst through the fraying screen door of her Gran's kitchen, her nostrils filling with the sting of starch wafting from beneath a hot iron, and overlaid with the sweet aroma of sugar, cinnamon and cooking apples, the girl spied her would be savior. "Help me, Ella! Help me!" she cried, tears beginning to roll down her plump, dirty cheeks.

1

Ella, her Gran's maid, set aside the steaming iron. "Baby girl, what you cryin' 'bout? Why you needin' ta hide?" Ignoring the questions, the frightened child cast her eyes frantically around the small, hot kitchen, past the mounds of unironed sheets, beyond the apple shavings on the kitchen table, searching for a place, any place, that would shield her from her tormentor.

Before the little girl could answer, or hide, an explosion of sound shook the room. A man, red faced, fists clenched, and exuding anger so black it could be seen, thundered at the terrified child "If I have to pay for rabies shots I'm going to beat your ass!" The little girl cowered on the floor, arms circled for protection over her head, as the man took an enraged step and raised his hand to strike down and hard at the child. "Stop, Mr. Matthew! Stop!" cried Ella, stepping between the two. "Get outta' my way, Nigger!" screamed the man, shoving the maid harshly against the sink. "This is none of your concern". But the maid's plea had been sufficient, her crumpled body willingly accepting the rage intended for the child. Staring at his victims, the man shook his head, turned and left the house, leaving behind the sound of soft weeping.

Jesus, God. Allison sighed, *Where the Hell did that come from?* She hadn't thought of that day in her

Gran's kitchen in years. *Can't worry about it now, either. No need to resurrect shit that can't be changed.* Dispelling the unwanted thoughts with a shake of her head, Johnson & Merritt's only female partner focused her attention on the pile of legal files currently camouflaging the top of her desk. Petite, slight of build, with covergirl good looks, Allison's physical traits had initially lulled the mostly male legal community in Ft. Charles into misjudging the young lawyer as a lightweight. Within a few years though, a string of courtroom successes had carried Allison's reputation outside Ft. Charles' small legal community, and as a result Allison's book of clients had quickly rivaled those of several of the male partners in her firm. Begrudgingly, Ben Johnson, Johnson & Merritt's founding partner, had offered Allison an ownership share in the all male firm. Allison Parker had come a long way from the terrified child hiding in her grandmother's kitchen so many years ago.

Opening the manila file marked "McNair Investigative Report" Allison smiled as she perused the documents marked "Confidential". When Sherry McNair had approached Allison about taking her case, Allison had politely informed Sherry that she only represented employers and offered to recommend a couple of local plaintiff's lawyers for Sherry to contact.

"No, Ms. Parker" Sherry had replied. "I know your reputation. If anyone has a chance of winning, it's you."

Thinking that allowing Sherry to vent her emotions would be the quickest way to bring the meeting to a conclusion, Allison had replied "Why do you say that, Sherry?". Fifteen minutes later, any thoughts Allison had of sending Sherry's case to another lawyer had vanished. If the firm's intake committee gave its approval, Allison had informed the anxious woman, Sherry McNair's sexual harassment case would be Allison's first plaintiff's case.

Allison had carefully crafted the memo recommending the McNair case to the intake committee. Johnson & Merritt was primarily a business defense firm. Allison could only remember one other plaintiff's case the firm had accepted in the past five or six years, and that had been a case for an existing and well paying business client. Taking the McNair case would cost the firm money unless Allison won at trial or obtained a good settlement for her client. But Allison had been persuasive, and approval to take the case had been given. Three months ago Allison had filed a complaint against Miller Industries and its president Steve Miller. This afternoon most of the documents occupying the top of Allison's desk related to that case.

"Hey, Allison. Got a minute?"

Concentration broken, Allison smiled as her favorite partner settled his lanky frame comfortably into the one chair not covered with books, files, and other as yet unidentified important stuff. David Jackson was always Allison's first choice when two lawyers were needed on a case. Easy to work with, not hampered by the typical trial lawyer ego, and one of the brightest minds in the firm - certainly an anomaly in a profession known for backstabbing, a behavior common to most of the other partners in Johnson & Merritt. What you saw with David Jackson was what you got. Allison thought that transparency was probably one of the major reasons David had such a natural rapport with juries, a fact Allison had used over the years to the advantage of her corporate clients.

"I spent some time last night looking over the statement Sherry McNair gave to the EEOC." David laughed. "This is the first time I've seen anyone claim to be sexually harassed because the boss was screwing someone else." The EEOC, or Equal Employment Opportunity Commission, was the Federal agency where all sexual harassment claims had to be lodged before a case could be filed in court. Allison's first step after being retained by Sherry McNair had been to obtain the McNair investigative file from the Commission.

"It's more complex than that" Allison retorted. "Sherry says the woman who slept with the boss was given the biggest raise in the office, even though she had only been with the company for two years. The woman got the best assignments, got to work with the most senior people, even though her tenure and experience didn't support those sort of assignments. It's sort of like reverse sexual harassment. Sherry was penalized by not being the boss' squeeze. And it doesn't matter that the boss never asked." Allison leaned across her desk, handing David a slim volume. "Look at this treatise. There's not much caselaw on claims like this, but there is some, and it's been recognized by the courts as actionable". Allison paused. "Best of all, because the issue has never been litigated in our jurisdiction, we'd be presenting - and winning - a case of first impression."

"Damn it, Allison. Winning this case is a long shot and you know it." David barked. "You've made your reputation as the best gun an employer can hire. Why risk torpedoing your reputation by taking a plaintiff's case like McNair? Really, I don't know why the committee agreed to let you take this case."

"What difference does it make why I took the case?" Allison was irritated. "It's my ass on the line if the firm loses money on it, not yours. And besides, do you really think I'd take a case like this if I didn't think I could win it?" Pushing her chair back from her desk, Allison crossed her legs. "Are you going to work this case with me or not, David?"

"Of course I am, Allison" snorted David, glancing over his shoulder as he left Allison's office. "But before we get to trial maybe you'll be honest with me and yourself about why you've taken this case. It might make a difference in the outcome".

Listening to David's retreating footsteps, soft shushes on the firm's lush carpeting, Allison considered David's words. Why was she taking this case? Was she trying to prove a point? If so, to whom? She had graduated near the top of her law school class. Law Review and Moot Court adorned her resume. She had made partner in one the best firms in the state the first time she was eligible, and next year would chair the Women in the Profession Committee of the Alabama Bar Association. Her client satisfaction rating was the highest in the firm based on surveys Johnson & Merritt commissioned every few years. No, Allison thought, she hadn't taken the McNair case to prove her skills to the state's legal community.

Allison gazed out her office window, slowing her breathing, letting her mind run unconstrained, her thinking and her sight unfocused and loose. Although Allison had first encountered the mental discipline as a relaxation technique, she had quickly discovered that it also allowed solutions to rise to the surface of her mind when she seemed unable otherwise to solve a problem, or, as now, to reach a truth she had hidden in her subconscious. As Allison's awareness of her surroundings faded, another memory arose…

The smoky scent of cigars and loud male voices rose from the den below, disrupting the solitude of Allison's bedroom.

"That's quite a collection you've got there" commented one of the men. "Don't believe I've ever seen anything quite like it".

Allison sighed. She knew what had gained the men's attention. The Wall. Rice's wall. A ten by twenty foot expanse of sheetrock plastered with every newspaper article or award Rice had ever received. And there were plenty. Which award would her father talk about first this time?

"Here's the News Press article when Rice was named All State." bragged Matthew Parker pointing to a large framed article. "His coaches expect him to be named All American this year. Not many high school quarterbacks pass for 1000 yards in a season."

"Impressive" agreed one of the men. "We're always interested in athletes who can put up those kind of numbers".

"Rice is exceptional, gentlemen. He's the complete package. Football and baseball. Three year letterman in both sports." Matthew Parker enthused. "The college that signs my son will be signing a star."

"That's why we're looking at Rice, Mr. Parker" offered another voice. "We know he's a superb athlete. Our only concern is his height. 5'10" is a bit small for a SEC quarterback. Even if we don't make an offer, and at this point I'm not saying we won't, Rice will have plenty of opportunity at smaller colleges."

"Height's not an issue" retorted Matthew Parker dismissively. "Don't make it one. We aren't interested in small colleges. Rice is SEC material. Period."

"*Any other aspiring stars in the family, Mr. Parker?*" *inquired another voice Allison thought was tinged with a trace of sarcasm.*

"*Nah. Just Rice*".

A tear slipped down Allison's cheek as the memory faded. The dynamic in her family of origin had never changed. Top grades, class honors and awards, professional achievement. Nothing had mattered to Matthew Parker. Surely she had not taken the McNair case to try, yet again, to garner recognition and approval from her father? What was it she had seen on a Facebook post? Something about doing the same thing over and over again and expecting a different result?

Did it really matter why she had taken the McNair case? Allison asked herself as she packed her briefcase and headed out the door. No, it didn't. Winning the case for her client was all that mattered now.

CHAPTER TWO

"Jim" Allison called, broadcasting her voice over the roar of her hairdryer. "Don't forget I've got that hearing in Franklin at 3:00 this afternoon. You'll have to be home by 5:00 so Sharon can leave".

"I know" replied her husband, walking into the room. "And I haven't forgotten Charlotte's practice at 6:00, either" he added, giving Allison a quick kiss on her cheek. "It's on my calendar at the office. All I have today are a few arraignments. I'll be home well before time for Sharon to head out."

Being married to a judge certainly had its benefits, Allison reflected, not the least of which was that Jim could decide when his work day would end, even if he were presiding over a trial. Allison had met her

husband during her third year in law school. As a local sitting judge, Jim Kaufman had been asked to give
a lecture on courtroom procedure to the law school's
trial practice class Allison was taking. No one was
more surprised than Allison to receive a call from Jim
the next week, asking her if she would be interested
in meeting him for coffee one day. A fifteen year age
difference hadn't mattered a bit, and they were married a week after Allison graduated from law school.
Now, just like so many of their friends, Allison and Jim
juggled parenting two small children while engaged in
busy, full-time careers.

"Thank goodness one of us has some semblance of
control over our schedules" laughed Allison slipping
on her favorite power pumps.

"You must be worried about your hearing today"
observed Jim. "You're wearing your Louboutins".

Allison smiled. Her black Louboutin pumps had
been her reward for winning the Johnson Management
case last year. The plaintiff, a regional human re-
sources director who had been terminated for sexually harassing African American female employees,
had sued Allison's client alleging pretext, claiming he
had been fired as punishment for questioning some of
the company's safety regulations. A lot of money had
been on the line if Allison's client had lost the case,
and the facts hadn't been the best with which to work.
But, bringing in defense verdicts in difficult cases was

what had made Allison's reputation. Allison wore her Louboutins when she needed visual armor, and today was going to be one of those days.

"What's the hearing about"' inquired Jim reaching past Allison to retrieve his half empty coffee cup from the bathroom counter. "It's in the McNair case, right?"

"That's your third cup of coffee this morning." Allison lectured, taking the cup out of Jim's hand and pouring its contents down the sink. "You know the doctor told you to cut back on caffeine after you got that stent" Allison reminded her husband, referring to the unexpected results of a heart catheterization Jim had undergone a few months earlier. Adding a subdued clip to her french-twisted hair, Allison returned to the topic. "Yes, it's the McNair case. I've filed a Motion to Compel. The defense has refused to provide some of the documents we asked for in discovery."

"On what grounds?" asked Jim, his judge hat now firmly in place. "Has that case turned nasty already?"

"Already?" Allison snorted. "This case got nasty the minute I filed the complaint against Miller Industries and Steve Miller. Those guys think they are above the law. It's been one roadblock after another".

Picking up her suit jacket from the bed, Allison gave her husband a knowing look. "I can't wait to kick their arrogant little asses".

Entering Judge Lee's courtroom, Allison was once again reminded of the sound of nothing. No talk. No whispering. Not even the sounds of breathing. How could one room be filled with people sometimes, she thought, and still be so empty? Maybe it was the fright factor of the room itself - enormous paintings of previous and now mostly deceased Federal judges hanging down both sides of the richly paneled room, casting their judgmental demeanor on all who entered, while thick red carpet blanketed the floor. Today the quiet was amplified by the lack of inhabitants. While trials often morphed into a sort of spectator sport, the days when only the lawyers made appearances, commonly referred to in lawyer lingo as 'motion days' where counsel argued mostly dry and boring issues, never attracted the Perry Mason wannabe crowd. Courtroom groupies wanted excitement. Verbal fireworks. Smoking guns. All that ludicrous BS found on every lawyer show on television. In reality, Allison knew many cases were ultimately won at trial due to successful legal arguments on motion days such as this one.

Her black Louboutins made soft squeaky sounds as she walked through the short swinging gate that separated the spectator section of the courtroom from the lawyers, the judge, and when appropriate, the jury.

"*Crap!*" Allison thought. "*Why didn't those shoes squeak like that at home this morning?*" Pushing the thought of annoying shoe sounds to the back of her brain, Allison adjusted her suit jacket. Squeaky shoes were the least of her problems today. Nope, her primary problem was sitting five feet away at the defense table. Jack Striker. Arrogant, good looking, and brimming with self confidence to the point of narcissism, Jack Striker had been Allison's rival for high end corporate clients for the past ten plus years. Steve Miller, CEO of Miller Industries, seated in the chair next to Striker, acknowledged Allison with a nod.

Odd, thought Allison. Having a client actually attend motion day was quite unusual. *What's Steve Miller doing here?*

"When did you start slumming, Allison?" smirked Jack turning his chair in Allison's direction.

Take a deep breath, Allison counseled herself. *Ignore him.*

"You know as well as I do that your client is a lying piece..... pun intended." Jack smiled salaciously. "I intend to kick Ms. McNair back into the same gutter she crawled out of."

Turning towards the defense table, Allison detected the slightest smirk resting on Steve Miller's face.

"Jack, Jack" purred Allison. "I didn't know you had such strong feelings for Ms. McNair. Sure you don't want to change sides?"

"Really, Allison" replied Jack. "If defense work is boring you, I can think of better ways for you to recharge your batteries than taking a loser case like this one."

Allison laughed, humorless eyes telegraphing her true feelings. "The day Jack Striker cares about my well being is the day I expect Hell to freeze over".

A loud knock resounded in the courtroom announcing Judge Lee's imminent appearance.

Leaning towards Jack, Allison whispered with a smile. "And you're the only lying piece I know".

By the time she got back to the office it was well after 6:00 p.m., and the firm was deserted. Riding the elevator to her office, Allison replayed the afternoon's courtroom drama and wondered what she was missing about the day's events. As the so-called moving party, court procedure dictated that Allison would make her argument to Judge Lee first, then Jack Striker would argue why Allison's motion should be denied. Many times and particularly for discovery motions like the one Allison had filed, Judge Lee would stretch the rules a bit to allow each side to give a further brief argument, and then render his decision from the bench instead of issuing a written opinion at a later date.

Almost none of that had transpired today. Instead, as soon as Allison had concluded her initial argument, Jack Striker had risen from counsel table and advised Judge Lee that his client had decided not to contest the motion. Allison had been stunned, and Judge Lee royally pissed.

"And why are you just now deciding this, Mr. Striker?" Judge Lee had inquired angrily. "Do you enjoy wasting the Court's time?"

Striker had claimed a miscommunication with his client, replying that Mr. Miller had withdrawn his objection to producing the requested documents after hearing Allison's argument. Allison hadn't believed any of it, and although Judge Lee had accepted Striker's explanation, she didn't think Judge Lee had believed him either.

Why would Striker do that? Allison wondered. *Why antagonize Judge Lee over a document request?* Whatever she thought about Jack Striker's character, Allison admired his legal abilities. Striker was a very smart attorney, and one of the best defense lawyers in the region. He was not her biggest competition by accident. There has to be an ulterior motive, a reason that his client would fight so hard not to turn over the documents she had requested through discovery, and then after hearing her argument, instruct Striker to "confess" the motion. Not for a single minute did she buy the miscommunication excuse. Men like Steve Miller didn't build successful businesses without paying attention to details.

Reaching into her briefcase, Allison retrieved her Iphone, hitting an auto dial for David Jackson's home number.

"David, it's Allison. Got a minute?" Allison inquired, barely giving David time to utter a quick hello.

"Yeh, what's up? How'd the hearing go?" David inquired.

"That's why I'm calling. It was weird - Striker confessed the motion. Why in Hell would he do that?" Allison asked in a puzzled tone. "I thought Judge Lee was going to read him the riot act. Striker didn't even make an attempt at an argument - blamed it on a client misunderstanding."

"Ha! Nothing like blaming the client" David laughed. "Wonder how Striker's going to explain the billing charge for his court appearance."

"That's just it, David. Steve Miller was right there. I think he and Striker had this planned." Allison replied. "Why risk alienating Judge Lee over a routine document request? It doesn't make sense. I've got to be missing something."

"Maybe we're looking at this the wrong way" offered David. "Maybe risking Judge Lee's ire by confessing that motion was worth more than we know. Maybe this isn't about the document request at all."

"Maybe..." Allison acknowledged. "But I can't see Jack knowingly committing a fraud upon the court, which is exactly what this would be if he were in cahoots with his client."

"So, if Jack was as surprised as you and Judge Lee were, what does that prove?" David asked. "And in the overall scheme of things, what difference does it make? You got the documents you wanted."

"I don't like it" Allison fumed. "Miller took a risk opposing my discovery motion. Judge Lee could have easily found him in contempt of court, and I wouldn't have been surprised if Jack Striker had fired Miller as his client before they left the courtroom."

"So Jack Striker has a client who is a, either totally stupid or b, smart enough to be two steps ahead of him." David offered. "I repeat: in the overall scheme of things, what difference does it make?"

"I swear, David" Allison retorted "sometimes I wonder how you got through law school. If Miller's actions were deliberate, the only thing that makes sense to me is that Miller wanted to buy himself time for reasons he couldn't share with his lawyer."

"The desire to be a whipping boy for a smart-ass female lawyer is what got me through law school" David laughed recognizing the sort of commentary that accompanied Allison's thought process when in full investigative mode. "Why would Miller need to buy time in a sexual harassment case? That just doesn't make any sense."

"Agreed. And sorry for the crappy comment" Allison tossed in an apology. "Maybe time to conceal some sort of evidence or information that will make our case and lose his." Allison's voice became serious. "I don't know what's going on with Steve Miller, but I sure as Hell am going to find out."

Severing the connection and gathering some files to take home, Allison contemplated an initial game plan as she drove from her office. First, she'd talk to her client again. As Executive Assistant to the company's CEO, maybe Sherry McNair had inadvertently seen or heard something she shouldn't have and hadn't realized its importance. Next, Allison would do a more thorough investigation of Steve Miller. So far she had focused her attention on Miller Industries. Maybe she should focus on its CEO instead. Miller Industries was a privately owned corporation, and Steve Miller its largest shareholder. Allison had heard rumors that the company was getting ready to go public. While an adverse decision in a sexual harassment suit would cause some bad press, it would only be temporary, and it certainly would not affect the price of a stock offering. Steve Miller wasn't worried about a sexual harassment suit. It had to be something else.

Twenty minutes later, her car's headlights illuminated the white, lowcountry cottage Allison shared with her family. Following the winding driveway past a large pond, Allison reflected on how fortunate she was to have found this place of refuge. Only fifteen miles from downtown Fort Charles - close enough for a decent commute, but far enough into the country to create an emotional haven from the often overwhelming pressures of an active trial practice. Built originally in the late 1800's, numerous additions had enlarged the once small stone cottage into a comfortable and rambling house. Although far larger than a cottage, the home had managed to maintain its cottage roots, beckoning all who saw it to rest on one of the rocking chairs lining the front porch.

Allison and Jim had worked hard to maintain the home's initial integrity, balancing the need for a modern update with a desire to keep as much of the original house and its several additions as possible. The ten acres that Jim and Allison had purchased surrounding the cottage's original two had prompted them to name their home "The Farm" although the only farming that occurred there was when Jim mowed the property on his tractor. No matter how stressed from trial or dealing with a cantankerous client, coming home to The Farm always energized Allison.

"Hey, guys." Allison called to her family as she entered the back door. "Did anyone save me some supper?" She was glad to be home.

CHAPTER THREE

1977

Helene glanced furtively through the bedroom window. *Hurry,* she admonished herself silently. *This may be your only chance.* With a focus born of desperation, Helene hurriedly threw clothes - her own and those of her two children - into the large suitcase she had pulled from the attic. Matthew almost never left her alone in the house. Helene suspected Matthew had given their housekeeper Alice instructions to report Helene's comings and goings to him on a daily basis. But today, Alice had gone home sick. There was no time for Helene to plan, only time to act. She didn't know where they would go. The destination wasn't important. Getting far away from Matthew was all that mattered. How could she have been so blind all those years ago? She had thought his money would buy her happiness. All it had bought was her imprisonment.

Depositing the suitcase by the front door, Helene turned towards her children's bedrooms. Four year old Rice, Matthew's spitting image, was sprawled on the bedroom floor, busily building a Lincoln Log house. "Rice, honey, let's go. Mama's got a surprise for you and Allison."

"Don't wanna" Rice whined in reply, ignoring Helene.

"Come on, Rice." Helene forced a smile. "We're going for ice cream.

"No." Rice screamed, throwing one of the toy logs at his mother. "Go away."

Just leave him. The thought rose unbidden in her mind. *He's the one Matthew wants. He won't follow you just for the baby.* Torn by indecision, Helene crossed the hallway to Allison's room. Undisturbed by her brother's outburst, two year old Allison slept peacefully in her crib. Thankful that her daughter was still asleep, Helene gently lifted her from the crib and turned to leave the room.

"What the fuck do you think you are doing, Helene?" demanded Matthew Parker, blocking the doorway. "We've been over this before. You're not leaving and neither are my children."

Clutching Allison tightly to her chest, Helene began to weep. "Matthew, please let me go. I'll leave

Rice with you. Just let me take Allison. We'll disappear. You don't have to give us money or anything."

"Put the baby back in her crib, Helene" Matthew ordered moving menacingly. "Now."

Helene's hesitation was costly. Snatching Allison from her mother's arms, Matthew tossed the now screaming child into her crib, then slammed his fist into Helene's face.

Standing over his wife's crumpled body, Matthew growled "Helene, if you ever try this again, you'll find yourself in the sanitarium. For life. You know I can make that happen. And you'll never see your children again. Ever."

Soft footsteps entered Helene's consciousness.

"Why is mommy on the floor?" a plaintive voice asked.

"Your mother hurt herself doing something bad." As if from a distance, Helene heard her husband's voice as her mind lost its grip on consciousness. "She won't do it again."

CHAPTER FOUR

Present Day

"Your father called." Allison's secretary Donna Pevey reported as Allison returned from lunch. "Can't be good news". Allison sighed. "No telling what his agenda is this time".

"He said it's urgent - wanted me to track you down instead of leaving a message." Donna handed Allison a slip of paper. "This is the number he left for you to call."

It's always something, Allison thought, settling into her orthopedically sculpted desk chair. Like all of the partner offices at Johnson & Merritt, Allison's private office enjoyed an expansive view of the city. Some of the offices, like her partner David Jackson's, faced the river, while others, like Allison's, beheld a view of distant low mountains. Associates - baby lawyers who had not yet "made" partner - were relegated to interior offices, along with paralegals and other support staff. Only secretaries, placed strategically near their assigned partner's office, had a glimpse of the outside world during the work day.

Being hired by Johnson & Merritt, one of the most prestigious law firms in the state, had been a feather in Allison's cap. Between her second and third years of law school Allison had spent six weeks as a summer clerk for the firm. When the offer of an associate position had come her way in her last year of law school, Allison had eagerly accepted. It wasn't until she overheard a conversation her first year in the firm that Allison began to wonder if she had been hired because of her relationship with the man who had became her husband rather than on her own merit. Determined that no one ever think that to be the case, Allison had devoted herself to becoming one of the best employment litigators in the city. Twelve years later that was exactly who she had become.

What do you want this time, old man? More bragging about Rice's latest get rich scheme? Irritation clawed at Allison as she dialed the unknown number.

"Matthew Parker." Allison was surprised to hear her father's voice answer.

"Daddy. Where are you?"

"Dr. James' office. You remember him." her father replied.

Allison certainly did remember Dr. William James. The doctor who had turned a blind eye to the bruises, contusions and broken bones as he treated Helene Parker over the years. The doctor who, just incidentally, had been on the board of her father's bank for thirty years.

Her father continued. "Bill wants to talk to you."

"Good afternoon, Allison". Dr. James' calm voice brushed Allison's ear. "I'm glad we could catch you before Matthew left my office."

What in the world is going on? Allison didn't think she was going to like where this conversation was headed.

"I know you haven't been home since your mother died" Allison noted the disapproval in Dr. James' voice, "so you haven't seen your dad in a couple of years."

And you know why, don't you, you self-righteous prick, Allison wished she dared retort.

Dr. James continued, "Your dad has not been feeling well for the past couple of months. He came in last week for an appointment and we ran some tests." He hesitated. "It's bad news. Stage 4 liver cancer."

What goes around comes around Allison thought but did not say. "Define Stage 4 in layman's terms, doc." She asked. "How long does he have?"

"It's hard to say definitively, Allison, but given his labs, overall declining health and progression of the disease to his lungs, I would be surprised if Matthew has more than a few months."

"And you are calling me, why?" Allison struggled to keep her tone civil.

"With Helene gone, Matthew has no one to care for him...." Dr. James hesitated.

Civility fled before Allison's reply. "Well, he should have thought about that before he killed my mother."

Allison was the one who had found Helene Parker's body. An odd tone in her mother's voice during their last conversation, something Allison couldn't quite put her finger on, had prompted the trip. She had gone alone. Charlotte had a gymnastics meet, so Jim had assumed home duty, encouraging Allison to make the five hour trip to set her mind at ease.

"I'm sure your mother's fine." Jim had assured Allison. "You know she gets in these slumps every so often, but before you know it, she's back to the old Helene."

"Something's different this time." Allison fretted. "I could hear it in her voice. I'm worried."

"Then drive up there Saturday morning, Allison. I know Helene would like to spend some private time with you. A surprise visit will do you both some good."

So she had gone.

The drive had been interminable. Allison had called her mother multiple times during the long trip, hearing only a soft "This is Helene. I'll call you back soon. Leave a message."

The coroner's report listed the cause of death as suicide. An empty bottle of Valium lay on the bed next to Helene Parker's body. Some sort of liquid, wine according to the later autopsy report, had filled the nearby glass, the moisture from its contents already marking the bedside table with whitish rings by the time Allison had arrived. A crumpled piece of stationery, the initials "H C P" etched at the top of the page, was found in Helene's delicate fist. The vision of two words, starkly black on the cream page, would remain with Allison forever. Her mother's legacy: "no more".

"Allison Cecile Parker". Dr. James thundered. "How dare you say such a vile thing. What is wrong with you?"

"What is wrong with you, Dr. James, that you would think for even a minute that I give a shit what happens to my father. Let him call Rice. Rice can take care of him. I'm not interested." Allison disconnected the call.

＝◦＝ ＝◦＝

By 4:00 Allison had refocused her attention on the five inch stack of computer generated printouts containing transcripts of Steve Miller's texts and emails from the past year. Reviewing pages and pages of mostly mindless and irrelevant chatter was usually relegated to one of the firm's paralegals. Having a one hundred and twenty-five dollar an hour litigation paralegal summarize documents rather than wasting three hundred fifty an hour for a partner to do such trivial work was a generally accepted practice in the legal community, and one that Allison utilized regularly. However, unlike many lawyers, Allison did not fully rely on the paralegal's work product. Instead, she used the summary as a sort of legal Cliff Notes, examining the original text when something of interest in the summary piqued her interest or raised her litigator's antenna.

People are so stupid Allison reflected. Nothing was secret anymore, certainly not an electronic communication like a text or email. Anyone who watched NCIS or CSI ought to know that little tidbit. But no. People continued to leave electronic fingerprints left and right, dropping clues like Hansel and Gretel dropped bread crumbs. *Maybe stupid was too harsh.* Allison reflected skimming over a text entry from March of the previous year. *More of the "it won't happen to me" mind set.* If she were lucky, Steve Miller would have been lulled into complacency, perhaps leaving a crumb for her to find.

A sharp buzz from her office phone diverted Allison's attention. Recognizing the familiar number on the phone's display pad, Allison depressed the speaker icon. "Hey, honey. Have you adjourned for the day?"

"The parties settled the case right after lunch." Her husband's deep voice filled the air, referring to a civil case that had been tried in his courtroom for most of the week. "I had intended to spend the rest of the day reviewing several pending motions, until I got a call from your brother." Clearing his throat, Jim continued. "And after listening to Rice, I spoke with your dad's doctor for almost an hour, and then finally with your dad." He paused. "Allison, you can't ignore the situation with Matthew."

"I am not having this discussion, Jim." Allison retorted, anger quickly elevating her voice. "I told Dr. James to let Rice deal with Daddy, and I meant it. It's time Rice did something other than take Daddy's money."

"It's not that simple, baby." Allison heard the lecturing tone in Jim's reply. "Rice isn't equipped emotionally to help Matthew, and you and I both know he can't be trusted to handle Matthew's finances." The soft hum of the cellular connection filled the silence before Jim added the words Allison had heard earlier in the day. "Matthew doesn't have anyone else."

"What are you suggesting, Jim?" Allison warily replied. "Surely not that Daddy live with us?"

"I think that's the only realistic option." Jim's tone prefaced a prepared argument. "I don't like your father any more than you do, Allison. The man's a real piece of work. I hate how he's treated you, I hate how he treated Helene - God knows Matthew Parker doesn't deserve a single kindness." Jim hesitated. "I'm not asking you to do this for Matthew's sake. I'm asking you to do this for your sake, because you are a good person, a better person than your father, and because this is the right thing to do."

"I just don't know if I can." Allison replied, a catch in her throat as she contemplated the burden Jim was asking her to assume.

"You can do anything you put your mind to, baby." Jim's soft encouragement flowed over the open line. "And you won't be doing this alone. We'll do it together."

"Did Dr. James suggest this?" Allison asked unconvinced. "Was this his idea, or Daddy's?"

"Actually, it was Matthew who suggested the move." Jim continued. "And I think that speaks volumes. Matthew doesn't have much time, and he knows it."

"What did Rice say?" Allison was sure the answer would be no surprise.

"You know Rice." Resignation tinged Jim's response. "All he wanted to know was what was in this for him, although I'm sure that's not how he sees it."

"He actually used those words?" Allison inquired.

"Not the actual words, no, but that's what he meant. He wanted to know when we were closing up Matthew's house and what we were doing with its contents."

"Let me guess." Contempt coated Allison's words. "Rice has offered to help move Daddy. Better get out your snow boots, because some place really hot is about to freeze over."

"No need to worry about strange weather, Allison. All Rice wants is some of the furniture." Jim explained. "He said he had been promised several antiques. Guess he wants to make sure they don't end up in our house."

"Well, having one's priorities in place was never Rice's strong suit." Allison opined. "Let him have whatever he wants. Next time he's out of work they'll end up in the pawn shop. I don't have the energy to deal with his entitlement issues."

"So, are we agreed on Matthew?" Jim waited for Allison's decision.

"I'll think about it" Allison sighed.

CHAPTER FIVE

That fucking bitch, Steve Miller cursed under his breath. *That cunt.* Slamming his fist on his antique mahogany desk, Steve Miller tried to calm himself. *No matter....no matter. It's just a hiccup, a glitch. Get a grip.*

Everything was going according to plan. The IPO launching Miller Industries was set for five months out. He'd be a rich man by the end of the year. What was he thinking? He was already rich. By the end of the year he'd be more than rich. He'd be untouchable - so much money he could do whatever he wanted for the rest of his life. And then Sherry McNair had decided to get pissy. If she had just hired one of those hacks that usually bottom fed off plaintiff's cases.....Instead, she got that bitch from Johnson & Merritt.

Steve Miller knew all about Allison Parker. Tenacious, focused, driven. He'd actually heard her work ethic likened to a dog worrying a bone. Once she got her teeth in a case, there was no stopping her. Aggressive, smart and willing to push the envelope, Allison Parker was a litigant's worst nightmare - unless of course she was representing you. She'd even been recommended to him a few years ago when Miller Industries had a Family Medical Leave claim filed against them. *Shit, I should've hired her for that one* Miller lamented. *Then she'd have had a conflict and wouldn't have been able to take Sherry's case.*

Of course, it wasn't the sexual harassment claim that was worrying Steve Miller. Like many men who had made it to the top of the corporate mountain, Miller considered employment claims to be nothing more than legalized extortion by disgruntled employ-ees. Miller Industries never settled an employment case. To do otherwise, Miller thought, simply encour-aged more of the same. Steve Miller had no doubt Jack Striker would handily dispose of Sherry McNair's claims if the case proceeded to trial. Unfortunately, Miller thought, other circumstances - much more important circumstances - might force Miller Industries to settle the McNair case before a jury heard the first witness.

Miller stared at the bottle of Bushmills he had pulled from his desk drawer. Pouring a healthy three fingers into the Waterford tumbler on his desk, Miller watched the golden whiskey sparkle against the faceted crystal. *Might as well get this over with.* Appreciating the rich burn as the liquid caressed his throat, Miller dialed a private number.

"Speak" a quiet voice commanded.

"Jesus, Jeff." Steve exclaimed. "What's with this "speak" shit? Do I need to bow, too?"

"Well, well, well - if it isn't Mr. Rich." humor edged Jeff Bishop's reply. "Are you slumming now, Stevie boy?"

"Very funny, ass hole" Steve retorted. "I read the papers. You're doing just fine. How many auto repair shops do you have now in Alabama?"

"Never enough, Stevie, never enough." Jeff laughed. "And I read the paper, too. Looks like you're doing just fine as well. Not bad for two guys who should have ended up in Huntsville." Jeff added, referring to the location of one of the state's maximum security prisons.

"Yeh, I know. It's a damn miracle." Steve replied. "Most of the guys from the old neighborhood have seen the inside of that place at least once."

"Well, Stevie boy, they didn't have your balls or my brains" Jeff chuckled. "But I'm sure you didn't call to compare bank accounts or to reminisce. And, since you're calling instead of emailing, I assume this is an off the books discussion?"

"It is, indeed." Steve soberly replied. "You still in the business of granting favors?"

"Depends on what it is and who is asking."

"You know I'm getting ready to take my company public?" Steve continued. "A small glitch has appeared. It's like this…..".

"Not a problem" Jeff declared after listening to Steve's request. "In fact, I know just the person to handle this."

※ ※

Through perseverance and intense determination, Ben Johnson had built the perfect life. Although born to ignorant and uneducated tenant farmers in rural Arkansas, by the time he was ten years old, every teacher at Greenwood Elementary knew that Ben Johnson had won the intelligence lottery. Some of the teaching staff joked among themselves that aliens must have inseminated Ben's mother. How else could such a preternaturally bright child come from the likes of Thelma and Bull Johnson? Ben's fifth grade teacher, Betty Parrish, had been Ben's ticket out of Greenwood. Childless and widowed, Betty had persuaded Ben's parents to allow him to live with her during the school year. By the time Ben graduated Valedictorian from Greenwood High School he had not seen his parents in three years.

Ben had attended the University of Arkansas on an academic scholarship, graduating Phi Beta Kappa. Betty Parrish had urged Ben to pursue a career in law, and obedient to the woman who Ben now considered his true mother, Ben had applied to, and been accepted by, Cumberland School of Law in Birmingham, Alabama. When graduation day arrived three years later, Ben's resume had added Editor of the Law Review, membership in Order of the Coif, and a Federal clerkship to his many honors.

Two months after Ben started his clerkship with Judge Bartlette, Betty Parrish died. At Betty's funeral Ben had been approached by Macon Hubbard, Greenwood's sole lawyer.

"Ben, so sorry for your loss" Macon had intoned. "Betty loved you like a son, you know."

"Thank you Mr. Hubbard" Ben had replied. "I am surely going to miss her."

"She was so proud of you" Macon had continued. "You need to come by the office before you leave tomorrow. There are some matters that I need to discuss with you."

Ben had done just that, and had been shocked to discover not only had Betty Parrish left her entire worldly belongings to him, Betty Parrish had been rich. Really rich. All those years of living with her, watching Betty clip coupons, buy her clothes at Walmart and second hand stores, living in a modest house in a low income neighborhood - and Ben never had a clue. Betty Parrish died with seven hundred fifty thousand dollars in the bank, four million dollars in blue chip stocks, and ownership of several prime pieces of commercial property in Atlanta and Birmingham.

"How did she have all of this?" Ben had asked Macon Hubbard.

"Inherited every bit of it" had been the lawyer's reply. "Old family money. Not from here. From Charleston."

"She told me all her family was gone" Ben replied. "Why would she have told me that?"

"Couldn't say" the older lawyer had replied. "I didn't realize any of this until she came in to make her will last year. Betty couldn't have loved you more if you had been her birth child. She wanted to make sure everything she had would go to you."

Ben told Betty's lawyer to sell the house. He wasn't coming back to Greenwood. He would add the proceeds from the sale of the house to the rest of the money, and hire a financial advisor to help him manage the stocks and commercial real estate. Driving away from Greenwood, Ben had shed tears of gratitude for all that Betty Parrish had done for him.

Upon his return to work, Judge Bartlette had invited Ben to dinner.

"I know you are grieving your mother" Judge Bartlette had said to Ben. "Come over to the house for Sunday dinner. You need to be around people at times like these." Ben had accepted the invitation, declining to correct Judge Bartlette's misconception about Ben's parentage. Years later Ben wondered if the invitation had been a set-up, for it had become clear upon his arrival at the Bartlette residence that the true purpose of the dinner invitation had been to introduce Ben to the judge's daughter, Linda. Before the end of his clerkship, Ben and Linda had married. When his year was up, they had moved to Fort Charles, close enough to Birmingham for Linda to stay in touch with her family, and far enough for Ben to tell himself he would be his own man. Being Judge Bartlette's son-in-law had given Ben's legal career a boost money could never have bought, while his inheritance from Betty Parrish enabled him to establish office space in one of the newer buildings in Fort Charles while he launched his own firm.

Where had the years gone, Ben wondered sometimes. Although God had only blessed Ben and Linda with one child, their daughter Sarah had given them nothing but joy. While espousing all the politically correct commentary about women's independence and equality, Ben had been relieved when Sarah married David Jackson, one of the young partners at Johnson & Merritt. Ben would make sure David made enough money to keep Sarah at home, where she could raise their children and be a proper Christian wife. Appearances were important.

At 65, Ben was just entering his firm's mandatory phase down. Over the next three years Ben would reduce his practice, eventually transferring all of his clients to hand picked successors within the firm. Along with the relinquishment of clients would come the relinquishment of control over the firm, making the way for the next generation of young bucks. Ben hated to think about it. Johnson & Merritt was his creation, his fiefdom, and - along with the windfall from Betty Parrish- the vehicle which had granted him access to the ranks of Fort Charles' social and business elite. True, Ben reflected, he was nothing more than a big fish in a relatively small pond, but the status he had attained over the past forty years was more than gratifying. It had defined who and what he wanted the world to see - twice president of the Chamber of Commerce, membership at the Fort Charles' Country Club, a large home with pool and tennis courts in the city's most exclusive neighborhood, new Mercedes every other year, and founding father of one of the state's most prestigious law firms. Someone very different from the man Ben Johnson had tried so hard to extinguish.

A soft hum from Ben's cell phone permeated his thoughts. *Who in the Hell has that number?* Ben mused, noting the absence of an identifying ringtone. The "blocked number" display illuminated the phone's keypad. Ben answered warily "Hello?".

"Listen carefully, Mr. Johnson" a harsh male voice instructed.

"Who is this?" Ben demanded.

Ignoring Ben, the voice continued "My employer needs a favor. A favor only you can provide."

"Just who do you think you are?" Indignation coated Ben's response. "Whoever your employer is can call my secretary and make an appointment like everyone else." Ben fumed. "How did you get my private number?"

The unidentified voice sighed, then continued. "My employer says to tell you, and I quote, 'A favor done demands a favor in reply.' "

Ben Johnson cringed as the words he had prayed never to hear crawled into his ear. He had always been careful. Never in Fort Charles. Never in a city where anyone knew him. Never in a public park or bathroom. Ben had guarded the secret of his sexuality as tightly as Queen Elizabeth's guards watched over the crown jewels in the Tower of London. He knew he was damned. He'd known that since he was twelve years old and realized he wanted to suck Sammy Deal's cock. The Bible said homosexuality was a sin, and there was no getting around that fact. Ben had tried. He had really tried. He forced himself to date girls in high school and college, hoping somehow that he could change, could somehow rid himself of his sin and be reborn a real man. Ben had married Linda with the same fervor a drowning man grabs a life preserver. Surely, he had thought, marriage would cure him. He loved his wife, and he loved his daughter, but his sexual need for men had never left him.

Over the years Ben had learned how to find the high end clubs frequented by men like him. Men who lived a straight life, who couldn't afford, for whatever reason, to live openly as a homosexual. Living a double life had turned out to be easier than Ben had initially thought. Out of town business trips were the perfect cover, and one night, or one hour, stands had provided Ben sufficient relief to quiet what he referred to as his inner demon.

Until Atlanta.

"What is the favor?" Ben knew he had no choice but to ask.

"Your firm is representing a woman named Sherry McNair in a lawsuit against Miller Industries and Steve Miller."

Ben knew the case. His son-in-law David and Allison Parker were representing the plaintiff. He hadn't been too happy when David and Allison had reported the new matter on the firm's weekly report. Plaintiff's work was so declasse' Ben thought. Not at all the caliber of work Johnson & Merritt normally handled.

"Yes. What about it?" Ben waited.

"Get rid of it."

"What do you mean, get rid of it?" *It's just a sexual harassment case* thought Ben.

"My employer suggests a good first step would be pulling the Parker woman off the case."

"I can't just pull one of the firm's partners from a case, especially not without the client's consent," Ben argued.

"You're a smart man, Mr. Johnson. You'll think of something."

"This may take a while to accomplish..." Ben started to say.

"No excuses." The empty phone line buzzed quietly.

Ben Johnson had cancelled all of his afternoon appointments. He had to think, to clear his mind of all the "why" questions. Why would Jeff Bishop call in the favor over a sexual harassment case? Was it the case or the fact that Allison Parker was handling it? Why would that matter? She wasn't that good, was she? Maybe it wasn't Jeff. But who would know about

Atlanta other than Jeff? No, none of that mattered. All that mattered was his compliance. His secret had to be kept, whatever the cost.

CHAPTER SIX

2011 - Rice

Rice Parker was supremely irritated - his life was supposed to be better than this. Closing in on forty, he would have just finished his pro football career, he'd have millions in the bank, a couple of homes, and one of those trophy wives. With his looks and charisma, a post football career as a sports announcer would have been his for the taking. Instead, he was stuck with that bitch Mary Louise and three ratty kids. Hell, he wasn't even sure that last one was his.

It could have been worse. He could have been stuck in that eat-shit apartment he and Mary Louise had to move to after they married. Matthew had been furious

when he found out Rice had gotten Mary Louise preg-
nant. "What were you thinking?" Matthew had bellowed. "And she's a fucking nigger loving Catholic."
Rice could still hear his father screaming. "Make her
get an abortion." For the life of him, Rice didn't know
why he hadn't followed his father's orders. Thinking
with his dick was all he could figure now. Back then he
had thought he was in love.

Rice wasn't sure whether it was the birth of his second child, a daughter, eighteen months later that had
softened Matthew Parker's heart, or whether his father's
obsession with appearances had temporarily overcome
his disdain for Mary Louise. Whatever the reason,
when the two-story brick colonial in Westover came on
the market, it hadn't been hard to manipulate Matthew
into buying the house for Rice and his young family.
All Rice had to do was take advantage of Matthew's
fixation on status by pointing out how bad it looked for
the son of the bank president to be living in an apartment after three years of marriage and two children.
It had never occurred to either Matthew or Rice that
the residents of Sumner, Tennessee, likely could care
less about where Rice Parker lived, or why. Matthew's
only caveat had been that title to the Westover house
be in his name, not Rice's. Matthew Parker was a man
who was used to being in control. He wasn't taking any
chances that his daughter-in-law could get her hands
on the Westover house or, for that matter, any of Rice's

other non-existent assets. "Women," Matthew had told his son, "can never be trusted."

The years after high school had been hard for Rice. The football career Matthew had promised would come his way had never materialized. None of the SEC schools had wanted him, and he wasn't about to play for some rinky dink second tier college. Begrudgingly, Matthew had paid for Rice to attend the state university - no football scholarship paying the way - where Rice had struggled to figure out who he was if he wasn't a football star.

Knocking up Mary Louise had put an end to higher education, although if Rice had the capacity to be honest he would have had to admit he didn't do much the two years he spent in Knoxville other than drink, drug and screw. In the early years of their marriage the few times Rice had attempted night classes Mary Louise had pitched a fit, complaining about having to take care of the children by herself. Rice had hoped the Westover house would have made a difference, that Mary Louise would be satisfied, but no, things only got worse. And it hadn't helped that Rice couldn't keep a job. Mary Louise didn't like living hand to mouth, even if Matthew made up the slack for Rice's meager and erratic income, and she never let Rice forget what a failure he was as a husband and provider.

All that woman's ever done is sit on her ass and bitch thought Rice, thinking back. When Mary Louise gave

up all pretense at marriage, and began openly committing adultery with one, then two, prominent business-
men in Sumner, Rice had stood helplessly by, listening
to his friends talk behind his back, but unable to take
any action. He wished he had the guts to divorce Mary
Louise, but Rice was afraid to risk his father's wrath.
"Divorce doesn't happen to a Parker" Matthew had
intoned when Matthew had appeared time and again
at his parents' house, lamenting Mary Louise's public
behavior. "You're embarrassing this family. Get your
wife under control."

Thus, reality had intruded, usurping the life of
wealth and fame Rice had been promised for as long
as he could remember. Three children and a philan-
dering wife later, Rice Parker was miserable. But, he
had a plan.

"Sumner Community Bank" his father's secretary
answered the number Rice had dialed. "Matthew
Parker's office."

"Hey Charlene, it's Rice. Is my father around?"

"Why Rice, how nice to hear your voice. How are
Mary Louise and the children?" *What a suckup*, Rice
thought to himself. *Like she really cares.*

"They're fine." Rice responded shortly. "I need to
speak with my father."

"He just got back from lunch, hon" Charlene replied, oblivious to Rice's rude tone. "Let me see if I
can find him."

Rice waited, Kenny Chesney's voice filling his ear via the bank's phone system. Although his father hated country music, Matthew Parker knew the bank's client base - mostly rural customers, gun owners and hunters, conservative to the core. People whose taste in music, if they had any taste at all, ran exclusively to country. "Give them something familiar, make them think you are just like them, and you can do anything you want." Rice smiled remembering Matthew's words. He intended to use Matthew's philosophy against him.

"Rice" Matthew bellowed. "Make it quick, son. I've got a board meeting in ten."

"You remember Jerry Evans? One of my fraternity brothers at UT?"

"He that kid from Jackson?"

"Yes, that's the one. Well, he runs a successful investment firm over there. Took it over from his dad after he graduated."

"What about him?" Matthew's impatience sounded in his reply. Rice knew that tone. He needed to make his pitch now - his father was about two seconds from ending the conversation.

"Jerry's firm has some inside information about a new start-up company, says it's gonna' be another Microsoft." Rice hesitated. He needed to careful about what he said next. "Based on Jerry's intel, I can pre-buy stock in that start-up and then sell it for five times the investment the day the stock hits the board" Rice replied, referring to the New York Stock Exchange. "Apparently the sales price has already been set."

"Why is Jerry telling you about this? I know you sure as hell haven't got any money to put in the stock market." Matthew laughed. "Have you even seen him since you left Knoxville?"

"Oh, we've stayed in touch" Rice replied glibly. And they certainly had. Jerry had been Rice's source for weed and pills during his two years at UT, and the relationship had continued after Rice married and moved back to Sumner. Only now, the weed and pills had been replaced with cocaine, a much more expensive habit. Jerry hadn't dealt in the hard stuff, so he had introduced Rice to those who did. Effortlessly, Rice had traded up to cocaine, weed and pills discarded as an afterthought. At first it had just been recreational, a little toot here before a dinner party, a little toot there before tailgating. No harm done, Rice had told himself. But bit by bit, the infrequent rush had become a daily necessity.

For a while Rice had managed to scrounge enough money to pay for his habit. His mother had been an easy mark, always willing to give him cash, and selling some of the jewelry Mary Louise kept in their safety deposit box had been a stroke of genius. When other sources of income had run dry, Rice had justified cashing in his children's savings bonds by telling himself his children would never miss the money. Now,

Rice was into his dealer for over fifty grand and the opportunity Jerry was offering him was one Rice really couldn't refuse. "There's nothing to it man." Jerry had assured Rice. "I'll be making the trade in your name. No one will know we're splitting the profits." Rice was pretty sure what Jerry proposed didn't pass the smell test, and might even be illegal, but Rice also knew there would be painful personal consequences if he didn't come up with the money he owed. The possibility of jail worried Rice far less than the possibility of bodily harm.

"It's a once in a lifetime opportunity" Rice explained to Matthew. "I can use the profit from the stock sale to start my own business here in Sumner. I just need some upfront money from you."

"I financed the last business you started, Rice, and as I recall it took you less than two years to run it into the ground."

"Now, Dad, wait…."

Matthew continued "Do you have any idea how much money I've shelled out to support you and your family the last ten years?"

"This is different" Rice interjected.

"No, it's not. I'm not interested in playing your version of roulette, Rice. The answer's no." Changing gears, Matthew concluded the call. "I've signed you up for the shotgun match at the club in two weeks. I needed a partner. I'll have Charlene call you when I know our tee time. Get some practice time in. I don't want to be embarrassed."

CHAPTER SEVEN

Present Day

R ain pelted the plate glass windows in Allison's office, a staccato melody overlaid with ever increasing crashes of thunder as lightning illuminated the dark sky. *Good Lord*, thought Allison, startled by the closeness of the latest crack. *It's as dark as night out there.* Allison loved thunderstorms. Always had. She wondered sometimes if part of the reason was because the violence of those storms had drowned out the ugly sounds of her parents' fights when she was small. Strange, Allison thought, that such violence in nature had provided her an emotional respite from the domestic violence that had shaped her early years. Instead of bringing back dark memories, thunderstorms produced a calming, almost lulling effect. Allison had long ago quit trying to figure out the psychology of her attraction to thunderstorms in lieu of accepting the pleasure they gave her. Allison smiled. *It's cheaper than prozac.*

The computer on Allison's desk chirped a notice of an incoming email. Turning her attention to the screen, Allison noted the sender's identity, then skimmed the message.

"Client complaint necessitates removing you from the McNair case, effective today. Make the appropriate arrangements with David Jackson. He'll handle the case going forward."

What the hell? Reaching for her office phone, Allison angrily punched the numbers for Ben Johnson's extension.

"What do you think you are doing?" Allison demanded as soon as Ben answered. "I know Sherry McNair hasn't complained about how I'm handling her case. What client has complained about me?"

"It's a confidential matter, Allison. I'm not at liberty to share particulars with you."

"This is bullshit, Ben" Allison was hot. "If there has been a complaint against me that's serious enough for me to be removed from a case, I'm entitled to know the charges and defend myself."

"This isn't a formal Bar complaint, Allison." Ben replied, referring to the state agency which regulated lawyers. "And I don't intend for it to get that far. Removing you from the case will satisfy the client, and the problem will go away."

"Have you talked to the board about this?" Allison inquired. The firm's governing board was made up of five of the firm's partners. "I can't believe the board would support this action."

"I don't need to talk to the board." Ben's voice turned hard. "I still own 51% of this firm. It's my decision. Anyone who doesn't like it can leave. And that includes you."

Allison sat unmoving, the buzz of the phone line signaling the call's termination. She wasn't sure what had just happened. In her twelve years with Johnson & Merritt she had never known of a partner to be removed from a case. Never. Sure, there had been a few client complaints over the years, usually someone grouching about a final bill, or disgruntled about an outcome that didn't meet the client's original expectations. None against her, thank God, but client complaints weren't that unusual, even in firms like Johnson & Merritt, and especially when money was at stake.

As Johnson & Merritt had grown in size the firm had incorporated for tax benefits and, as importantly, to shelter individual partner income in the event of a large malpractice claim. The by-laws provided for a managing partner, similar to a corporate CEO, with a governing board comprised of five partners, each serving three year terms on a rotating basis. In addition to a governing board for business matters, Johnson & Merritt also had a compensation committee which determined partner income each year. Selection of the partners for the board and the compensation committee were made by vote of the partnership. While the firm's structure gave the appearance of representative governance, Ben Johnson had made certain the by-laws provided that the managing partner would be a standing member of both the board and the compensation committee. Johnson & Merritt was his creation, and Ben had had no intention of relinquishing control. Thus, when voting shares had been divvied up, Ben had retained 51%. Ben had remained managing partner from day one, and as a result he had never rotated off either the compensation committee or the board.

Like many firms, Johnson & Merritt had an internal procedure for dealing with client complaints. If a complaint was lodged against an associate - a non-partner lawyer - the associate's supervising partner handled the investigation into the complaint, and then reported his or her recommendation to the board. To Allison's knowledge, the board had uniformly rubber stamped a supervising partner's recommendation without any serious dialogue or discussion. Not so if the complaint were against a partner. In those rare instances, one of the board members was designated to investigate the complaint by meeting with the partner against whom a complaint had been lodged to discuss in detail the allegations and to allow the partner to respond. Sometimes other firm lawyers or paralegals were interviewed, depending on the seriousness of the charge. Once the internal investigation was completed, the entire board reviewed the findings before deciding what, if anything, needed to be done. A report of the board's decision was then disseminated to each partner as part of the weekly partner report.

Allison pulled a slim file from her desk drawer. Flipping through the sheets of paper, Allison separated the board reports entitled "Client Complaint Determination." Over the seven year period that she had been a partner, there had been three client complaints, two against partners, and one against a firm associate. The complaint against the associate had been a common one - failure to return the client's telephone calls. The associate had been reprimanded and ordered to make a written apology to the client. The complaints against the partners were more serious. One claimed the partner had settled the client's lawsuit without approval. The other claim, against a different partner, had alleged misconduct during trial. If true, the partners could have faced action by the state bar commission, possibly resulting in suspension of their law licenses.

The board's investigation on both partner charges had been thorough and lengthy. Both partners had been given the opportunity to examine the charges and to provide a response. The board had recommended reducing one of the partner's compensation for one year, finding that while the client had been aware of and had, in fact, approved the settlement, the manner in which the partner had handled that client's case had not met the standard required in the firm. The board determined that the claims of misconduct against the other partner were unfounded. Ben Johnson had not intervened in either case.

Shakespeare had it right, Allison thought. Something was rotten in Denmark. Or, more accurately, something was rotten about the McNair case. Allison was willing to bet it didn't have anything to do with Sherry McNair's claim, either. Even though the sexual harassment claim was not your typical run-of-the-mill claim, Allison couldn't see any reason the case itself would cause anyone heartburn, not even Steve Miller. Even if a jury found in favor of Sherry McNair, under the facts of the case and current law, the most the award could be would be mid six figures - hardly enough money for a company like Miller Industries to worry about. Then again, what was with that business in Judge Lee's courtroom the other day? Jack Striker had vociferously resisted producing the requested documents, only to roll over in front of Judge Lee with barely a whimper. And now this. Removing her from the case. Something kinky was definitely going on with the McNair case, Allison thought, but it wasn't sex.

"Donna" Allison called towards her office door. "Can you come in here for a minute?"

Allison's secretary appeared at once. Donna Pevey was one of the best secretaries in the firm. By sheer luck, Donna had been assigned to Allison three years earlier when Allison's previous secretary moved to another town. Lots of legal secretaries were wary of working for female lawyers, claiming that female lawyers were demanding, unreasonable and impossible to please. Allison liked to think she was the exception to the rule, and she made a concerted effort to treat all of the firm staff as her equal regardless of their status within the organization. Her attitude had paid off, resulting in an unforeseen benefit: not only did Allison and Donna have a great working relationship, most of the staff at Johnson & Merritt would do anything Allison asked of them. The ultimate winners were, of course, Allison's clients, and happy clients were loyal clients, bringing repeat business to Allison as well as new clients.

"What do you need Allison?" inquired Donna.

"I've been removed from the McNair case."

"What?" Donna stammered. "You what? ….Ok, you got me. Very funny."

"I'm serious, Donna. I've been removed from the case and ordered to turn everything over to David Jackson." Allison continued. "I need you to box up the McNair files and see that David's secretary has all the documents by tomorrow afternoon."

""This isn't fair. It's your case" Donna was hot. "Can't you do something about this?"

"I am going to do something about this, just not what you think" Allison replied. "That's why I called you into my office." Settling back in her chair and turning her phone to silent Allison looked at Donna. "Close the door, would you? Let's have some privacy."

Donna leaned against the closed door. "You thinking about doing something that might raise some eyebrows?"

"Probably more than eyebrows." Allison glanced out the window gathering her thoughts. "What I am considering - no what I am going to do - could cost both of us our jobs."

"Something illegal, huh?" Donna grinned.

"Not illegal, technically" Allison responded. "More like investigative work."

"Who are you planning on investigating? If it's putting our jobs on the line it ought to be somebody pretty big, and therefore something pretty interesting, too."

"I've got a couple of targets. Steve Miller is number one. Miller Industries is number two."

"That's nothing new or dangerous" Donna interrupted. "We investigate opposing parties all the time."

"My third target is Ben Johnson." Allison replied. "If we get caught, I figure Ben will fire both of us, and anyone else in the firm who helps me."

"Why Mr. Johnson?" Donna asked. "I understand why you'd want to take a closer look at Steve Miller and his company, but why Mr. Johnson?"

"None of this passes the smell test, Donna. The McNair case is peanuts to this firm. Miller Industries is a pretty good sized business, and I've heard Steve Miller is taking the company public next year." Allison added, referring to the process of selling shares in a privately owned company, and having those shares traded on the world stock exchanges. "But there is no reason -legitimate reason, that is - that I can envision even in my wildest dreams that would cause the managing partner of this firm to remove me, or any lawyer, from a case without presenting the matter to the board."

"That is definitely weird" Donna admitted. "Well, I'm in. I never liked that man anyway" Donna admitted. "If you're not a partner in this firm, Mr. Johnson acts like you don't exist. I bet he doesn't even know the names of half the staff."

"Don't let your personal feelings about Ben Johnson get in the way" cautioned Allison. "I intend to take a long, hard and very invasive look at Ben Johnson. You need to be sure you are well aware of the consequences to you if I screw up."

"I'm a good legal secretary. I won't have a problem finding another job if I need one." Donna smiled. "Shall I give Frank Martin a call? If anyone can find dirt on someone, it's Frank."

"See if I can meet him at his office some time tomorrow". Allison rose from her chair, giving Donna a brisk hug. "I owe you."

CHAPTER EIGHT

Atlanta 2009

It was after 11:00 p.m. when the cab dropped Ben Johnson and his companion at the Atlanta Ritz Carlton. As a long time customer, he was regularly upgraded to the Club Floor, where the accommodations and the extra perks of cocktails and heavy hor d'oeuvres provided a welcoming end to a long day of business. Staying at the Ritz stroked Ben's ego. "Hello, Mr. Johnson", "Do you need anything, Mr. Johnson?" "How can we be of service Mr. Johnson?" In Ben's mind, being the recipient of obsequious behavior was exactly as it should be.

The staff at the Atlanta Ritz was nothing if not discreet. Discretion cost money, and given the price they were paying for their accommodations, guests at the Ritz expected the upscale version of the expression "What happens in Vegas stays in Vegas." Nevertheless, Ben had never brought anyone back with him to the hotel.   A man of usually extraordinary caution with regard to his extracurricular sexual activities, Ben had always found his assignations in club bathrooms, parked cars, or dark alleys.   Yes, those assignations were somewhat distasteful in Ben's mind, and probably dangerous to a degree, but they were totally anonymous. None of his sexual partners knew who he was, and he never saw them again. Safety in anonymity.

But this one was different. Younger than Ben - he didn't want to know, really, it would make him feel old - Ben's companion stood about six feet tall, maybe one hundred eighty pounds.   Blond hair, curling over his collar, deep green eyes, a Hugo Boss jacket over a white shirt unbuttoned just enough to show a tanned and smooth chest.   Their eyes had locked across the bar in the Omni Hotel where Ben had stopped for a drink after his late afternoon business meeting.   Not the regular place for a pickup. Somehow, a casual hello turned into dinner and drinks in a corner booth. Chris Cannon was a banker, he said. In town for a regional banking convention. Wife and infant daughter at home in Richmond. *Safe*, thought Ben as the quiet messaging Ben understood filtered through their dinner conversation. By the time after dinner brandy was served hands had touched under the table, then hands to thighs. Ben had become so excited he could barely carry on a coherent conversation. A simple, anonymous fuck would not be enough.

The door to Ben's suite was barely closed before Ben was pulling off Chris' shirt and jacket, frantically tugging at Chris' belt.

"Let me suck you" Ben had pleaded, holding Chris' rock hard member in his hands. "I've been wanting to do this all night."

Pushing Ben to the floor, Chris positioned himself over Ben's upturned face, shoving his cock deep into Ben's mouth with quick, thrusting motions. Ben moaned in ecstasy, hands tightly gripping Chris' buttocks, frantically trying to consume the hot, throbbing rod in his mouth. And it had been just the beginning. Ben had fucked and been fucked all night long. He couldn't remember when he had wanted or desired a man as much as he did Chris. He never wanted it to end.

But, morning had come. Ben had ordered room service for them - eggs, bacon, grits, biscuit and hot coffee. A typical Southern breakfast. They had laughed over coffee, perused the Atlanta paper, and talked of when they would see each other again.

"Let me take a quick shower" Ben remembered saying. "I don't have to check out until later this morning. Enjoy your coffee and I won't take long."

"Take your time" Chris had smiled in reply. "I'll be right here."

Only Chris hadn't been there. When Ben got out of the shower, and returned to the suite's sitting room to remind Chris about a new book he had thought of, Chris was gone. And so were Ben's wallet, all his money, all his credit cards, his briefcase and his suitcase full of clothes. Ben stood dumbfounded, wrapped in his bath towel. *What have I done?*

A month passed. No charges appeared on Ben's credit cards. Of course he had immediately canceled all of them, telling the credit card companies he had lost the card. Same story to the DMV so he could get a new license. Explaining the loss of his briefcase and all of his clothes to Linda had been tricky, but she had bought his story about a hotel theft. Fortunately, Brooks Brothers had saved Ben from public indecency by delivering underware, slacks, socks, shoes and a shirt to Ben so he could leave the hotel.

And then came the call.

"Hello Ben. You miss my cock?"

A strangled grunt was the best reply Ben had been able to make.

"We have some business to conduct Ben. In fact, I think we are going to have a very long term business relationship."

"What do you want?" Ben's voice was a whisper.

"Ten thousand by this Friday is a good start. Small bills, nothing larger than $100. Have it delivered by private messenger to 45 Park Lane Drive, Birmingham. Suite 15. Leave the package with the receptionist."

"I don't have that kind of money."

"Don't shit me, Ben. I've done my research. This is a drop in your big, fat bucket. Any word to the police, the FBI or anyone else, life as you know it will be over " Chris laughed. "What do you think about my cock now, you fucking faggot?"

"Why are you doing this?" Ben cried over the phone line.

"It's just business, Ben." Chris had replied coldly. "Just business."

CHAPTER NINE

Present Day

Allison watched the woman approaching her on the sidewalk. *She's not from around here,* thought Allison, eyeing the stranger's white shoes. Although early October, the weather in Fort Charles generally remained warm until around the first of November. More years than not, children could trick or treat in costumes unencumbered by coats or sweaters. Cold weather seemed to know it needed to wait, to give little ones that last outdoor opportunity before fall and winter winds forced everyone indoors for a few months. Nevertheless, while fall temperatures in the south might mimic summer, there wasn't a female older than five or six who didn't know the rule about white shoes after Labor Day.

Once upon a time Allison had actually done some research on what she referred to as the "Wearing White Rule". She had been surprised to learn that the habit of not wearing white after Labor Day was birthed in the late 1800's and early 1900's as a way for the wealthy to distinguish themselves sartorially. If you were a member of the lucky sperm club, born into wealth and privilege, you would automatically know how gauche and plebeian it would be to wear white after Labor Day unless you were (1) a bride, (2) a debutante, or (3) at a resort. Otherwise all that was white would be relegated to the closet until Easter. Of course, rules were made to be broken, and if you were a famous celebrity or international phenomenon, you could not only break the rules but become a fashion icon along the way. *Just look at Coco Chanel,* thought Allison. *She wore white whenever she felt like it, and didn't give a toot what anyone thought about it.*

Allison wasn't sure when the wearing white rule migrated from the uber wealthy to the middle class. Maybe it only migrated to Southern families. She'd never had this conversation with a Yankee, a Cowgirl, or a New Ager from California so she didn't know. But there was no doubt that Southerners of a certain social class would rather be caught dead than be seen in white shoes or carrying a white purse after Labor Day.

Allison laughed at the memory of the shock and horror expressed when Princess Fergie arrived in Texas wearing white pumps after Labor Day. Allison couldn't remember whether it was the Dallas or Houston paper, but whichever one it was - and maybe it was both - ran a huge picture of poor Fergie standing at the door of the Royal airplane, her white shoes an irrevocable social faux pas.

It's funny the lessons we learn and the messages we carry from childhood, Allison thought, nodding politely as the unknown woman passed by, rule breaking shoes tapping on the pavement. *Too bad she didn't get a primer on Southern social mores* thought Allison as she turned down Bull Street towards Frank Martin's office. *Little things still matter here. Whether they should or not is a discussion for another day.*

1590 Bull Street housed an nondescript brown brick building. Two stories high, with a low slung roof reaching out over small second floor windows, Frank Martin's office building looked like a tired old man. Even the large bayfront windows and oak colored door failed to brighten an otherwise rather dingy facade.

I'm not here to talk about architectural design Allison thought as she pressed the buzzer by the right of the front door. *I wonder if the security is for show or by necessity?* Allison contemplated the possible answers to her question as she waited to see who, if anyone, would open the door.

As Allison pressed the buzzer for a second time, the oak door opened, only to be replaced by a man of seemingly equal size.

"What's on fire, missy?" boomed the giant. "Or do you just have no patience?"

"Uh, excuse me." Allison replied startled. "I'm looking for Frank Martin's office. I must have the wrong office."

"And why might you think you're at the wrong office?" the giant inquired, a smile creeping from the corner of his blue eyes.

"Well, you're not quite what I expected" Allison replied, adding "Mr. Martin."

The giant laughed and extended a huge hand for Allison to shake. "Got that pretty fast Ms. Parker. Come on in. You're right on time."

The interior of Frank Martin's office looked nothing like the exterior of the building which provided its four walls, floors and roof. Soft lighting illuminated a well appointed, wood paneled reception area. What appeared to be an oriental rug covered the wide plank flooring, anchored on one side by a leather sofa and by two chintz covered club chairs on the other. An attractive, smallish desk sat unobtrusively to the side, a computer and telephone crowding its small top. A door at the far end of the area led, Allison presumed, to additional office space. Allison thought the room looked more like a family living room than a private detective's office.

"I gave my secretary the afternoon off" explained Frank Martin. "When Donna said you didn't want to meet at your office I figured privacy might be important."

"Very perceptive, Mr. Martin."

"Call me Frank." Martin replied, gesturing for Allison to sit. "Makes for a better relationship."

"Only if you call me Allison. Keeps us on even footing." Allison replied, sinking comfortably into the nearest chair.

"So, what can I do for you Allison." Frank Martin inquired, making himself at home on the large sofa.

"First, I need to know if there is any reason you can not undertake an investigation of any of the partners at Johnson & Merritt."

"Anyone in particular?"

"Yes" Allison replied handing Martin several folded sheets of paper. "But first, please review this list. All of the partners at Johnson & Merritt are listed here, as well as the names of their spouses, if any, and their children. I've also listed the parents and in-laws for each of the partners." Allison paused. "Have you performed any services for any of the persons listed?"

Martin's eyes scanned the pages once, then again more slowly. "I've not been retained by any of these

individuals for personal matters" he replied. "However,
I did a couple of preliminary venire investigations for
Sammy Smith a few years back" Martin added, referring to the "venire" or pool of potential jurors sum-
moned for trial cases. "Sammy always liked to know as
much as he could about prospective jurors before his
trials started."

"This matter does not involve Sammy" Allison replied. "But I need to know whether that prior work for
Sammy would prevent you from investigating another
partner in the firm."

Martin's gaze was direct. "I owe no loyalty to
Johnson & Merritt, nor to Sammy Smith, nor do I see
my previous work for Sammy as a conflict of interest
in accepting an investigation of anyone in that firm."

"Alright" Allison nodded her agreement. "I have
three targets: Steve Miller, Miller Industries, and Ben
Johnson, the managing partner of my firm." Pacing
the room, Allison described the McNair case, the legal
issues surrounding the sexual harassment claim, and
her subsequent removal from the case by Ben Johnson.

"What am I looking for?"

"I'll know it when I see it." Allison reached into the
briefcase she had earlier placed by her chair. "Here's
what I've already pulled on Miller and Miller Industries
from the internet and public filings. Nothing suspicious that I can see. Certainly nothing to make Ben
Johnson unilaterally pull a partner from a case."

"What do you know about the type of work I do, Allison?" Martin asked quietly.

"I know you get results. That's all I need to know." Allison continued "The information I need will be hard to find and is probably well hidden. You may need to utilize some unusual or slightly questionable techniques. So long as you stay on the clean side of the law, I don't care how you handle the investigation."

"How far back do you want me to go?"

"As far as you can" Allison stood to shake Martin's hand. "There's got to be a connection between Miller and Ben Johnson. I just don't know what it is."

CHAPTER TEN

The past few weeks had passed quietly. Handling routine matters for a couple of her regular corporate clients had kept Allison fairly busy as had the planning, decorating and production of the annual costume party Allison and Jim hosted at the Farm the Saturday before Halloween. What had started as a simple get together for a few couples with small children when Charlotte and Mack were toddlers had now, just a few years later, somehow blossomed into a full blown affair for their children's classmates and parents, as well as for neighbors and friends.

Although Hallowe'en was certainly a child's holiday, Allison was pretty certain the grownup attendees had as much fun "dressing up" as did the children. This year Allison had favored the classics, donning a tired but true Alice in Wonderland costume, replete with a live white rabbit courtesy of their next door neighbor, while Jim, to the delight of the younger attendees, gave a nod to current fiction as Albus Dumbledore. Hayrides on the tractor, pony rides on her children's Shetlands, apple dunking and general running around mayhem preceded a dinner of hotdogs and hamburgers for both children and parents, with 'smores heated over a small campfire as dessert.

Taking a sip of her morning coffee, Allison glanced through the breakfast room window, surveying the leftover decorations littering the pasture before reaching for the paper and settling in to her Sunday morning routine. With rain forecasted ahead of an incoming cold front, everything would be a soggy mess by mid afternoon. *Looks like my morning is planned out for me* Allison thought. *Maybe after one more cup of coffee.*

"Morning, babe" Jim called as he wandered into the room. Dressed in faded jeans and grey t-shirt, dark hair still damp from his morning shower, he leaned down to kiss the top of Allison's head as he headed towards the stove. "Think I'll make pancakes. Want some?"

"How can you be so chipper this early in the morning?" Allison inquired. "I'm doing well garnering enough energy for a second cup of coffee."

"You need to learn to enjoy your parties more instead of being the worker bee the whole time" Jim gently reprimanded. "No one's grading your performance."

"I know, I know. Old habits are hard to break". Laying the paper aside, Allison continued "Not that anything I did was ever good enough."

"If you're referring to Matthew, consider this. I don't think you'd have either the work ethic or the drive to succeed if you hadn't had to fight for recognition in your family. In a convoluted and weird-ass way, Matthew did you a big favor."

"Maybe."

"He sure as hell didn't do any favors for Rice. Pulling his ass out of one financial problem after another, buying that house for him and Mary Louise, never making Rice deal with any consequences of his bad choices." Laying a plate of steaming pancakes in front of Allison, Jim added "The politically correct term for how Matthew has treated Rice is probably "enabling". Frankly, I think he cut off Rice's balls years ago. Your brother is pitiful and pitiable. It's a blessing Matthew wasn't interested in you."

"Until now, you mean." Allison paused to sample her pancakes. "Oh, these are really good. How about a couple more?"

Jim spooned several scoops of batter onto the sizzling griddle. "What do you mean?"

"Now he wants me to take care of him while he dies."

Allison ate in silence while Jim finished cooking. After a few minutes and settling himself at the table, Jim quietly asked "Well, are you? I didn't want to bring this up yesterday before the party, but I got another call from Dr. James. Either Matthew comes here or Dr. James is going to admit him to residential hospice in Sumner. If we bring Matthew here Dr. James can order in-home hospice. A nurse would be here every other day to check on him."

"We'd still have to have a full time sitter. And maybe someone to help with his meals given our schedules. I can't ask Sharon to cook for Daddy. She's busy enough with Charlotte and Mack."

"It's doable, Allison. The guest house is perfect for Matthew and his sitters. Dr. James said Matthew isn't eating much anymore, so I'm sure the sitters can fix light meals that he can tolerate." Jim hesitated. "This is as much for you as for Matthew. I don't want you to have any regrets when he is gone."

Allison sat quietly. How was it, she wondered, that the memories of so many years ago could still hurt her so badly that she would turn her back on a dying man? *I'm better than that* she told herself.

"Alright. I'll call Daddy tonight and see when we can get him moved. First thing tomorrow I'll contact that sitting service Sheldon Alston used for his mother. He said they did a great job."

"You're doing the right thing" Jim assured his wife.

Clearing the morning dishes from the table, Allison thought *I sure hope so.*

⇒⊹ ⊹⇐

Matthew Parker slowly lowered his body into the wicker rocker on the front porch of his daughter's guest house. Glancing at his hands he noted the sallow yellow skin, underlaid with bluish veins. *Old man hands* he thought grimacing in pain, a soft moan escaping his lips. He had lost so much weight that the simple act of sitting was torture. No matter how soft the cushion, he couldn't find a position that didn't make his bones ache. Still, he was grateful to be alive, even in this condition. Everyone else might think he was in imminent danger of dying, but Matthew knew differently. He wasn't going anywhere. Not yet.

A trim woman in white scrubs appeared in the doorway. "Mr. Matthew, I heard you groaning. You ready for some pain medicine? It's been four hours. You can have your next dose now."

"No. It makes me foggy. Bring me that black notebook in there by my bed, would you? And a pen, too." Matthew repositioned himself in the chair. *Damn this disease.* Matthew complained silently. *I don't have time for this.* But he knew he had nothing but time, and damn little of it. Two months ago he had been sitting in his office at the bank, planning his next take-over - that small bank in Clarksville - when he got the call from Doc James. Cancer. Not only cancer, but fucking metastasized cancer. Too far progressed for any treatment.

"Get your affairs in order, Matthew" Dr. James had urged. "You've got three months, four if you're lucky. If we'd caught this sooner, maybe….." Dr. James had added. "But, you're on a short leash here, Matthew. Not much time left at all."

Matthew and Bill James had been friends since their first years of college. Fraternity brothers, each had been the other's best man, and godfather to each man's first born. By the time Bill had finished his medical residency and returned to Sumner to open a general medical practice Matthew was already a vice president in his family's bank. Five years later, thanks to the early demise of Matthew's father, Matthew had become president of Sumner Community Bank. One of first things Matthew had done was name his friend Bill James to the bank's board of directors. Things were getting difficult at home, and Matthew needed an ally who would have a vested economic interest in keeping his mouth shut.

And so it had begun. Matthew had lost track of how many times Bill James had covered for him after he had beaten Helene. Broken nose, broken arm, stitches under her eye, dislocated shoulder - only once had Bill insisted Helene be admitted to the hospital for treatment of her injuries, the other injuries he had treated at the Parker residence. But their friendship had suffered. After Helene committed suicide Bill had resigned from the bank's board of directors, and Matthew had not seen him either personally or professionally. Not until Matthew had figured out he was sick, and fear had propelled him to Bill's office for an appointment.

Matthew knew what Bill had meant when he told him to get his affairs in order. Helene hadn't been the only one he had hurt. Taking up the pen Janice had brought to him, Matthew began laboriously to write in the black notebook.

CHAPTER ELEVEN

Frank Martin began every investigation the same way. At the beginning. If he was investigating a person, he started with the day the person was born, and worked forward. If he was investigating a company he would search for the incorporating documents, and then investigate all the incorporators. Thirty years ago when Frank had obtained his private investigator's license and opened up shop, gathering in-depth intel on a target required weeks, and sometimes months, of mind numbing work which might or might not produce usable information. *Thank God for Al Gore and the internet* Jack thought, laughing at the vanity of a Washington politician claiming to have invented the internet. Personally, Frank didn't care who invented the internet. The internet now existed, and Frank loved it. Investigation via internet search engines had cut his research time on a case by ten-fold. No longer did Frank have to know the exact question he wanted to ask. Now Frank could type in different words or phrases and Google, Safari or Dolphin did the work for him, offering up multiple avenues for him to explore. Once he found what he wanted, it didn't take much ingenuity to access supporting documents. Instead of pounding the pavement for hours on end, Frank could enjoy his coffee and cigar in the comfort of his office, Chopin and Bach offering soothing melodious support. True, there were still times that personal surveillance was necessary, or one-to-one interviews the only way to credibly assess information. Frank knew he would likely need to utilize both of those investigative tools in order to provide Allison what she wanted. Not a problem. What most people didn't realize, and what now helped Frank so immeasurably, was the extraordinary amount of personal information available in cyberspace. Big Brother really was watching. Not much was private anymore.

As helpful an asset as the internet had become, there was a limit to what it could uncover. Fortunately, Frank had learned early-on the value of personal contacts in his line of work. The woman at the IRS; the guy with Homeland Security; Frank's cousin at Immigration, not to mention contacts in various state and local agencies. The list went on and on. Frank had helped each one of his contacts solve a thorny problem - some personal in nature, some professional - most of which would have had career ending consequences had Frank not been able to provide damage control in the form of information. Even if unable to help on a particular matter, Frank's contacts had been instrumental in opening doors for him that might otherwise have remained closed.

In the end, however, the secret of Frank's successes could be traced to one stellar personal characteristic. Frank never gave up. Ever. Even when the client was satisfied that no stone had been left unturned and terminated the investigation, if a question remained in Frank's mind, as far as Frank was concerned the case remained open. On more than one occasion Frank had contacted a client months later, handing over additional information beneficial to the client's original issue. Word had traveled quickly in the business community of Ft. Charles and beyond, that Frank Martin was a man who got results, no matter how difficult the job.

Frank's desk chair groaned, emitting a complaint as it struggled to support Jack's two hundred and eighty pounds. Placing his cowboy booted feet on his desk, freshly lit cheroot in hand, Frank contemplated the significance of what he had just heard. Steve Miller had a juvie record. And not just any juvie record. In 1984 when Steve Miller was sixteen he had been arrested on a charge of conspiracy to hire for murder in Limestone County, Alabama. Normally criminal charges or convictions for juveniles - those people under the age of eighteen - were either sealed or expunged by court order once some sort of restitution was made or juvenile sentence served. It was almost unheard of for juvenile records to be accessed absent court intervention, and sometimes not even then.

The key to this discovery had started inadvertently, and fortuitously it now turned out, during his initial background search of Miller's family, friends and known associates. Steve Miller had grown up as a ward of the State of Alabama. From the age of eight, when he was removed from his single mother's custody, until his arrest at age sixteen, Steve Miller had lived with three different foster families in rural Limestone County. As with many rural couples who fostered wards of the state, the families where Steve Miller had lived had also fostered other children. More children meant more help in the fields in addition to the extra monthly income paid by the state for room and board. For families struggling to make ends meet, foster parenting was an easy way to make money from free labor.

Frank knew all too well how the system worked. He had grown up in it. To Frank's way of thinking, foster care was a roll of the dice, and he had rolled a lucky seven. His foster parents had been extraordinary people, hard workers, overflowing with love for children, kind individuals who had raised him in loving strictness, saving all of the money they were paid as foster parents so Frank would have money to start his own life when he turned eighteen. But for as many foster parents as there were like his own, there were others out to make a buck, who didn't give a shit about the children who had been entrusted to them, and who in more instances than not saw a good beating as the answer to effective child rearing. Based on what he had read about Steve Miller's three placements, Frank was pretty sure he knew what kind of hell Steve Miller had faced.

What was unusual, though, about Miller's case, and what had eventually led Frank to Miller's juvie record, was the boy who had lived with Miller in all three of the foster homes. Frank knew that foster children were moved to new families for a variety of reasons, but by far the most common reason for a move was behavior. Bad behavior. Frank couldn't think of any reason why Miller and Jeff Bishop, a foster kid three years older than Miller, would have been moved together unless they were related, but Frank hadn't seen anything to indicate a tie by blood or marriage. Conversely, if Miller and Bishop had been discipline problems, the Department of Human Services would have separated them, sending each boy to a different home, likely as far away from the other as possible. Frank had decided to place that question in the unanswered file for future contemplation. He might need to revisit it again.

Jeff Bishop had graduated from the state foster care system in 1983. Wondering if the friendship between Miller and Bishop had continued, Frank had googled Jeff Bishop's name along with the words "Limestone County, Alabama". Sure enough, in less than an eyeblink, several links to information on Jeff Bishop had appeared. In 1984, one year after leaving foster care, Jeff Bishop and an unnamed minor had been arrested on serious criminal charges. Frank had skimmed the articles. Best he could tell from the cryptic reports, a homeless man in Athens, Alabama claimed that Bishop and another person had offered the man money to "bump off" a local thug. The District Attorney had jumped on the case, obtaining arrest warrants for Bishop and his alleged accomplice, the unnamed juvenile. Information was scarce on the ultimate outcome of the charges, but from what Frank could tell, it looked like Bishop had served just six months at the county penal farm. For such a light sentence Frank figured the case must have fallen apart, probably due to either the disappearance of the star witness for the prosecution, or that witness's inability to sober up for trial. Otherwise Bishop would have ended up with serious prison time. Six months on the penal farm smelled like a plea bargain. There was no mention about sentencing, or adjudication, for the juvenile accomplice. Frank needed more information, and he knew who could get it for him. Locating the number he needed, Frank had made his call.

"Sullivan. Department of Human Services. How may I help you?"

"Is this the lovely Stella? Heart throb of all fifteen year old boys?"

"Frank Martin! You old reprobate. Where have you been keeping yourself?"

"Working, Stella. Just like you. Not enough hours in the day sometimes." Frank shifted the phone to his other ear, and reaching for a pen and paper continued "If you've got a minute I'd like to ask you about an old file. I'm trying to connect the dots on an investigation."

"How old?"

"1984 and '85. Records for a Steve Miller. His social is 416-424-4876."

"Frank, I've told you before. I can't just willy nilly pull old files."

"I don't want you to pull his whole file. He was in the system from 1976 to around 1986 or so. But I think he got in trouble with the law in '84. I need to see if Miller's file says anything about an arrest or plea agreement."

"Don't you have any sources in the courthouse, Frank? Let someone else do this for you. I may be a fixture around here, but I can still get in a heap of trouble for giving you back channel information."

"It's not local, Stella, and I don't know anyone well enough to trust in Limestone County."

Frank waited. The grandfather's clock in the corner of his office ticked five full minutes before he heard Stella's reply.

"On October 3, 1984, Steve Miller pleaded guilty to a Class C Misdemeanor of Conspiracy. He was sentenced to six months of community service, with probation until he reached the age of eighteen. The record should have been eligible to be sealed or expunged sometime in late 1986 or early 1987. I can't tell from the file whether that ever happened. You'll have to check the court records in Limestone County." Thanking Stella, Frank had disconnected the call.

Interesting Frank thought, blowing cigar smoke towards his office ceiling. *Very interesting, indeed.* Laying the cheroot in an ashtray, Frank typed "Fort Charles Journal" into the search bar on his computer. When the front page of Fort Charles' weekly business paper filled the computer screen Frank clicked on archives, and then entered the words "Miller Industries". *I thought so* Frank remarked. The September 23 edition had run an article on Miller Industries and its upcoming public stock offering. Steve Miller had been interviewed for the article, and it was clear from the tenor of the piece that the stock offering was expected to be quite successful, increasing not only the company's value substantially, but Miller's personal wealth as well.

Is that it? Frank asked himself. It made sense that Steve Miller would want to hide that part of his past. Investors were a skittish group. It wouldn't take much to taint Miller Industries' stock offering. Lots of money potentially lost. But what was the connection to the McNair case? Or to Allison Parker? These were additional questions for Frank's unanswered file. Their answers would come, Frank knew, in due course. They always did. In the meantime, he would prepare a status report for Allison, bringing up her to speed with his current progress, and the surprise discovery in Steve Miller's past. Frank would let Steve Miller's past percolate while he turned his attention to Allison's third target, Ben Johnson.

CHAPTER TWELVE

Rice Parker was about at the end of his rope, fig-uratively speaking, although if he couldn't fig-ure out a solution pretty damn quick Rice knew that literally being at the end of a rope might be his only out. For the past two years, Rice and Jerry Evans had enjoyed the profits of a perfect, if albeit questionable, enterprise. Simple, really. Rice had opened a trading account with Jerry at Merrill Lynch in Jackson. Based on insider information that Jerry would periodically receive, Jerry would enter a purchase order in Rice's name for new issue stocks. That part of the partner-ship was totally legit. Brokers were always permitted to give those sorts of "bennies" to good customers. After all, the brokerage business was about making money.

Give the client a profitable tip, and the client would continue to invest. End result? More commissions for the broker and the brokerage house. The Securities and Exchange Commission knew all about those sorts of deals and didn't have a problem with them.

But that wasn't exactly the arrangement Rice and Jerry Evans had made. As the old saying went, Rice didn't have a pot to pee in, and Jerry Evans had taken total advantage of that fact, helped along by Rice's constant indebtedness to some very nasty people. It had sounded so simple when Jerry proposed it to Rice.

"Look man" Jerry had explained, "this is fool proof. As far as Merrill Lynch is concerned, it's all legit. I'm simply giving a preferred customer - you - a tip on a new stock issue. I enter the order at the pre-issue price the day before the stock hits the exchange. As soon as the market opens, I buy the stock for you at the pre-issue price, and then immediately sell it at the increased market price. You'll get the check for your profit within forty-eight hours. Bring me my half in cash, and there's no paper trail at all."

"How much money are we talking about upfront?" Rice had asked. "I'm not that liquid."

"Not a problem" Jerry had replied. "Just give me your personal check so I can claim I've been paid for the purchase order. I won't run it through our system until you've deposited the sale proceeds. No one will be the wiser."

At first, Rice had been cautious. It made him nervous to give Jerry a check he knew wasn't any good. Enough of his father's banking knowledge had rubbed off for Rice to know that what Jerry had proposed was illegal check kiting. Rice could go to jail if he were caught. He was pretty sure Jerry would go to jail with him, but that was slim consolation.

If he had been able to kick the cocaine habit maybe things would have been different, Rice sometimes thought, but that had never happened. Cocaine had become his confidant, his lover, his only escape from the realities of life. No, Rice thought. He could not imagine a life without it. In short order Rice had locked away his doubts and fears, plunging full ahead with Jerry's scheme. The partnership had allowed Rice to finance his ever increasing habit and to put enough money in Mary Louise's checking account to keep her happy and off his back.

The crux of Rice's dilemma had originated six months earlier. As a result of regulatory oversight Merrill Lynch had been required to change some of its internal procedures. One of those changes, the one that was causing Rice considerable heartburn, required Merrill Lynch brokers to deposit client checks into the firm's trust account prior to entering a purchase order. No longer could Jerry Evans hold Rice's bad check until Rice had cash in the account to cover it.

At first Rice had enough cash on hand in his account at Sumner Savings Bank to cover smaller stock
orders, and it seemed that he and Jerry would continue, just with smaller purchases. But, one thing had
led to another - braces for one of his kids, a diamond
bracelet Mary Louise had bought, coupled with a rise
in the price he was having to pay for his coke - and Rice
had found himself tapped out. Rice had not asked
Matthew for help, knowing his father would ask questions Rice either would not, or could not, have wanted
to answer. Same with his sister Allison. All he'd get
from her would be a lecture on responsibility.

And then Rice had thought of Charlene, his father's secretary. A spinster nearing seventy, Charlene
has worked for Matthew from his start as a young bank
officer through his rise to the presidency of the bank
and chairmanship of the Board. She had refused to
retire, and with all the federal age discrimination laws,
neither Matthew nor the bank had pushed the issue.
Charlene would do anything for Matthew Parker, and
she would protect his reputation whatever the cost.
Rice knew Charlene would help him. And she had,
covering his bad checks, breaking all sorts of banking rules, helping Rice so her beloved Matthew would
not be embarrassed by his son. Then two months ago
cancer had forced Matthew to resign from the bank.
Distraught over Matthew's diagnosis, Charlene had declared herself unable to remain at the bank without

him. Matthew was gone one day and Charlene the day after, leaving Rice to his own devices, one step ahead of his creditors and his dealer.

Rice was out of options. If he couldn't find another source of income Rice was a dead man. His dealer had made that painfully clear last night. Two broken fingers were nothing compared to what was coming if Rice didn't pay up. The antiques Rice had picked out of Matthew's house would help temporarily. The English linen press and the antique English pine chest had brought eight grand from the Atlanta dealer at Scott's. Rice had done his homework, researching the value of his parents' collection of furniture, silver and china. Georgian mahogany pieces his parents had bought on multiple trips to London, a Louis XVI armoire from Paris, his mothers' French and Scandinavian porcelain, two Persian rugs - Rice couldn't believe what he could get for those- who would have thought that raggedy carpet in the dining room was worth seventy-five thousand bucks? Matthew's gun collection alone ought to net him another hundred thousand or so. If only his father hadn't given his sister Helene's jewelry. Rice was pretty sure his mother's jewelry collection would have brought a good price, but Matthew had maintained the Southern tradition of passing jewelry down the female line. If Allison said anything about the silver service and flatware, something else that generally passed to one of the daughters in a Southern family, he'd have to figure a way around that. Good thing for him Allison hadn't argued about him taking most of the furnishings when they had closed up Matthew's house. Rice needed all of it. Every single bit.

Parking his car outside Allison's house, Rice mulled over what he was going to say, oblivious to the natural beauty around him. The Farm's guest cottage was located behind the pool, some distance from the main house, on the far side of a garden. Silky Pearle D'Or rose petals, light brown edges curling delicately from an early frost, waived in the breeze on a huge bush nearer to the main house, while the vibrant red Dortmunds adorning the picket fence enclosing the garden remained unscathed, sparkling with morning dew. The garden itself, filled with fall blooming perennials, offered a wash of color.

Rice hated coming to The Farm. Totally lacking in self awareness, Rice Parker could not understand why his sister had achieved the professional and financial success that had eluded him his entire life. When *Always Alabama*, the state's semi-society magazine, had published a five page story, complete with color pictures, about Allison, her husband and their gardens Rice had been so pissed he'd sent a nasty email to his sister. *What makes you so special?* he'd asked. Just thinking about that story made Rice mad all over again. And here he was, walking through that damn rose garden. Rice spit on the nearest bush. *Maybe they'll all get black spot* he thought viciously.

He'd have to keep a watch on his temper, Rice reminded himself, walking along the meandering stone path. Rice had deliberately waited until Allison and Jim left for work. *What they don't know won't hurt them.* Rice laughed, envisioning his sister's future surprise. *At least not until it's too late for them to do anything about it.* Matthew was getting weaker by the day. If Rice was going to be able to manipulate Matthew at all, now was his chance. The day nurse might be a problem, but Rice figured if money didn't buy her silence, a threat against her family certainly would. All he needed was Matthew's signature.

Matthew Parker, wearing a heavy sweater, knees covered with a blanket, rocked in an old chair on the cottage porch. Steam rose from a heavy mug, placed strategically on a small table close to his right side. "Rice. Didn't expect to see you this morning. You looking for Allison?" Matthew sipped from the steaming mug, raising an eyebrow as a followup to his question.

"No, as a matter of fact I was looking for you, Dad."

"That's a surprise." Setting down the mug, Matthew questioned "What's on your mind?"

"How much pain medication does Dr. James have you on now?"

"Not that much. Why?"

"You'll have to start taking more before too long, Dad. Doc said your pain levels were going to get pretty bad." Trying for a look of concern, Rice continued "I'm worried about someone taking advantage of you once your pain meds are increased."

"No one's taking advantage of me. Don't you worry about that." Pulling the blanket tighter around his shoulders, Matthew's eyes hardened. "What's really on your mind, Rice?"

"Just you, Dad. Really. I'm worried about you." Reaching into the satchel he had brought with him, Rice pulled out a small sheaf of papers. "This is a Power of Attorney..."

"I know what a Power of Attorney is" Matthew replied sharply.

Ignoring the interruption, Rice continued. "I had Sam Kelly prepare this. Letting someone else handle your affairs for you in your final days is one less thing for you to worry about."

"Do you take me for an idiot?" Matthew harumped. "The first thing I did after Bill James told me I was dying, and dying soon, was get my estate matters settled. I should have done it years ago, but I kept hoping I wouldn't have to put restrictions on your inheritance."

"What are you talking about, restrictions on my inheritance?" Rice's voice quavered, an undertone of fear brushing the surface of his words.

"I had hoped you'd get your act together, Rice, learn to be responsible, take care of your family, but that has never happened."

"I don't know who you've been listening to" Rice sputtered, "but I've been doing very well the last few years."

"Cut the crap, son. Charlene came to see me three weeks ago. She told me everything she'd been doing for you, covering your checks, keeping you out of trouble. Said her conscience had finally gotten to her, so she had come to me to confess."

"I can explain, Dad." Rice interjected. "It's not what you think."

"Don't bother with an excuse. When I die, your half of my estate will be placed in a Trust I've set up. Allison and Jim are the Trustees. They will provide you sufficient funds to support yourself and your family in a reasonably comfortable lifestyle for as long as you live. Upon your death, any money remaining in the Trust will be divided among your children. Mary Louise can take care of herself if she's still alive."

"Nooooo!" Rice screamed leaping to his feet. "You can't do this to me! You can't!"

"Get a grip, boy" Matthew yelled in reply. "It's my money and I can do what I damn well please with it."

"She won't give me enough" Rice whined. "That bitch and her sanctimonious prick of a husband think they know everything." Advancing towards his father, Rice growled "I bet she put you up to this, didn't she?"

Matthew struggled to raise himself from the chair. "I may be dying, but I'm not senile. No one put me up to anything. Until this very minute I worried if I'd made the right decision about that Trust." A harsh laugh escaped from Matthew's lips. "Not anymore." Turning his back on Rice, Matthew paused at the cottage door to make a final observation. "You should have been the girl. Your sister's more a man than you'll ever be."

Two hours, several scotches and a snort of cocaine had calmed Rice enough for him to examine his options.

Rice had been certain that the Trust business had been Allison's idea. Leaving Matthew, Rice had phoned Allison from his car, demanding to know if she had prepared the Trust documents.

"No, Rice, I did not. That would have been a conflict of interest. I referred Dad to Williams, McConnell and Foster. They handle most of the estate work in the area, and I knew they would do a good job."

"Have you read it?" Rice asked, unable to believe his sister hadn't had some input.

"No. Dad told me he'd have Mike Williams send a copy to me and to you next week."

Rice hadn't believed Allison for a minute. *Lying Bitch* he murmured, remembering their conversation. *You think you're so smart.* Rice ground his teeth thinking about his sister. God, he hated her, and that prick judge she was married to. Well, he'd have to deal with her later. Right now he had bigger problems.

Selling Matthew's antiques and collections would net him enough cash for a couple of months, maybe more. He'd have to rein in Mary Louise's spending, and cancel that shopping trip to New York she had been planning, but it couldn't be helped. Rice cringed thinking about the crap Mary Louise would give him over that. Well, he'd just put his foot down, and Mary Louise would have to go along with it. It would take some time for him to figure some way around Matthew's plan to deprive him of his rightful inheritance.

CHAPTER THIRTEEN

David Jackson twirled his Montblanc pen on the smooth surface of his mahogany desk. The expensive pen had been a gift from his father-in-law when he made partner at Johnson & Merritt. A waste, David had thought, and gross display of conspicuous consumption, but he had known to keep his opinion to himself. His wife Sarah adored her father, and while she understood David's more ascetic leanings, David had come to suspect over the years that where his wife's affections were concerned he ran a distant second to his father-in-law. At first it had bothered him and he had spent many a sleepless night wondering if his marriage was over. After a while, he had just accepted things as the way they were. He didn't have a bad marriage. Sarah was a gracious hostess and a good mother to their two children. To anyone looking at his family, David knew, nothing would have seemed awry. And most people would have traded places with him in a New York second, warts and all. So, David had settled, determined to find meaning in his career, like so many other men before him. Only lately had David allowed himself to admit that his career was not enough, that no matter how well he did at Johnson & Merritt, he would always wonder if the financial rewards which came his way were Ben Johnson's way of keeping Sarah close and dependent.

And then four weeks ago the McNair case had landed on his desk, courtesy of his father-in-law, with an accompanying directive to settle the case as soon as possible. David wasn't sure what concerned him more - how he had ended up in charge of this case or why he was being ordered to settle the claim. None of it had made any sense. He knew he should have immediately contacted Sherry McNair, tried to find out why, or even if, she wanted to settle the case, but he had delayed. And he should have pressed Allison harder for an explanation. All she would tell him was that Ben had removed her from the case, claiming a client complaint. Allison told him she didn't want to talk about it. If he had a question about the case itself, fine, but she wasn't discussing her removal by Ben.

Then today Ben had called him, wanting to know why the case was still on the firm's active case list. The conversation had been troubling, to say the least.

"I told you a month ago to settle this case." Ben had stated in a cold tone. "What did you not understand about that order?"

"I've been trying to get in touch with our client" David fibbed. "I can't see anything in the file indicating that the Defendants have even made a settlement offer. I think settlement at this point may be premature."

"When I want your assessment of a case I'll ask for it" Ben thundered. "Pick up the fucking phone and call Jack Striker. He'll be happy to give you a demand. Get rid of this case before the end of this week. "

"Ben, wait. This isn't like you". *What is going on here?* David thought, hearing the tension in Ben's voice. "I can't settle a case without the client's approval. You know that. I've got to contact our client, and even if I recommend a figure, I can't make her accept it if she doesn't want to."

"That's your problem. I want the case settled and off our books by the end of the week. Make it happen."

Giving a final twist to his Montblanc, David picked up the McNair file and headed to Allison's office. Whether she liked it or not, Allison was going to give him some answers. He might not like what he was about to hear, but David couldn't tone down the warning bells that had started going off in his head. Something was not right about the McNair case, and something sure as hell wasn't right about Ben Johnson's behavior.

Passing by the firm's plush reception area, this afternoon occupied by several clients awaiting appointments, David's eye was drawn to the large oil painting of the firm's founder prominently displayed in the center of the room. David had always thought Ben to be above reproach, but now he wondered. Too often temptation of one sort or another had been the downfall of a successful man. Had something like that happened to Ben? The very thought troubled David, but it seemed the most likely explanation for Ben's insistence on settling a case like McNair which was, in terms of cases, pretty pedestrian. No, David was convinced, there was more here than meets the eye.

"Hey, Donna" David smiled. "Allison granting audiences?"

"You're a hoot, David Jackson" Donna Pevey laughed in reply. "She's working on the brief in the Fairhope appeal. Given the sounds I've heard coming out of her office this afternoon I'm sure you'll be a welcome break."

An hour later David Jackson looked at Allison and quietly sighed "Mother of God. Have you lost your mind? The minute Ben finds out you are investigating him your career is over. Jim being a judge won't help you. No firm in the southeast, much less Alabama, will touch you. Why are you doing this?"

"I'm doing this because it's the right thing to do. Because not only does Sherry McNair not deserve to have her case railroaded, there's something really, really wrong going on here. I know it and so do you."

"Look, I'm bothered by Ben telling me, no ordering me, to settle the McNair case, but I'll make sure our client gets a decent settlement. You don't even know the woman that well. Let it go."

A car horn sounded, interrupting the silence that had overtaken the two partners. Allison crossed to the window, looking over the stalled traffic below, her back to her partner.

"I never took you for a coward, David. Maybe the Johnson money means more to you than having a clean conscience. Just do me one favor. Let me know before you rat me out to your father-in-law." Allison turned, casting a sad look towards her partner. "Now, get out of my office."

⇒⊹ ⊹⇐

The only sound in the Jackson house was the ticking of the old clock on the wall. Glancing up from his seat at the kitchen table, David was startled to see the time. Sarah had gone to bed around ten, and his kids had been down well before that. Unable to sleep, David had been alone with his thoughts for hours, his sole companion the family's yellow cat asleep at his feet.

This business with the McNair file was disturbing, no doubt about it. Ben kicking Allison off the case was inexplicable. David hadn't been a partner very long, but he knew the firm's procedure for handling client complaints, and that Ben Johnson was a stickler for following the rules. David was also bothered by Allison's reaction. Why hadn't she brought this matter to the board? Did any of the other partners know about this? It wasn't like Allison to back away from a fight.

Well, she isn't backing down, is she? he thought, awareness flashing in his mind. *She's just doing it off the grid.*

The question for David, and the reason for his insomnia, was both simple and complex. What was he going to do? Settling the McNair case was something he thought he could live with, particularly if he could get Sherry McNair a good amount of money. Most employment cases settled before trial, so this one would be no different in that regard. He would call Jack Striker in the morning and make a demand.

But what about Ben? What did any of Allison's suspicions matter if David were able to get their client a favorable settlement? So what if Ben had removed Allison from the case? All that mattered was the client, right? But no matter how David posed the question, no matter from which angle he addressed the problem, he couldn't make the red flags disappear from his conscience. What Ben had done not only violated firm policy, it was so completely out of character for the man that David had to wonder if Ben had removed Allison from the McNair case under some sort of duress. Although Allison had been circumspect about what Ben had actually said to her, David had gotten the strong impression that Ben had threatened Allison in some fashion.

If Ben were not his father-in-law, David thought he would not hesitate to assist Allison, at least to some degree. Maybe not all the way to investigating another partner, but he would certainly have urged her to take the matter to the board. Or would he? Had he become so professionally and financially comfortable at Johnson & Merritt that he would have allowed one of his partners to be the victim of what was becoming, in David's mind, a gross abuse of power?

Who are you, buddy? David asked himself. *Has that moral compass of yours been so easily replaced?* A great weariness seemed to bear down upon him, but David had his answer. Whatever the consequences, if Allison asked for help he would give it.

CHAPTER FOURTEEN

The spectacle in the Calhoun County Circuit Court had been amazing. Normally Allison wouldn't have bothered watching a criminal proceeding, and certainly not one in state court. Most of Allison's cases involved violations of civil Federal laws, and so were tried in the Federal District Court in Birmingham. But the Ernestine Senter case had caught her attention, particularly since her husband would be the presiding judge.

Ernestine Senter was eighty years old, a widow, living twenty miles outside Ft. Charles in a mostly rural area. Early last summer Mrs. Senter had been awakened in her bedroom by an intruder who announced to Mrs. Senter his intent to rape her. Allison knew from the news reports that Ms. Senter had defended herself royally, and the would be rapist was soon apprehended. For some reason, unknown except in the feeble mind of the accused, a plea bargain had never been reached in the case, so yesterday Allison's husband Jim had convened court in the case of The State of Alabama vs Chockwe Robinson. The jury had been selected, and opening statements made by both sides before Jim had adjourned for the day, telling the prosecution to be ready to call its first witness at 9:00 the following morning.

Word had travelled fairly quickly as happens in towns the size of Ft. Charles. Every seat in Judge Kaufman's courtroom was taken by 8:45, leaving standing room only for the tardy. Fortunately for Allison, her husband's courtroom deputy had saved her a seat at the end of the first row of spectators. While the Baliff announced "All Rise" Allison had quietly slipped into her seat.

As expected, the prosecutor called Mrs. Senter to the stand as the first witness, starting with the usual mundane questions - name, where she lived, was she married, and so forth. Boring but necessary prerequisites to set the stage for the the meat of Mrs. Senter's testimony. And juicy meat it was, indeed.

According to Mrs. Senter, Chockwe Robinson had broken into her home around one in the morning, stepped into her bedroom naked and had announced his intent to "rob yo' house afta' I fuck yo' skinny white ass." Unfortunately for Chockwe, he had underestimated his victim.

"I got it" Mrs. Senter told the jury. "I grabbed, yanked and twisted that dong all at the same time." Pointing towards the Defendant, Mrs. Senter continued. "He was smacking me this way and that, trying to choke me, but that just made me madder." Turning back towards the jurors, some of whom were now leaning forward in their seats, Mrs. Senter continued. "I grabbed hold of his balls with my other hand and started twisting them the opposite way. It was like turning two faucets. I turned his dong one way and his balls the other." Nodding, Mrs. Senter added "He was screaming pretty good by then."

For the next fifteen minutes an entire courtroom of people sat mesmerized as the white haired octogenarian proceeded to testify about how she had hung onto her attacker as he tried to flee down the hallway of her house towards the locked front door.

"He kept begging me to let him go, but I wasn't born yesterday" Mrs. Senter explained. "I said to him, do you think I'm stupid enough to let you go inside my house?"

After forcing Chockwe to unbolt the two deadlocks on the front door, Mrs. Senter testified that she had given his package another hard twist and pushed him out of her house. "Then, I ran back to the front closet and grabbed my daddy's shotgun. I got off two good shots as he ran out my front yard."

Applause had filled the courtroom at the end of Mrs. Senter's testimony, forcing Allison's husband, who was trying hard to repress a grin, to pound his gavel more than once in order to regain control of his courtroom.

Defense counsel had wisely elected not to cross-examine Mrs. Senter, and the prosecution had continued to call its remaining witnesses. An emergency room doctor from Ft. Charles General had testified that the Defendant had appeared at the hospital's emergency room on the evening in question with buckshot wounds to his buttocks. A county deputy told the jury about responding to Mrs. Senter's 911 call, and described the evidence found at Mrs. Senter's house, including pants and a shirt later identified as belonging to the Defendant. A forensic specialist testified that the tire tracks found in the dirt road beside Mrs. Senter's house matched the tires on the Defendant's 1987 Ford truck. By the time her husband adjourned for the lunch recess the State had rested its case.

Knowing Jim would not have time to eat with her, Allison headed back to the office, confident that justice would be done in the Robinson case, and probably before the end of the day. She doubted there was much the defense could provide to counter the evidence already in front of the jury. In fact, if the jury was out more than thirty minutes before rendering a guilty verdict she would be surprised. She'd find out tonight when Jim got home.

Stopping by the Corner Deli on her way to the office, Allison picked up a gyro and a bag of chips, feeling guilty as she bypassed the cottage cheese and fruit salad. *Next time,* she promised herself. If Allison wanted to stay a size four a bit longer she knew she would have to adjust her eating habits. Thirty-five had brought the first changes to Allison's metabolism. Now, three years later, regular mornings at the gym were a necessity, and desserts a thing of the past. Her husband could eat a package of Oreos and not gain a pound. *What was it with men and their jack rabbit metabolisms? It wasn't fair* Allison lamented.

Back in her office, Allison unwrapped her lunch and hit the play button on her phone to retrieve the waiting message the blinking light indicated.

"Allison, it's Frank Martin. I have some materials I think will interest you. Let me know how you want to handle this."

Allison yawned. She hadn't been able to look at the report on Steve Miller until almost ten, and now it was past midnight. Having a home office allowed Allison to put in extra hours away from the firm, but unless she was in the midst of a trial Allison never picked up a work file until her children were in bed and she and Jim had enjoyed at least thirty minutes of one-on-one time over a cup of decaf coffee or tea. Family time was too important. This evening Jim had shared the afternoon's proceedings in the Ernestine Senter case, including the twenty minute record breaking time taken by the jury before returning a guilty verdict. Now, looking over the pages she had picked up from Frank Martin's office on her way home, Allison reflected on what she had read.

Steve Miller's criminal background was, and was not, a surprise. Miller would hardly be the first man to have had a run in with the law as a teen. Allison knew a couple of boys from Sumner who had gotten in trouble over minor vandalism when she was in high school. Both had grown into decent, law abiding men, one after a stint in the Marines, and the other after a few more lessons in the school of hard knocks. What was a surprise to Allison about Steve Miller's past was the nature of the crime for which he had been arrested. Murder for hire was a serious crime. The fact that Miller had pled to a lesser charge told Allison that while there hadn't been enough evidence for a conviction, there had been enough evidence to prevent Miller and some guy named Jeff Bishop from walking free.

Reviewing the report's concluding paragraph a second time, Allison pondered Frank's suggestion that public knowledge of Steve Miller's past could negatively impact the upcoming public stock offering for Miller Industries. Allison tended to agree with Frank's assessment. Investors might be leery of buying stock in a company whose CEO had tried to have someone killed, even if he had been a punk kid of sixteen at the time. Leopards didn't change their spots, and investors were a nervous bunch. If a guy didn't blink at murder for hire, surely he wouldn't blink at stock fraud. Yes, thought Allison, that kind of information could be very detrimental to Steve Miller and his company.

Assuming that's what Miller is trying to hide, how in the world is this connected to the McNair case? Allison asked herself. *And why would Ben Johnson kick me off the case?*

The name Jeff Bishop sounded familiar. Had she seen that name somewhere before? Surveying the stacks of different colored folders littering the floor of her workspace - complete copies of the entire McNair file courtesy of Donna Pevey's after hours work - Allison retrieved a pale green folder marked "Miller Text Communications". *Maybe in here*, she thought.

A hand on her shoulder caused Allison to jump.

"Babe, it's 1:00 in the morning." Jim gently massaged Allison's neck and shoulders. "You need to come to bed."

"I know. The time just got away from me. I didn't mean to keep you up."

Moving his hands under Allison's shoulders, Jim cupped Allison's breasts. "Speaking of being up, maybe you could help me with that."

"You're such a devil" Allison laughed. Turning to meet her husband's embrace, Allison pressed her body against the length of Jim's bulging erection, her mouth seeking her husband's lips.

"Are you objecting, counselor?" Jim inquired.

"Never, my love" Allison whispered, as they moved towards the bedroom. "Never." She'd figure out who Jeff Bishop was another time.

CHAPTER FIFTEEN

2010

B en Johnson paid the first ten thousand Chris Cannon demanded. He paid the second, and then the third. But when the demand for thirty thousand came Ben knew he had to do something. At this rate there was no way he could hide the payments from his wife, and besides, who was to say the next demand wouldn't be for even more? The problem, Ben acknowledged, was how to stop the blackmail without revealing his secret life.

The solution had presented itself to Ben one morning in February while reading the Sunday paper. Ensconced in slippers and his favorite plaid bathrobe, morning coffee in hand, a fire crackling in the keeping room fireplace, Ben's eye was caught by a headline on page 2: "*Body Found in Woods*". Although the victim had been identified through dental records as a man missing for three years, the remains had been so decomposed that authorities had no way to determine cause of death, or whether the man had died where his remains had been found or the body dumped there post mortem. All the investigation had revealed was that the man had lived in Rome, Georgia at the time he was reported missing. Calls to the Rome police had been dead ends. The deceased had been an insurance salesman with a wide territory in north Georgia. No known enemies. No estranged wife or jealous husbands, so far as anyone knew. The manner and reason for the man's death would likely remain a mystery.

Perfect thought Ben. *Absolutely perfect.*

The fact that he was contemplating murder caused a twinge in Ben's conscience, and Ben wondered if he could really commit such an atrocity. *No*, he answered, he knew he couldn't pull the trigger, but he also knew he was more than willing to pay someone else to do the deed for him. Too much was at stake to worry about morality now. Considering the risks of failure, Ben knew his plan would need to be impeccable and completely untraceable to him. Chris Cannon's body would need to be disposed of far from Ft. Charles, far from Birmingham, maybe even far away from Alabama. The assassin would have to be patient locating, tracking and then ambushing the target without drawing attention at any point in the assignment. There were professionals who would take this sort of job. Ben just needed to find one. A job like this would be expensive, Ben was sure of that, but paying a hundred grand or more to rid himself permanently of his blackmailer would be worth every single penny.

To Ben's surprise and relief, it had not taken more than a couple of weeks to locate the right man. Afraid to plant even the tiniest seed of suspicion in the mind of his fellow lawyers, Ben had looked outside the Ft. Charles legal community to make his initial inquiries. What he needed was a contact in the criminal network, someone who could be trusted to make discreet inquiries, someone who would keep silent for a price, someone who crossed the ethics line when need or cash required. And then Ben remembered Dickie.

Dickie Lott was a Mississippi criminal trial lawyer. Raised on the wrong side of the tracks on the Mississippi Gulf Coast, Dickie had been one of Ben's classmates at Cumberland School of Law. Dickie's ticket to higher education had been a sharp intelligence, and he had graduated near the top of his class just like Ben. And, like Ben, Dickie had become a wealthy lawyer. However, where Ben had assumed the quiet but understated life of the wealthy gentry, Dickie had flaunted an opulent lifestyle in Biloxi, Mississippi, complete with yacht, private jet and cattle ranch in Wyoming.

Hiring Dickie Lott cost a bundle. No run of the mill criminals graced the offices of The Lott Firm. A retainer started at fifty grand, depending on the nature of the crime Dickie's client was alleged to have committed. The final bill presented to a client of The Lott Firm typically exceeded half a million dollars. No one complained. Juries loved Dickie Lott. His win rate was near 90% and even the worst of Dickie's clients had escaped the death penalty.

Although impossible to substantiate, Dickie was rumored to have ties to the Mississippi Mafia, an organization thought by law enforcement to control many of the illegal gambling and prostitution activities that had financially supported the Gulf coast area before the advent of legalized boat gambling. After the Mississippi Legislature had made boat gambling an extra source of state revenue, the Mississippi Mafia had expanded its drug trade to compensate for its loss of gambling income. Even the criminal element understood the need to diversify in a changing economy. If such an organization actually existed, Ben was certain Dickie Lott could open the proverbial door for him. For a price.

Although almost forty years had passed since Ben and Dickie had attended law school together, their paths had continued to cross every few years at law school reunions, legal conferences, and political fundraisers on the national level. Getting access to Dickie would not be a problem. How to couch his request to give Dickie plausible deniability - should the need ever arise - would require some thought. Ben spent several days devising, and then discarding, elaborate cloak and dagger scenarios of the approach and pitch he would use to ensure that if anyone ever inquired, Dickie could truthfully swear that he and Ben had only discussed some interesting criminal cases one afternoon over cocktails, rather than the names of possible assassins for hire. Finally Ben realized that the safest course was the one that should have occurred to him at the very start. He would simply hire Dickie as his lawyer, effectively shielding any conversations he might have with Dickie under the protection of the attorney-client privilege. No matter what Ben said to Dickie, no matter what Dickie said to him - no court could or would compel Dickie to reveal what Ben had said to him. Chiding himself for being a bit paranoid - after all, Ben thought, the odds of him or Dickie being caught or prosecuted for murder would be one in a million - having the attorney-client protection added an additional level of insurance. Fifty grand was a lot of money, but Ben figured he would get his money's worth and more. Being rid of Chris Cannon was worth a bundle.

A few minutes on his computer easily yielded Dickie's phone number.

"The Lott Firm. How may I direct your call" a pleasant female voice asked.

"This is Ben Johnson from Johnson & Merritt in Ft. Charles, Alabama. Put me through to Dickie, please."

"May I tell Mr. Lott the nature of your call Mr. Johnson?" the voice politely inquired.

"No, you may not" Ben brusquely replied. "This is a personal matter."

"One moment please" came the unruffled response.

Tapping his fingers on the desk in front of him, Ben sulked. He didn't like being in the position of supplicant, which was the exact feeling he had gotten from Dickie's receptionist. Did she really think he would tell a telephone operator the nature of his business? A click on the line and hearty hello interrupted Ben's inner dialogue.

"Ben Johnson. To what do I owe this honor?" Dickie chuckled. "The last time I saw you was at the ABA conference in L.A."

"That was two years ago, I think. Hard to keep track of time anymore" Ben worked hard to keep his voice light and his tone upbeat. "I've got a matter I think you might be able to help me with, Dickie." Ben paused, *Come on Ben, don't chicken out now.* "I'd like to retain you for a particular matter, and I'd like to set up a meeting with you next week in Chattanooga to discuss it."

"Chattanooga? Why there" Dickie asked in a puzzled tone. "What's wrong with you coming to Biloxi? That's a hell of a lot closer for you, or me for that matter, than Chattanooga."

"This is a matter of utmost delicacy. Highly confidential. It's imperative that I not be seen at your office, or you at mine." Ben continued. "I've got business in Chattanooga next Tuesday. I'll book us a private dining room at the Mountain City Club."

Checking his calendar Dickie agreed. "Not a problem, but my travel costs in the King Air will be added to your retainer. See you Tuesday."

Chartered in 1889, The Mountain City Club was one of the oldest private clubs in the country. As with so many of the clubs of its sort, membership was by invitation and restricted to "men only" members until a prominent Chattanooga business woman broke that particular glass ceiling in 1992. The building housing the original club had been demolished some forty or so years earlier, and was now replaced by a well appointed brick structure patterned after the governor's palace in Williamsburg, Virginia. A place of quiet and dignified repose, members were circumspect and discrete, making the club the perfect setting for private meetings. As a member of The Summit Club in Birmingham, Ben had used his club's reciprocity agreement with The Mountain City Club on several occasions to host dinners or conduct private meetings when in Chattanooga on legal business. Ben felt certain that one of the intimate dining rooms in the Chattanooga club would provide him complete privacy, and anonymity, for his meeting with Dickie.

Ben had been right about the privacy. A single, discreet waiter had served them a delicious grilled salmon, perfectly cooked to a warm pink, accompanied by roasted asparagus and a wild rice casserole. Conversation during the meal remained light as the men discussed the fall football season for their respective state universities and lamented the lack of leadership in Washington. Only after coffee and key lime pie had been served, and the waiter dismissed, did the conversation turn serious. To Ben's surprise, and relief, Dickie acted as if people contacted him regularly for the names of assassins for hire. *Shit, maybe they do* Ben thought, trying to match Dickie's nonchalance.

"Here's a billing statement for today's meeting" Dickie explained, handing Ben an invoice prepared on stationary bearing the imprint *The Lott Firm*. "I've opened a client matter number for you. There won't be anything in the files other than a copy of this statement reflecting our meeting today."

"Good" Ben folded the invoice and placed it inside his suit jacket. "That will be sufficient to invoke the attorney-client privilege." Noticing Dickie's grin, Ben retorted "I know you think I'm being paranoid. I'm not." Pushing away from the table and retrieving his briefcase Ben added "I'm just being careful. Jail does not interest me."

The steeple bell on St. Paul's Church, a few blocks away on Seventh Street, rang two o'clock as the men exited the club. Surveying the packed parking lot, Dickie remarked "It's a good thing I took a cab from the airport. Is this the usual lunch crowd?"

"No." Ben replied. "The maitre'd told me there's a meeting of the board of directors and executive officers for the Tennessee Bankers Association here today. Meetings all day, and lunch in the main dining room." Ben laughed. "Maybe I should ask one of the members for a loan."

"Yeh, right" Dickie replied. "What would you say when they asked you why you needed the money?"

"Here comes your cab" Ben responded, ignoring Dickie's question. "Have a pleasant flight back to Biloxi."

Twenty minutes later, heading down I-24 towards Ft. Charles, Ben reflected on the day's meeting. Dickie had provided him two names and numbers, name two as a backup if the first choice declined the job. Both men were professionals. Both knew the consequences of getting caught. No matter which man took the job, Ben knew he would not have to worry about being given up to the authorities in the event the man was ever caught for Chris Cannon's murder. The amount of money Ben was paying for this service ensured that his name would never be mentioned. Ever.

CHAPTER SIXTEEN

Present Day

D arkness came early these days for Matthew
Parker. Time was running out for him, a reality the rapidly shortening November days served only
to reinforce. Bill James had been right - Matthew's
strength was fading quickly, seemingly in reverse proportion to the increasing pain in his gut. The narcotics helped him get a few hours of sleep at night, but
taking them all the time wasn't an option for Matthew.
No, he needed a clear head for the task in front of him.

Glancing at the black notebook lying open on the
kitchen table, Matthew reflected on what he wanted to
say. So many regrets. So many should-haves. Looking
back now was almost unbearable. Laying aside his

unlit pipe, Matthew watched his trembling hand reach for the ever present cup of black coffee. *Caffeine and nicotine* thought Matthew. *A dying man's amphetamines.* Matthew knew he owed Helene the biggest amends of all. If God really existed, and heaven and hell along with Him, Matthew doubted he'd have an opportunity to make that amends to Helene in the hereafter. Matthew didn't believe for a minute that Helene's suicide would have foreclosed her from heaven. Helene had been a gentle soul, and he had pressed the life out of her as surely as if he had poured the pills and wine down her throat. If there was anything across the veil other than a dark, cold grave Matthew was pretty certain he and Helene wouldn't be in the same place.

Why had he been such a shit all his life? That was the million dollar question that had begun to haunt Matthew's waking hours. And not just to Helene. His daughter despised him, and his son had lost his way. Matthew hated to admit the truth, but a terminal diagnosis had that sort of clarifying effect on a man. Matthew had failed as a husband and father. All that had mattered to him had been his own status and wealth. He had manipulated, punished, ridiculed and rejected everyone who failed to meet his own selfish needs. Matthew sighed. He knew he was powerless to change the past. But maybe, just maybe, he could do something about the future, even if he didn't have much time left to live in it.

Setting up a Trust for Rice had been a start, although Matthew knew Rice didn't see it that way. Matthew had known about Rice's drug habit for a long time. Only Matthew's long standing relationship with the Sumner County Sheriff, and a ten thousand dollar contribution to the Sheriff's re-election campaign, had prevented Rice from being arrested. That knowledge, coupled with what Charlene Ellis had recently confided to him about Rice's check kiting and involvement in the stock scheme with the Evans boy in Jackson weighed heavily on his mind. Matthew had lost count of the number of times he had paid Rice's creditors or supported Rice's family after Rice lost yet another job. Hundreds of thousands of dollars spent over the past twenty years, just so he would not be embarrassed by Rice's failures. *I have ruined my son*, Matthew thought gazing out the window at the brown pasture grass, barely visible as the autumn sun slipped towards the horizon. *And it's too late to change him.* At least Rice would never starve, and no matter what else happened to him, Rice wouldn't end up on the street. Allison and Jim would take their responsibilities seriously, regardless of what they thought about Matthew, or for that matter, what they thought about Rice.

But he still had a chance with Allison, didn't he? After all, she had agreed to let him spend his last days at the farm. That had to mean something. Of course, Matthew reflected, Allison understood about duty.

That was why he had chosen her and Jim to manage Rice's trust. Was that why she had finally acquiesced to his request to move to the guest house? Was duty Allison's only motivation? Matthew couldn't bear to think so.

"Janice." Matthew called to the nurse in the adjacent room. "Bring me my cell phone, would you? I need to call my daughter."

Allison didn't know what to make of the afternoon's call from her father. He hadn't said much, just asked her when she would be home.

"Is there something you need, Daddy?" she had inquired. "Are you okay?"

Allison heard the intake of labored breathing, then a weary "I'm fine. I just wanted to know when you'd be home."

"I probably can't get out of here until six or so." Distant alarm bells had begun to ring in Allison's head. This sort of conversation was so unlike Matthew. "Are you hurting? Where is Janice?"

"Can't a man want to spend some time with his only daughter?" Matthew's gruff reply and tone had reassured Allison. "Everybody acts like I'm going to die any minute. I'm not going anywhere anytime soon."

"I'll see you before seven, Daddy" Allison replied as the conversation ended. *What in the world is going on?*

Four hours later, standing in the dark on the guest house porch, Allison paused to gather her thoughts. Conflicting emotions swirled in her mind and heart, love and hate competing for first place in her affections, or lack thereof, for the man who had given her life. *Whatever it is, just accept it* she told herself. *Don't get angry. Just let it go, no matter what.*

"Come in" Matthew called in response to Allison's quiet knock. "That you, Allison?"

"It's me Daddy" Allison replied bending to kiss her father's cheek. "Janice, why don't you go on and leave now?" Allison suggested to her father's nurse. "Lorraine will be here at eight. I'll sit with Daddy til she she gets here." Whatever her father wanted to say, Allison knew he wouldn't talk in front of Janice. Allison doubted even a terminal illness could change Matthew's penchant for privacy.

"Thanks, Allison" Janice replied. "This will give me a chance to run by Walmart on the way home before it's too late."

Waiting for Janice to gather her belongings, Allison settled into one of the room's large clubstyle chairs. A cozy blend of consignment store treasures and a few pieces from Allison's grandmother, the guest house seemed to wrap its arms around its inhabitants. Out of town guests or local friends who needed to stay over rather than drive home after parties proclaimed the farm's guest house to be the best B&B around. *I'll have to have it cleansed after he passes* thought Allison. *It would be just like Daddy to hang around after he's supposed to have passed over.* Smiling wryly at her superstitions, Allison waited for her father to speak.

"I want to talk to you about your mother" Matthew began after Janice had bid him goodnight. "Hear me out, Allison." Matthew raised his hand to stop Allison's objection. "I know you blame me for your mother's suicide. And probably rightly so. But I want ..." Matthew hesitated, "no ... I need to talk to you about your mother and me. About how it was a long time ago. Before things changed."

No words came to Allison's lips. Blinking back tears, both of anger and sadness, all Allison could permit herself was a nod of the head.

"I can still remember when I first saw your mother. There was a dinner dance at Castle in the Clouds on the back of Lookout Mountain, near Chattanooga. Your mother had a date with one of my old fraternity brothers. She was wearing a yellow dress....."

"Who is that gorgeous gal in yellow dancing with Earl McClannahan?" Matthew Parker inquired, taking a quick drag on his cigarette. "She's a knockout."

"That's Helene Cecilio" Jack Hutchison replied. "She's here visiting her cousin Mamie Kitchens."

Matthew sipped his bourbon, watching keenly as his old fraternity brother Earl monopolized Helene's attention, one dance after another. Earl can't be that funny, Matthew thought, as Helene tossed her head in laughter, apparently in response to some remark her partner had made. *Enough of this*, Matthew concluded, walking towards the couple. "Mind if I cut in, Earl, old buddy?" he asked, taking Helene's hand.

Leading Helene away in a graceful waltz, Matthew addressed his startled partner.

"I believe introductions are in order. I'm Matthew Parker. An old friend of Earl's." Matthew smiled "I couldn't let Earl keep all this beauty to himself."

"Are you always this forward?" Helene replied, her smile softening the mild reprimand in her question.

"Only when I am compelled by someone as lovely and intriguing as you, Helene Cecilio."

"Ah. I see you know my name." Helene's dark hair swung from her shoulders as Matthew executed a dip. "What else, pray tell, do you know about me, Mr. Parker?"

"Nothing, other than the date of our wedding." Matthew laughed, seeing Helene's look of surprise. "Don't be so shocked" he had added. "I can be very persuasive. And I usually get what I want."

And persuasive he was. Not a day passed that Matthew did not see or talk to Helene, even after he returned to Sumner and she to Sweetwater. Matthew sent so many flower arrangements to Helene's house that soon there were no flat surfaces on which to display them. "That boy certainly is persistent" Helene's mother had correctly observed. Thirty days after Matthew had first glimpsed "that gorgeous gal in yellow", Helene Cecilio became Mrs. Matthew Parker.

"I know you and mom only dated for a month before you married. Did you really love her, Daddy, or was she just another thing to be collected?" Matthew heard the bitterness in Allison's question. "I know she tried to leave you when I was a baby. …. Didn't know I knew about that did you?" she added, seeing the startled look on her father's face. Allison felt anger rising inside herself. "If you really loved her, like you claim, why did she want to leave? What really happened?"

"I don't know." Matthew's head sagged. "Honest to God, I don't know." Raising himself slowly from his chair, Matthew shuffled to the kitchen to refill his cup with coffee. "I got jealous, I guess. Everyone loved your mother, and she loved everyone else. Always helping at the church, volunteering at the homeless shelter."

Matthew turned to face Allison, his eyes seeing another scene. "I couldn't share her. I just couldn't."

"You suffocated her." A deep grief filled Allison as she grasped an inkling of understanding. "No one could have lived like that, Daddy, not even someone who loved you."

"I know that now" Matthew's answer was barely a whisper. "Why couldn't I have known it then?"

Helping her father to his chair, Allison reached for Matthew's hand. *Skin and bones,* she thought, startled by the brittle fingers that wrapped around her own. "I don't know how to answer that question, Daddy. I guess it doesn't really matter anyway."

"Yes, it does" Matthew replied, anguish and sorrow almost palpable in his voice. "It has to."

CHAPTER SEVENTEEN

The worn hinges creaked as Frank Martin opened the heavy oak door and stepped into his darkened reception area. *Gotta get those suckers oiled* he thought wryly. *Worn hinges for a worn out old man.* Frank wasn't that old - only fifty-seven - but the years of PI work had taken their toll. Sometimes, when his knees and back ached like they did this morning, Frank felt like he was a hundred years old. Still, he wouldn't have traded his career for any others he could think of. No sitting behind a desk all day for Frank, even if the trade-off meant cold nights on surveillance duty. Frank thrived on solving puzzles, and being a private investigator had provided him that opportunity on a regular basis. Over the years Frank had more than once remarked to a few close friends that being paid to do work he loved seemed almost wrong. Almost.

The office security system chirped as Frank punched in the alarm code and pressed one to disarm the system. In his line of work, client files were highly confidential, particularly given how Frank often obtained his information. More than one P.I. office in town had been burglarized, with nothing other than one or two client files being removed each time. Taking extra precautions in the field had saved Frank on more than one occasion. He saw no reason not to extend that philosophy to guarding the secrets maintained in his office filing cabinets.

Walking into his office proper, Frank tossed his overcoat over the dark blue chair closest to his desk. The chair's twin, on the far side of the desk, overflowed with green accordion files Frank had abandoned the preceding night. A brown leather sofa hugged the wall opposite, years of client repose, and Frank's afternoon naps, evidenced by its sagging springs and gently worn demeanor. Early morning light above a battered credenza behind Frank's desk offered the room's only illumination.

Frank had always been an early riser. The quiet and solitude of five a.m. had often provided the perfect stimulus for a mental breakthrough on a case. While he waited for the coffee maker to finish perking the morning's first pot, Frank considered the information before him. If the internet searches, legal magazines, and newspaper articles were accurate, Ben Johnson was the poster boy for hard work and success. Starting his legal career as a sole practitioner, Ben Johnson had spent the next forty years building one of the southeast's most prestigious full service law firms. Consistently ranked in the top five of regional business firms, Johnson & Merritt's client list was a who's who of Fortune 500 names. No hint of scandal, impropriety or malpractice had sullied either Ben Johnson or his firm. Johnson & Merritt was rock solid.

Likewise, Frank's research on Ben Johnson's private life had been equally unproductive, at least as far as providing anything unusual or questionable. Long term and apparently stable marriage to the daughter of a Federal judge, active on community civic boards, deacon at First Baptist Church, member of Ft. Charles Country Club - all to be expected of a successful businessman in Ben Johnson's position.

Hell, Frank thought, sipping his coffee, *no one is that squeaky clean. What have I missed? Something before Ft. Charles?*

Once again, Frank skimmed the papers before him. Nothing, absolutely nothing, looked out of the ordinary. Nothing at all until Frank's inner eye began to see a tiny red flag waving at the periphery of his field of vision - Ben and Linda Johnson's wedding announcement in the Ft. Charles Gazette. How had he missed that before? Although Linda's lineage was prominently displayed in Gazette's announcement, there was no similar mention of Ben Johnson's family - no parents, deceased or living, no siblings, no grandparents - and no indication of Ben's hometown or life before Ft. Charles. Such a lapse in the listing of heritage or place might not be unusual in other parts of the country, but family and place of birth were as much a part of the south as shrimp and grits. Many a transplanted northerner had been surprised to hear a new neighbor ask "Who's your family?" or "Where are you from?" as a complement to the cake or fresh bread brought as a housewarming gift. So ingrained was this sort of societal marking that Frank couldn't remember ever seeing a southern wedding announcement that didn't include a listing of both the bride's and groom's family.

By noon Frank had called in favors from two old clients, both men skilled in "navigating" records normally considered confidential and generally unobtainable absent a court order. His next step would require travel, and he'd need to clear it with Allison.

"Hello, Frank" Allison answered after the second ring.

"You clairvoyant or something?" Frank inquired.

"Nope" Allison laughed. "It's caller ID. I can't believe you of all people wouldn't know about that little invention."

"I know, I know." Frank allowed. "I just can't get used to someone answering the phone and knowing it's me before they hear my voice."

"I'll remember to act surprised the next time you call." Allison chuckled.

"Are you where you can talk freely?" Frank asked, his voice conveying a more serious tone.

"Yes. What is it?"

"What do you know about Ben Johnson's family"

Allison thought for a minute. "Not much. I think his mother was a school teacher somewhere in Arkansas, or maybe Louisiana? I'm not sure about how I know that, just that he isn't from Alabama."

"I was at a dead end investigating Ben" Frank replied. "Everything I could find out about him just reinforced his public image. Good guy, upstanding citizen. And then I realized I wasn't seeing anything about his life growing up. No mention of family, or where he came from, or anything."

"Well, is that so unusual?" Allison questioned. "And anyway, what would that have to do with Ben throwing me off the McNair case?"

"I can't answer that question yet" Frank admitted. "But there was something not sitting right with me about Ben's past so I did some digging this morning. Ben was born in Greenwood, Arkansas. I've got his parents' names, and while they're almost surely dead, it's a lead on any siblings and other relatives. Maybe people still living there who knew him growing up"

"And you're thinking about going over there. Is that why you called?"

"Yes. It's your dime, but I think this is important. I don't know why yet, or how, but my gut tells me I need to look at Ben's past more closely."

"If you think you need to put boots on the ground, then do it" Allison replied. "That's why I hired you."

"I'll head out first thing in the morning." Frank replied, pulling up google maps on his computer. "I'll be there by early afternoon."

Located in the far western part of the state, Greenwood, Arkansas was a small town with big ideas. One of two county seats in Sebastian County, and with a population of less than ten thousand, Greenwood's current claim to fame was an outstanding AA high school football team. Not many schools as small as Greenwood High could boast of seventeen consecutive playoff appearances since 1996, nor of seven football championships in the same period. Frank remembered reading about some high school all-Americans from Greenwood who had been recruited by the University of Arkansas, one of whom, Tyler Wilson, had made it to the NFL. Football wasn't Greenwood's only claim to fame. A six foot tall bronze statue of a coal miner, complete with authentic coal car and two large slabs of granite, graced the town square, an everlasting tribute to the role coal mining had played in the early history of Sebastian County. Although most of the mines in Sebastian County had closed, two sites had remained active as recently as 2007. *Wonder if any of Ben Johnson's kin were miners?* Frank pondered as he drove into town. *That would be something Ben Johnson would likely be ashamed of, wouldn't it? But what would that have to do with Allison and the McNair case?*

Parking on a sidestreet, Frank headed towards the small cafe he had noticed on the square. Experience had proven that small town waitresses often provided a wealth of information. Settling into a corner booth, Frank perused the cafe's clientele. Two old guys at the counter, a younger couple in the far booth. At two in the afternoon, Frank was well past the lunch crowd and far too early for even the five o'clock diners.

"Hey, hon. What can I get you?" a white haired waitress inquired, pad and pen poised for Frank's order.

"Coffee, black, to start. Y'all have any pie left?" Frank asked in a friendly tone.

"Lawd, yes." the waitress replied. "We have the best pies in Sebastian County. Blueberry, apple, fruits of the forest, and key lime today."

"What's fruits of the forest?" Frank asked, visions of men in tutus dancing in the woods invading his imagination. "I'm almost afraid to ask."

"Oh, you!" Jack's waitress laughed. "That's just a pie with strawberry rhubarb, blueberry and cherry combined. We've only got one piece left. It goes fast."

"Okay. Bring her on" Frank smiled congenially. "Sounds good."

Frank lingered over his pie and coffee, engaging his waitress in small talk each time she refilled his mug. Gauging her age at early to mid sixties, Frank thought there was a good chance the waitress would have known Ben Johnson and maybe Ben's family. When she appeared to top off his coffee for the fourth time Frank ventured a question.

"Is Greenwood your home?"

"Sure is. Born and raised. My granddaddy moved here from North Carolina back when mining was the big industry here. What about you? Just passing through?"

"Yep" Frank lied easily. "On my way back to Ft. Charles, Alabama. Say, you wouldn't have known a guy by the name of Ben Johnson would you? He lives in Ft. Charles now and is from these parts."

"How old a man would he be?"

"Mid sixties. He's a pretty successful lawyer there. Got his own firm and all." Taking a sip of coffee, Frank added "I think his mother was a school teacher here."

The waitress frowned "Greenwood's a small place. I only remember one boy named Ben Johnson, 'bout my age if I rightly recollect. His family lived out in the trailer park off Highway 71. His mother wasn't no school teacher."

"I could have sworn I'd heard his mother taught at the high school" Frank prodded.

"Wait, now that you say that, I think Ben lived with one of the teachers his last couple of years in high school. Can't say which one, though. I wasn't much for school myself."

"Well, that sounds strange. Wonder why he did that?" Frank inquired.

Leaning across the table, the waitress lowered her voice. "He was a smart one, now that I think back on him. But, there were rumors about that boy too. Unnatural stuff. Mayhap his family kicked him out."

"Unnatural?"

"Him and another boy, Sammy Deal." The waitress placed Frank's bill on the table. "I shouldn't be carrying tales. Rumors is rumors, nothing more."

Frank had spent the rest of the day locating the high school, then settling into his motel room for some online research. If Ben Johnson and Sammy Deal had known each other in school, Deal would likely have been fairly close to Ben Johnson's age. Connecting to the motel's wifi Frank had run the name "Sammy Deal", limiting the search parameters to men between the ages of sixty-three and sixty-eight currently living in Arkansas.

Three hits had appeared. Thirty minutes later, after further research, Frank had narrowed his search to one. Sammy Deal, age sixty-four, hometown Greenwood, Arkansas, had to be his man. According to Deal's LinkedIn profile, Sammy Deal was the owner of The Limelight Club in Little Rock. A few more strokes of the keyboard, and The Limelight Club's Facebook page filled the screen. Although captioned as "a discreet and intimate atmosphere for those enjoying an alternative lifestyle" the pub style cover photo suggested more of a gentlemen's club atmosphere. The page was scarce. Just announcements about entertainment and club hours. There was no doubt, however, as to who the target audience might be.

Well, well, well. Frank smiled. *What do we have here?* Frank bookmarked the club's Facebook page. He would detour through Little Rock on his way back to Ft. Charles, a meeting with Mr. Deal added to his agenda.

Frank hoped his second day in Greenwood would be as productive as the first. The information he had uncovered about Sammy Deal definitely had promise, but Frank wasn't finished looking at Ben Johnson's early life. Today he planned to visit Greenwood High. It had been almost fifty years since Ben Johnson had been a student there. Frank doubted anyone working there then would still be there, but stranger things had happened in an investigation. Frank thought it much more likely someone might remember a teacher who would have taken a student into her home. A teacher who might have remained a school employee for many years after Ben had graduated. If he was lucky, Frank hoped, he would find someone who knew both Ben and the mystery teacher.

"Morning, ma'am" Frank nodded at the young woman behind the counter in the school office. "My name's Frank Martin. Is the principal available?"

"If you'll take a seat on that bench over there I'll check with Mr. Michaels. Can I tell him what this is about?"

"I'm working on a book about famous graduates from small town schools." Frank smiled benignly, "Just wondered if I could interview the principal. And maybe a few of the teachers."

People seldom turned down an opportunity to be interviewed. Frank had never quite figured out the attraction, but using the line about writing a book had always loosened the tongues of people who normally would not have shared information with a stranger.

The eager look on the face of the gray haired man approaching him indicated another willing interviewee.

"I'm Steven Michaels, principal of Greenwood High" the man introduced himself, shaking Frank's hand. "Sally tells me you're writing a book about some of our graduates."

"It's a book about small town schools in general." Frank replied "I'm looking at graduates from small schools across the south who have distinguished themselves in sports, academia and business. Sort of a heart of America type of story"

"How'd you pick Greenwood High?" the principal inquired.

Frank had prepared for this sort of question. "According to my research, Greenwood High has two very successful graduates. Tyler Wilson has made a name for himself in pro football with the Tennessee Titans and Ben Johnson has built a successful law practice over in Alabama. Wilson is a fairly current graduate, while Mr. Johnson would have graduated back in the sixties. I believe readers will be interested in both of these men's background stories."

"Bring us some coffee, would you Sally?" the principal called over his shoulder. Turning back to Jack, he motioned towards his office "Glad to help in any way I can."

Principal Michaels had been more than cooperative. So cooperative that Frank felt a twinge of embarrassment over the ruse he had used with the man. By the time Frank pulled away from the school parking lot he had interviewed two teachers, a cafeteria worker, and the football coach. The coach and one of the teachers had been a waste of time, but necessary for the charade since Frank was supposed to be writing about Tyler Wilson. The other teacher, Mrs. Schmidt, remembered Ben Johnson's family because she had taught one of his younger siblings.

"Complete trailer trash" Mrs. Schmidt had disdainfully commented. "I had just received my teaching degree and started here at Greenwood when I had the last of those hellions in my class. I had heard about Ben, the oldest brother. Smart boy. Hard to believe they were from the same family."

But Frank had hit the jackpot - no pun intended he thought - when he interviewed Della Mae Pickens. Della Mae had started her working career as a server in the school cafeteria when she was fifteen years old. Thanks to the age discrimination laws passed in the 1990's, an employer could no longer fire someone for getting old. Della Mae was still coming to work at the age of seventy-seven. Lean and dark haired, her barely lined face belied the years the calendar had marked as hers.

"I remember Ben Johnson." Della Mae had told Frank. "And I remember Betty Parrish, God Bless her soul. Miz Parrish saved that boy, sure as anything.

Took him into her home, treated him like her own 'chile. Talk 'round here was she left him all she had when she passed."

On his way out of town, Frank had stopped by the courthouse. Betty Parrish's will would have been probated and therefore accessible as a public record. The probate clerk had logged Frank's request and taken his money. "The Parrish file is in storage" the clerk told him. "Files from the seventies are paper files. Not computerized like today. We store those off site." It would take a few days to retrieve, she told Frank, but she would send him a copy of the file as soon as she could.

Punching a Little Rock address into the car's GPS, Frank considered all he had been told. *Okay, so he's from a bad family. Bad enough to lie about.* Frank strummed his fingers on the steering wheel. Ben Johnson wouldn't be the first person to be ashamed of where they'd come from. *What else? Something that might show up in Betty Parrish's will?* He'd have to wait until he got a copy of the probate file to see about that part of the equation, but if Della Mae had been right and Betty Parrish had left Ben Johnson her estate, so what? Hard to see how a young Ben Johnson could have forced the woman to do something like that. Whoever had prepared Betty Parrish's will would have seen through shenanigans such as taking an old woman to the proverbial cleaners. No, it had to be something else. *Time to talk to Sammy Deal* Frank muttered heading the car towards Little Rock.

CHAPTER EIGHTEEN

I can't ignore this any longer. David Jackson told himself for the umpteenth time. Judge Lee had issued a Case Management Order for the McNair case. If he couldn't get the case settled like Ben Johnson had demanded, David was going to have to start the pretrial discovery process to stay in compliance with Judge Lee's order. David wasn't sure what would actually be worse - facing his father-in-law's wrath or being held in contempt by Judge Lee.

Yesterday David had spoken with Sherry McNair.

"I don't want my job back". Sherry had been definite about that. "I'd work on a pig farm before I worked for that jerk again."

"That's a plus for us in settlement negotiations. Most employers balk at taking back an employee who has sued them."

"Allison never talked to me about settling. Is something wrong with my case? Is that why she's not handling it anymore?"

Hearing the concern in Sherry's voice, and wanting to avoid addressing Allison's absence from the case, David had quickly replied "No, no. Nothing is wrong with your case. I just think it's a good practice to see if we can settle up front before incurring expenses that you would have to pay down the line if we lost at trial."

David had hated playing the money card against Sherry, making her worry about incurring expenses in the case, but he hadn't had a choice. He needed her approval to settle the case. He would get her the best settlement he could, and deal with his guilty conscience later. The problem was timing. Going to Jack Striker at this point in the case, before any depositions had been been taken or written discovery exchanged, placed David in a weak bargaining position. He would be lucky to get his client thirty grand.

Well, start high. David told himself, dialing the number for Jack Striker's law office. *I can always come down. Better than leaving money on the table.*

"Hello, David. Good to hear from you." Jack Striker answered after his secretary had transferred David's call.

"Hey, Jack. How are you?" David replied. Although neither man particularly liked the other, professional courtesy demanded an exchange of pleasantries before getting down to business. Five minutes later, having assured each other of the health of their respective families, the conversation turned serious.

"I'm assuming you're calling on the McNair case?" Striker asked. "Has Allison lost interest? I told her that case was a loser."

"Allison is no longer handling this case. An unforeseen conflict has arisen." David hoped Striker wouldn't press for details. "I've been reviewing the file. Sherry has a strong case, and I'm confident we will prevail at trial."

"But" interjected Striker, "you're going to give my client a chance to settle. Is that it?"

"I'm giving your client an offer he can't refuse" David bluffed in reply. "One hundred fifty thousand. My client will sign a confidentiality agreement. Neutral reference for Ms. McNair should any prospective employer inquire."

Laughter exploded over the phone line. "You have got to be kidding. No way my client will pay anything close to a hundred and fifty K. Have you lost your mind?"

"Take the offer to your client, Jack." David tersely replied. "Miller Industries has until close of business tomorrow to accept."

———

Something was off. Jack Striker was sure of it. Steve Miller hadn't blinked when Striker told him earlier that morning what Sherry McNair wanted to settle the case.

"Draw up the papers." Miller had instructed. "Let's get this behind us."

"Steve, wait. That was just an opening offer." Striker had counseled his client. "David Jackson doesn't expect to get that kind of money for this case. It's just a starting point. If you want to settle you can get rid of this case for peanuts. Besides, why settle? I can win this case at trial."

"You don't know that, Jack. There are no guarantees with a jury."

"That's true, Steve. Jury trials always have an element of risk, but this case isn't worth a hundred fifty K. Hell, given what Sherry was earning, even if she won at trial a jury wouldn't award her that kind of money. And if they did, under the current case law, the judge would have to reduce the amount."

"I decide what this case is worth." Steve had replied, "Not you. The demand is accepted. Get it done."

"Why are you doing this, Steve?" Striker pressed. "Miller Industries has never settled an employment case. Why now?"

"The reason doesn't concern you, Jack" Steve had replied dismissively. "You're just a hired gun. Don't call me again until you've got McNair's signature on the settlement agreement."

All afternoon Striker had put off calling David Jackson with the news. Sure, it wasn't his money, and if Steve Miller wanted to piss away a hundred and fifty grand, what business was it of his? The terms of the settlement would be confidential, and Jack could publicly pitch the reason for the settlement in a way that wouldn't damage his reputation as a successful trial lawyer. No skin off his back. So, what was his hesitation in making the call? *Developing a conscience are you?* Striker chided himself. *I sure as shit hope not*, he thought, forcing himself to make the distasteful call. *Lawyers with a conscience end up poor.*

"David, old boy, this is your lucky day. Against my sage advice, my client has decided to pay your outrageous demand."

"Is that so?" David Jackson struggled not to sound completely surprised. "I guess Allison was right about this case all along."

"This doesn't have anything to do with Allison Parker" Striker retorted. "I think my client is paying too much, and I've told him so. But he says he's got better things to do than waste his time in court."

"I'll send over our standard settlement agreement, including a confidentiality provision" David advised. "If your client can sign off by Thursday I can present an order of dismissal on Friday. I've got a motion hearing with Judge Lee on another matter.

"Not a problem." Striker reluctantly agreed. "We'll send over the settlement proceeds via courier once Judge Lee signs the order."

Miscellaneous and routine matters for other clients kept Striker occupied for the remainder of the afternoon. By the time he turned off his computer most of the office staff had been gone for more than an hour. As with many successful law firms, Jack Striker's firm maintained a large in-house library. Until the early to mid nineties, the majority of lawyers in America still conducted research using actual books. By the end of the century, as the old guard retired and a generation of computer savvy young lawyers entered the legal field, even old line firms discovered that it was both more cost effective and quicker to conduct legal research online. No more manually digging through indexes, law books and journals. All a lawyer needed nowadays was a laptop and an online subscription to one of the legal search engines like Westlaw or Lexis.

Striker's firm was no exception. While hundreds of old law books lined the shelves of the paneled room, no new ones had been added in several years. When one of Jack's partners commented that all of the books reminded him of a gentleman's club he had visited in London - without chairs, cigars and brandy of course - the firm's managing partner had decided *why not*? In short order comfortable chairs and sofas had been added to the library, along with a well stocked bar, eventually giving the firm a much discussed reputation for post trial celebration parties as well as a unique and interesting space for hosting cocktail parties for firm clients.

"You the last one here, Mr. Striker?" a woman wearing a grey smock called from down the hall.

"Yes, Darla." Jack replied to the firm's cleaning lady. "I'm going to the library for a short one before I head home. Just lock up when you leave. I'll get the rest of the lights on my way out."

"The library." Darla snorted, voice low. "Looks like a bar to me."

"I heard that, Darla" Striker laughed, walking into the library. "Be careful going home."

Jack's "short one" had turned into several scotches before he figured out what had been bugging him all afternoon about the McNair case. Steve Miller's insistence on paying that ridiculous settlement had angered and upset Jack, mainly because Jack was concerned that settling the case so early would reflect badly on him. Jack prided himself on being able to handle his clients. Some might say "manipulate", but semantics weren't important. Jack knew what was best for his clients, and he had a talent for convincing them that they should always do as Jack recommended. Even when Jack's recommendations brought forth a bad result - something that rarely happened - Jack's personality was such that the client never blamed Jack for the unfortunate outcome.

Steve Miller had been different from the start, Jack now realized. Preoccupied, way too worried about the McNair case than he should have been. Employment cases were easy for an employer to defend, and Jack had tried to assure Miller that the McNair case would be an easy win. But no matter what he said, Miller was as twitchy as a Mexican jumping bean. Instructing Jack to delay providing information requested during discovery, and then changing his mind in court. Jack had been pissed about that little stunt. *Made me look a fool* he thought, remembering Judge Lee's anger. And this business with Allison Parker. Jack thought that was just plain ass weird. Once he had learned of Allison's reputation, Steve Miller had been adamant about getting her removed from the case. Jack told him that would never happen, that Parker was a good attorney and besides, there were no legal grounds on which to ask the court to remove her from the case, and then low and behold, the woman had withdrawn as counsel. What was that all about?

Steve Miller might be a strange bird, but he was a successful one. Jack had represented hundreds of successful men, and women for that matter, on all sorts of cases. His clients had not become successful by being afraid of litigation. To the contrary, most of the successful business people he knew would fight to the bitter end, settling a case only when it became apparent that winning in the courtroom was no longer an option. Regardless of what Allison Parker had claimed, winning the McNair case would have been a long shot, a fact which made Steve Miller's behavior all the more strange.

Unless. Striker set aside the empty glass and closed his eyes. Unless there was something in the McNair case that Steve Miller wanted to hide, something Allison Parker had found, or was going to find? Striker knew the answer was beyond his reach. Too many scotches tonight, but it would come to him. And as soon as Judge Lee signed the settlement order Jack was going to have a talk with Allison Parker.

CHAPTER NINETEEN

B est he could figure, Rice had less than sixty days of "working capital". He had sold everything he could get his hands on - the furnishings from his parents' house, Mary Louise's jewelry, his kids' savings bonds - and all he had left was twenty-five thousand dollars. Doing the math just about made him sick. The monkey on Rice's back was costing him five hundred bucks a day. At that rate, fifteen thousand of his reserve would be gone in a month's time. No telling what his credit card bill would be after Mary Louise got back from her New Orleans shopping trip. *I'll be lucky to have enough to pay the light bill,* Rice thought despairingly.

Getting Matthew to sign a Power of Attorney had seemed so simple. With unlimited access to Matthew's assets Rice's money woes would have been over with no one the wiser until the old man was dead and gone. But Matthew had outmaneuvered him, setting up that damn Trust. Then there was his bitch of a sister, always sticking her nose where it didn't belong, acting like her shit didn't stink. Rice couldn't figure out how Allison had become so successful. He was the one who was supposed to have had it all, not that cunt. *She must have fucked her way into that partnership,* an ugly voice spoke in Rice's head. *That and affirmative action.*

Thinking about his father infuriated Rice. *How dare you dictate how I spend my inheritance?* Rice reached for the blade to cut the white powder on the table before him. *This is all your fault, refusing to give me money last year for that new business,* Rice castigated a mental image of his father. *I'd be sitting pretty right now instead of scrounging for cash.* Rice sniffed, inhaling the last bits of the drug, then gently licked the razor blade for any residue of the white powder.

Reveling in the inflated sense of ego that a high always brought, Rice allowed his mind to wander. No matter what Allison said, Rice knew she and Matthew had conspired against him in setting up that Trust. *She's such a liar,* Rice thought. *Throwing me under the bus like that.* Cutting a new pile of powder with his blade, Rice leaned over to snort a short line. He would deal with Allison later, Rice promised himself, after he got some more cash, after he got rid of Mary Louise, after he....after he got rid of Mary Louise. Why hadn't he thought of that before? Rice was pretty certain the premiums were up to date on the life insurance policy he had taken out on Mary Louise and his children five years earlier. Five million on his wife, two million each on his children. Mary Louise was always on the road - like this trip to New Orleans, and the one last month to Birmingham. Her Lexus was getting old. Lord, did he know that. All his wife had done lately was nag him about getting her a new car. He'd have to check the service records, but Rice was positive the Lexus was overdue for new brakes. How sad it would be...... a fatal car accident. Nevermind the fact that his children would be motherless. Rice would be a rich man, and rid of that albatross to boot. A smile crept across Rice's face as he cut another line.

"What time are you leaving tomorrow?" Rice looked across the dinner table with a smile.

As soon as I am packed." Mary Louise replied, folding her napkin and laying it beside her plate. Melissa doesn't expect me at the beach house until mid afternoon, but I may want to stop in Point Clear on my way down."

"The TV says it's going to be in the 70's down there the next few days" Rice observed. "Hard to believe it's November. You and Melissa planning on any beach time?"

"Of course not, Rice." Exasperation tinged Mary Louise's reply. "I told you last week, we're going to the outlet mall in Foley. They've added some new stores."

"What could you possibly need that you don't already have?" Rice couldn't help asking.

"Just be glad I'm willing to shop at an outlet" Mary Louise sniffed, a pout pulling at the corner of her mouth. "I need a new cocktail dress for Diane Smith's party at the end of the month, and I might as well try to find something for the Everdeen wedding."

"Jesus, Mary Louise. You have an entire closet full of cocktail dresses."

"You can't seriously expect me to be seen in something I wore last year, can you?" Indignation dripped from Mary Louise's voice. "Besides, if you can spend money on toys like that jet ski you bought last summer, I can certainly spend money on a few paltry dresses."

Tossing back the last of his wine, Rice pushed away from the dinner table. "Okay, okay. Sorry I mentioned it." Taking a calming breath, Rice forced a smile. "And you're right. You should always to be the best dressed woman at the party." Giving his wife a peck on the cheek, Rice added "Don't pay any attention to me. You and Melissa just enjoy yourselves."

By ten o'clock Mary Louise had crawled into bed, turned on her sound machine, and pulled a sleep mask over her eyes. For once Rice was glad for his wife's ridiculous nighttime regimen. It would take an earthquake to wake his wife before morning. And thank the gods he had gotten himself under control at supper. All he needed was for his wife to back out of that trip.

Several hours later Rice heard the clock in the den softly strike the half hour, the only sound in the now quiet house. Rolling out of the bed, Rice grabbed his jeans and shirt from the corner chair and tiptoed from the room. It wouldn't take him long to finish the job he had started that afternoon. Telling Mary Louise he was taking the Lexus to have it serviced before her trip, Rice had instead taken his wife's car to an abandoned warehouse on the south side of Sumner. Rice needed a place where he could drain most, but not all, of the car's hydraulic fluid without being seen, or worrying about trace evidence being discovered later. The Price Cotton Gin was a relic of times past, used condoms and empty rolling paper wrappers now littering its dirt parking lot, indicators of its current value as a place for sex and drugs. Rice had spent several days researching various ways to cause brake failure.

Problem was, modern day cars had such good electronic warning systems that it was hard to sabotage a
vehicle. Rice grinned, remembering how he had aced
that little obstacle with Mary Louise.

"On my way to Firestone this afternoon the brake
warning light came on" he had reported to his wife.
"Fred looked at it and said it's just a computer glitch.
He's ordered some sort of software update for your car
to fix it, but he said your brakes are fine. Just ignore
the warning lights and bring it in after your trip."

"I told you I need a new car, Rice." Mary Louise
had complained. "I want you to trade this one when I
get back. There's a new Lexus convertible I want that's
on the lot at Trotter Motors."

The memory of Mary Louise's reply caused Rice
a nervous chuckle. *There won't be anymore cars in your
future, you demanding little bitch. Unless a hearse counts....*

Removing the tool he needed from its hiding place
in the garage, Rice rolled onto his back and snaked his
way under Mary Louise's car. He didn't think he would
need to puncture all four brake lines. Just getting the
back two wheels should be enough. Rice didn't want
the accident to happen until Mary Louise was well
out of Sumner. Better to have the wreck discovered
by some county yahoo instead of the Sumner police.
Tomorrow, after he dropped the kids at school, he
would dispose of the ice pick in a public dumpster. In
the unlikely event that the punctured brake lines were

discovered by insurance investigators after the wreck, Rice would provide the authorities with the threatening notes he had mailed to himself over the past weeks. *They must have meant to kill me,* he would cry piteously. Rice had it all figured out. No way the police would suspect him. He was a Parker.

Instead of returning to bed, Rice headed for his home office. Mary Louise did have an eye for decorating, he had to admit, looking around the wood paneled room. Bamboo shades covered the windows, framed by floor length, off-white linen panels hung on bronze colored iron rods. Two leather club chairs framed the fireplace, their navy color a nice complement to Rice's cherry wood desk, and a collection of original Gould bird prints were hung attractively about the room. *Well, I'll have plenty of money to hire a decorator* Rice told himself. *One that won't backtalk me, either.*

Grabbing a bottle from the small bar set up on a corner parson's table, Rice settled into the nearest chair and pulled a packet from his back pocket. Two oxycodone and a couple of bourbons ought to do the trick, he thought. Something to mellow him out - he didn't want to think too much about what he had just done, what he intended to happen. By the time the sun's rays peeked through the bamboo shades, Rice was dead to the world.

What the fuck is that noise? Rice's head was pounding, and some ungodly sound was making it worse. After a few seconds that seemed like an eternity, Rice shook himself awake enough to realize he was on the floor of his office, and that the pounding in his head was actually someone pounding on his front door. Why wasn't Mary Louise answering the door? Rice was having trouble clearing his head. *Shit.* Rice thought, seeing the empty bottle of Wild Turkey in the floor. *What time is it?*

The pounding from the front door was now accompanied by a shrill sound emanating from his desk. Ignoring the ringing telephone, Rice stumbled from his office. *Where is everyone?* Vaguely, Rice remembered he was supposed to take the kids to school this morning. *And who in the fuck is that beating on the freakin' door?* Whoever it was better have a good reason for being there at this time of the morning. Rice was going to give that asshole a piece of his mind. As he headed through the kitchen towards the front of the house, Rice noticed a note in Mary Louise's handwriting taped to the coffee pot. *Couldn't wake you, so taking the children to school on my way out of town. I'll be at Melissa's til Sunday afternoon.*

A sick feeling started in Rice's stomach. *Please God, no* he whispered as he opened the front door.

A uniformed officer stood stiffly on the brick sidewalk, hat in hand. "Mr. Parker? Mr. Rice Parker?"

"Yes." Rice replied.

"Can we sit down somewhere, Mr. Parker? I need to talk to you about your wife and children. " The officer hesitated. "There's been an accident."

CHAPTER TWENTY

A grief laden sigh escaped from Allison's lips. No matter how hard she tried to prevent it, to occupy her mind with work - Allison feared that the scene at the Sumner First Presbyterian Church would be forever and indelibly etched in her mind. Three small caskets, each adorned with a spray of white baby roses and a framed picture identifying the charred remains resting inside, had greeted the mourners as they had filled the sanctuary.

Mary Louise's body had survived the fiery crash, although she had been severely burned. Assuming she did not succumb to infection, a distinct possibility the doctors had warned Allison and her father, early brain scans indicated that Mary Louise would likely have significant mental impairment as well. *A blessing* Allison reminded herself. *Mary Louise will never know what happened to her children.*

The service had seemed interminable. What could a preacher really say to justify the loss of three innocent lives? When Rev. Haseldon said God must have needed three more angels Allison had wanted to scream. What kind of God would inflict a heinous death by fire on three innocent children just to get a few more angels? Was this visual supposed to comfort the family? Allison thought not. And then that line about funerals being for the living, not for the departed. Allison had heard that more than once, but what kind of life was left for Rice and Mary Louise? How could anyone possibly recover from this sort of tragedy? Would a parent want to?

Rice had been pitiful. Despite all their years of conflict and disagreement, Rice was family, and Allison's heart ached for her brother. It had taken both Allison and Jim to physically support a heavily sedated Rice as he walked to the family pew in the front of the church. According to Dr. James, who had been called to Rice's home by the Sumner police, Rice had collapsed upon hearing the news, howling an ungodly sound, and violently resisting efforts by the officers to calm and restrain him. Dr. James had sedated Rice, ordered an ambulance and admitted him to the hospital's psychiatric ward. Forty-eight hours had passed without Rice uttering a word. No one, including Dr. James, was certain what effect the funeral might have on Rice if he attended, but Allison had insisted. Rice had a right to bury his children. She and Jim would take him to the church, to the cemetery, and then return him to the hospital. And so they had. Two weeks had passed since they had laid Rice's children to rest near their grandmother in the Parker family plot at Greenwood Cemetery. The thought of Helene watching over her grandchildren provided only slight comfort to Allison, and likely none to Rice.

A steadily blinking red light interrupted Allison's sad reverie. Hoping to make progress on the stack of work she had mostly ignored since the accident, Allison had asked the front desk to send all of her calls that morning to voice mail. *Time to get back to work* Allison reminded herself as she punched the phone's replay button.

"Call me." Allison recognized Rice's voice. "It's important." Allison scribbled a reminder note for herself, then listened to the second message.

"Hey Allison. It's Frank Martin. I'm sending over the report on the Arkansas trip. I think you'll find it interesting. Give me a call after you've read it. I've got some ideas."

The third and last message was a surprise. "Jack Striker, here. Please give me a call at your convenience. There's a matter I'd like to discuss with you."

Picking up the phone Allison dialed her secretary's extension. "Donna, check with the runners, would you? Frank Martin is sending over his latest report. Have them bring it to me as soon as it arrives." Allison was anxious to see what Frank had to say. It was too much to hope he might have found the famous "smoking gun", but maybe he had found a few spent cartridges. At the very least, Allison knew she would have some interesting reading that evening after Charlotte and Mack went to bed.

The call from Jack Striker puzzled Allison. The McNair case had settled about the time of the tragedy with Rice's children. Why would Striker be calling her now? Allison knew the settlement proceeds had been paid. She had seen the entry on the weekly partnership operating report. Taking the McNair case on a contingency basis had resulted in a nice payday for David Jackson. Allison always thought the case a winner, but she had been surprised to hear that Miller Industries had rolled over so early in the litigation. Reaching for her phone, Allison dialed Jack Striker's number. Whatever Rice wanted would have to wait.

The Bread Basket was Ft. Charles' answer to Panerra Bread, a trendy light fare restaurant popular in larger Southern cities like Birmingham and Mobile. Friends of Allison's had opened the local knockoff last year, and the comfortable eatery had rapidly become a favorite with the downtown working crowd. Packed for breakfast and lunch, both eat-in and take-out, by mid afternoon The Bread Basket offered a much quieter venue for coffee. Sipping a cappuccino, Allison waited for Jack Striker to make his appearance.

A few minutes later Allison's patience was rewarded. Nodding a hello, Striker slid onto the bench opposite Allison in the booth she had selected for privacy.

"Want some coffee?" Allison asked, the ingrained offer slipping from her lips.

"No. Thanks just the same." Striker replied politely.

Well, aren't we Mr. and Ms. Manners?" Allison laughed. "Our mothers would be proud."

Laughing in return, Striker acknowledged the ritual that neither he nor any other child of the South could seem to shed. "I guess I'll be thanking the undertaker when he lays me to rest. Never let it be said that Jack Striker forgot his manners."

"I appreciate you meeting me on short notice." Allison smiled. Taking a final sip of her cappuccino, she added "Your message tweaked my curiosity. No offense, Jack, but it seemed rather out of character."

Striker sat silently for a few minutes, then addressed Allison in a lowered voice. "You have no idea. I've been debating calling you ever since you withdrew from the McNair case. I couldn't figure out why you handed the case to David Jackson, but figured it was none of my business." Stopping to glance around the coffee shop, Striker leaned towards Allison. "But when Steve Miller jumped all over that insane settlement offer I got a feeling something was going on that I didn't know about." Striker paused, then asked "Was there?"

Sometimes a decision had to be made in an instant. Allison pondered this reality as she struggled with whether or not to tell Striker about being pulled from the case, and about her own questions and actions that had arisen as a result. Jack Striker was a formidable opponent in the courtroom, but he was an ethical opponent. For him to have initiated contact with Allison, to have expressed his own reservations, to have agreed to meet her today - all of these factors tipped Allison's mental scale in favor of laying her cards, and her suspicions, on the table. Some of them, anyway.

"Ben Johnson pulled me off the case." Allison watched Striker closely. "He claimed there was a client complaint against me and he was removing me to protect the firm from a claim."

"Are you shitting me?" a stunned Striker asked. "Did he give you specifics?"

"No. That was part of the weirdness in the whole deal. Not only did Ben refuse to give me specifics, he hid the complaint from the board, and told me he would fire me if I didn't comply."

"Did you talk to Ms. McNair?"

"Yes, but I had to be careful about what I said. Based on our conversation, though, it was clear to me the complaint, if there was one, didn't originate with Sherry."

"Knowing you, Allison, I doubt you took this directive sitting down. Did you go to the board?"

"No. I'm handling this in a different way." Allison wasn't ready to play her entire hand. "Tell me what has worried you about the case. I know it's more than just a casual question or we wouldn't be sitting here."

"You're right. I'm walking a fine line here, Allison." A slight grimace marred Striker's attractive face. "Client confidentiality is a legitimate concern, but this case just doesn't pass the smell test."

"In what way?" Allison encouraged a reply.

"When Steve Miller pulled that stunt in Judge Lee's courtroom about the document production I was pissed. And rightly so. But I wrote it off as a fluke, some sort of miscommunication between Steve and my paralegal. After the hearing, though, I quizzed Cindy about her conversations with Steve regarding producing the documents you had requested. After talking to Cindy I was certain there had been no misunderstanding. What I couldn't figure, though, was why Steve had blindsided me in the courtroom."

"I was surprised by that as well" Allison allowed. "I even took another look at the documents after I got them to see if I had overlooked something myself."

"Find anything?"

"Nothing. But two days later Ben pulled me off the case. I don't think that was a coincidence."

Striker twirled the black fountain pen he had taken from his pocket. "That's not all that bothered me. After that hearing in Judge Lee's courtroom, Steve told me not to spend anymore time on the case. When I told him I couldn't control what the plaintiff did to move the case forward, or what Judge Lee might order, Steve just said everything had been taken care of. Then, when you resigned from the case and David Jackson didn't do anything to press the claim, like my Nana used to say, I decided not to look a gift horse in the mouth."

"So, why are we sitting here today?" Allison asked. "Your client must have been fine with the settlement amount. According to David, y'all didn't even make a counter."

"That's exactly why we are sitting here. If paying a hundred and fifty grand is having a case "taken care of" then something worth a lot more than that must have been at stake." Striker looked directly at Allison. "I don't like being made a fool of in the courtroom, but it's not something I can't handle. But I'll be damned if

I will be used to manipulate the legal system." Striker frowned. "When I came here today I had hoped to discover I was simply being a bit paranoid, but after hearing what you've told me, I am convinced my instincts were right."

"Are you aware of any possible connection between Steve Miller and Ben Johnson? Anyone or anything in common?" Allison asked. "I've done some looking and I don't think their paths have ever crossed, even in a town as small as Ft. Charles."

"Not that I can think of. Steve grew up in foster care in the north part of the state. No family to speak of. He never spoke much about his growing up years. From the little he shared with me, I got the impression those years were pretty bleak. He said he only had one friend, a guy a couple of years older than him. Jeff somebody." Striker paused. "Got to give the system credit though. Steve made something of himself despite a pretty terrible upbringing."

Allison glanced at her watch. "Maybe we can continue this discussion another time. I've got a 4:30 meeting I'm almost late for as it is."

"Definitely." Striker nodded in agreement. "I've got too many still unanswered questions."

So do I Allison thought, grateful once again for a genetic heritage that had blessed her with a superior memory. *Starting with why Steve Miller's cell phone records showed so many calls and text messages to someone named Jeff Bishop.*

CHAPTER TWENTY-ONE

2010

Anticipating the clandestine meeting with Jeff Bishop had unnerved Ben Johnson so badly that he almost backed out. *So many things could go wrong* he had worried. *What if this is a set up?* Trusting a criminal was risky, even a criminal referred by Dickie Lott. There was always a chance that the authorities were involved in a sting operation and Ben would be offered up by Bishop in some sort of plea deal. Multiple disaster scenarios rushed through Ben's mind as he made the drive to the pawn shop in the small town twenty miles from Ft. Charles where an unknown caller had instructed him to meet Jeff Bishop. But no scenario was more frightening for Ben than the thought of paying his blackmailer for the rest of his natural life.

Becker's Pawn and Gun had the shabby, seen-better-days look Ben associated with businesses frequented by the lower class. An older man in worn overalls, cigarette dangling from one hand, a beer clutched in the other, slouched on a bench near the shop's front door. What passed for a parking lot hugged one side of the shop. A black Ford pickup, ten years old if it were a day, sat beneath a weathered sign which declared "No Parking". A silver Corvette Convertible, the lot's only other occupant, reminded Ben of a debutante slumming on the wrong side of town. Pulling his Mercedes alongside the obvious interloper, Ben hoped he was not making a mistake.

"What can I do you for?" A gray haired man behind the counter asked, the slang southern expression rolling casually from his lips. "You looking for anything in particular?"

"I'm meeting a friend here" Ben replied cautiously.

"You Johnson?" the man asked.

Afraid to trust his voice, Ben nodded.

"Back there" the man indicated, pointing at a door. "You're late."

Ben wondered if this was the way Kirksey Nix felt when he ordered the hit on Judge Sherry and his wife in Biloxi back in 1987. Somehow he didn't think so. By the time Nix had ordered that killing he had already committed at least one murder of his own. Ben wasn't a murderer. Maybe if he told himself that enough times he's come to believe it. Opening the door behind the counter, Ben took a deep breath. There was no going back now.

⊫⊪

Driving home to Ft. Charles, Ben struggled to keep his composure as he remembered the events that had transpired in the back of Becker's Pawn & Gun. The man who had greeted him was not what he had expected. Conservatively dressed in a navy linen blazer, grey slacks, open collared shirt and leather mocs, Jeff Bishop's appearance had initially lulled Ben into a sense of comradery. Bishop had been cordial, too, inviting Ben to make himself comfortable at a small table and asking if Ben wanted something to drink while they discussed their mutual business.

The first thirty minutes passed quickly. Working out the terms of murder for hire seemed to be no different Ben thought from any of the other business deals he had brokered over the years. Terms of payment, details of the agreement, start and finish dates were negotiated as dispassionately as the purchase and sale of everyday goods and services. Ben would make the next payment to Chris Cannon, notify Bishop of the drop details, then Bishop would handle the problem from there. Ben didn't want to know the particulars. When the job was completed Bishop would let him know. *Nothing to this* Ben had thought until Bishop mentioned his final terms.

"One day I will ask you for a favor." The change in Bishop's tone had been noticeable. "That day may never come" he continued, "but if it does, you will do whatever it is that is asked of you."

Ben had quickly replied "Yes, yes of course. Not a problem."

"I'm not finished" Bishop had interrupted. "If you refuse to return the favor that is asked, if and when it is asked, I will ruin you. And your family."

"What? What are you talking about?" Ben had choked out the question. "What about the money I am paying you now?"

"Just a little extra insurance." Bishop smiled. "I have more to lose in transactions of this sort than the buyer does. Money alone hasn't proved to be a sufficient reward for the risks I take. Besides, what sort of favor could I possibly ever need from you?"

The porch lights on Ben's house beckoned warmly as he pulled up the brick paved driveway. Whatever he had to do in the future, whatever favor, he'd do it. Ben knew that with a certainty born of desperation. Anything to stop the blackmail. Anything to hide his true nature. He may have made an agreement with the devil, but like Scarlett O'Hara, Ben wasn't going to worry about it now. Heading towards the house he wondered what Linda had fixed for supper.

Two weeks after Ben and Jeff Bishop reached their agreement, Chris Cannon instructed Ben to have a runner deliver fifty thousand dollars to an office in downtown Birmingham. As agreed, Ben had contacted Jeff, making the call on the private line he had installed in his office at the firm.

"Our business should be concluded within the next few days" Bishop had assured Ben.

"How will I know when the matter is resolved?" Ben had asked. "Finally and permanently resolved" he added.

"You'll know" Bishop replied.

And so he had.

The envelope, marked Private and Confidential, had been delivered to Ben via courier. No return address identified the sender. Instructing his secretary that he was not to be disturbed, Ben retreated to his office and locked the door. Forty years earlier, when Ben had started his law practice, his wife had gifted him with an expensive brass and ivory letter opener. The almost antique now rested on Ben's desk, its practical use mostly a thing of the past since Ben's secretary opened ninety-nine percent of the mail he received. Ben picked up what he amusedly thought of as a decorative shiv, sliced the opening of the slim packet, and shook the contents onto his desk.

The eight by ten color photograph depicted both nightmare and salvation: Chris Cannon's lifeless eyes stared from the picture, a single gunshot wound to the center of his forehead the obvious cause of the large pool of crimson blood framing the blackmailer's head. Violent waves of nausea pulsed through Ben's body, a sheen of cold sweat dampening his brow, as he fought unsuccessfully to contain the contents of his stomach. Wiping the remnants of foul smelling vomit from his lips, Ben Johnson began to shake, but whether from fear, shock or relief he could not tell. *At least it's over* he told himself.

Ben cleaned the photograph as well as he could, then called his secretary.

"Terry, call the cleaning crew. I've gotten sick - must have eaten something bad at lunch."

Mr. Johnson, are you alright?" his secretary asked worriedly. "Do you need a ride home?"

"No, I can drive myself. I'll see you in the morning."

Ben stuffed the picture and envelope in his briefcase. He would burn them both on the way home. Tomorrow would be a new day.

CHAPTER TWENTY-TWO

Present Day

"Siri, call Rice, home" Allison instructed her cyberspace assistant. Her command acknowledged, Allison pushed the car's speedometer to 70. Stopping by the office after her meeting with Striker had been a mistake. By the time she returned several calls to opposing counsel who had insisted they "must" speak with her today she was an hour late getting on the road. Once again she had missed dinner with Charlotte and Mack.

Having children had been a difficult issue for Allison and Jim. Already forty years old when he and Allison married, Jim wanted to start a family right away.

"I'm just starting my career" Allison had countered. "I want to make partner before I have children."

"If we wait the five years you want" Jim had replied, referring to the earliest an associate might be considered for partnership in Johnson & Merritt, "I'll be on a damn walker by the time our children are in high school".

So, they had compromised. Charlotte had been born three years later, followed by Mack the year Allison made partner. Hands-on parenting had been another compromise. As a sitting judge, Jim had the luxury of ending his workday whenever it suited him. Allison's time, on the other hand, was constrained by client demands and trial court deadlines. As a result, it was Jim more often than Allison who arrived home first, started supper, and helped with Charlotte and Mack's homework. Over the years Allison had discovered that maternal guilt was a great motivator - that and the judgmental comments she overheard at firm parties from the non-working wives of many of her partners. As a result, Allison had perfected the art of what she referred to as "tunnel vision". By focusing intently on the day's work to the exclusion of lunch or office chit chat, Allison found she could accomplish in six or seven hours what many of her cohorts languidly produced in ten. Still, no matter how focused or organized, Allison's days were often longer than she wished.

Like so many working women with children, Allison struggled not to shortchange her children while still meeting the obligations of her profession. Whenever possible, Allison was home by six-thirty for the evening meal. Unfortunately, tonight had not been one of those evenings. At least Charlotte and Mack stayed up until 8:30 now. Allison wondered sometimes if she had made the right choice having a career, but she knew deep in her heart that she was a better wife and mother because she had a life outside her home. Not everyone agreed with her, but the life she and Jim had built together worked for their family.

"Hello?" Rice interrupted Allison's reverie, answering the call Siri had placed.

"Sorry I'm just now getting back to you." Allison apologized. "It's been one of those days."

"I need a favor."

What now? Allison thought, quickly reprimanding herself for being uncharitable.

"I got a call this morning from Nationwide." Allison heard the hitch in Rice's voice. "They're sending an investigator to examine the Lexus. Would you meet him at Powell's Garage tomorrow?"

"I've got a pretty busy schedule in the morning" Allison replied. "Why can't you be there?"

"I can't look at that car. Please, can you do this for me? The appointment isn't until three in the afternoon"

"Alright" Allison sighed. Seeing the burned out shell where his children had perished would be too much for anyone. "I'll be there. Who am I meeting?"

"Wilson Zentner. He left a contact number if you want it."

"Text me the number when we hang up. I'll message him in the morning to let him know to expect me."

"Thank you, Allison" Rice spoke words which rarely left his mouth. "I really mean it. Thank you."

The next afternoon Allison passed the two hour drive to Sumner thinking about Frank Martin's latest report. The back story Frank had uncovered on Ben Johnson had been illuminating. White trash parents, wrong side of the tracks, and in the closet if what Sammy Deal had shared with Frank was true - Ben Johnson had a lot to hide. Southerners were a peculiar breed. Personal success stories were publicly applauded, especially those where the underdog prevailed against overwhelming odds. Big bucks, charitable giving, and community service helped pave the way for acceptance in the business community. No one could fault Ben Johnson when measured by those criteria. But public acceptance was quite different from social acceptance. True acceptance, social acceptance, rested solely on the answer to the question "Who are your people?" With the right answer, even sexual preference could be overlooked. Lineage was everything, trumping money every time.

No matter how successful Ben Johnson had become, exposure of the lie upon which he had built a life in Ft. Charles would ruin Ben in all the ways that mattered to him, starting with his marriage. Old time Ft. Charles society would put up with quite a bit - a few years back one of its members had enjoyed an eighteen month government paid vacation at Eglin Air Force Base in Florida - but lying about lineage would result in permanent expulsion from the inner circle. No one made a fool of Ft. Charles society and survived.

As arcane as these unspoken rules might be, Allison understood that they would be unmercifully enforced against Ben Johnson. The fallout would be widespread, potentially affecting Johnson & Merritt. Yes, Ben Johnson had a lot to hide, but what in the world did any of that have to do with the McNair case? Allison had most of the puzzle parts now. Enough that a picture was beginning to take shape. But the key pieces were still missing. *There has to be a connection between Steve Miller and Ben Johnson* Allison thought. Switching the car's satellite radio to Vinyl Rewind, Allison drummed a rhythmic accompaniment to a Pink Floyd classic. Miller's arrest as a minor had been a real surprise. His alleged accomplice, a young man by the name of Jeff Bishop, had served a small sentence, while Miller had been given probation on a lesser charge. Allison agreed with Frank that public knowledge of Miller's criminal record could hurt the upcoming stock offering for Miller Industries. *I wonder if Miller disclosed his juvenile record to the Securities and Exchange Commission?* Allison would ask Frank to check out that angle.

The name Jeff Bishop had appeared in Frank's report on Ben Johnson too. Allison never asked Frank how he obtained Ben's private phone records, but now she was glad he had done just that. Absent Frank's report on Steve Martin, Allison would not have paid any attention to the calls on Ben's private line, but there they were - three calls from a number identified as belonging to a Jeff Bishop. The first call to Ben had come the day before she was removed from the McNair case, and the other two around the time David Jackson had settled the case. Allison did not believe in coincidences. *If it's the same guy, that's got to be the connection.* Did Ben Johnson and Jeff Bishop have a history that needed to be hidden? Allison would bet money on it.

Powell's Garage appeared in Allison's peripheral vision, drawing her attention to the reason for her drive to Sumner. Making a quick left turn, Allison pulled her SUV into the garage's parking lot. A white van, sporting a dark blue Nationwide emblem on its side panel was parked by the front door of the main building. The van's driver, sporting the same, albeit smaller, dark blue emblem on his white shirt nodded a greeting.

"You must be Mr. Zentner." Allison smiled, offering her hand.

"Yes, and you must be Ms. Parker." Zentner replied, grasping Allison's hand with a firm grip. "I understand your brother is not coming, is that right?"

"Right. He's having a difficult time of it, as I'm sure you can appreciate."

"Yes, I certainly can." Zenter tersely replied. "Are you here as a family member or in your capacity as counsel for Mr. Parker?"

"Given your question, I'm not sure how to answer." Movement near the garage caught Allison's attention. Two men in what used to be white coveralls were walking towards her and the insurance investigator. "Does my brother need a lawyer, Mr. Zentner?

Ignoring Allison's question, the investigator continued "In cases like this where large life insurance claims are being made Nationwide conducts a thorough and detailed investigation."

"I didn't know Rice had life insurance on his children." Allison forced herself not to appear surprised. "I thought the claim was on the vehicle."

"There is a claim on the vehicle. Obviously it is a total loss. Absent the size of the life insurance claims this would be an open and shut case." Zentner paused. "But the aggregate of the claims for the three deceased children is six million dollars. Your brother has a policy for another five million on his wife."

Stunned, Allison choked out a question. "Why was this inspection conducted before I arrived? It was my understanding that Nationwide wanted my brother to be here, or at least someone from the family to be here, for that very purpose. Are you telling me the inspection has already been completed?"

"In addition to conducting an inspection of Mrs. Parker's car we reviewed Mr. Parker's financial status..."

"You did what?" Allison asked indignantly.

"We didn't break any laws counselor." Zentner lectured in response. "Everything we examined was available either through public record or accessible via regulatory agencies."

"And?" Allison feared she was not going to like whatever she was about to hear.

"Based on our investigation of Mr. Parker's personal and financial circumstances, Nationwide determined that Mrs. Parker's car should undergo a forensic investigation. That investigation was conducted yesterday and today." Motioning towards the men Allison had noticed earlier, Zentner added "The brakes on Mrs. Parker's car had been disabled. Intentionally."

"I don't like what you are implying" Allison retorted. "My brother would never do anything to harm his children. How dare you make such an accusation."

"I've been in this business a long time, Ms. Parker, and I've seen the results of unforeseen consequences more than once." Zentner grimaced a tight smile. "Your brother should retain counsel as soon as possible."

"For the time being you can consider me his counsel." Allison handed the investigator one of her business cards. "I want a copy of Nationwide's investigative report on my desk within forty-eight hours."

Undeterred by Allison's directive, Zentner added "Internal policy will require Nationwide to refer this matter to the police. Your brother might want to hire a criminal lawyer, too."

⊷ ⊶

"Get everyone to bed without a crisis?" Jim asked as he flipped through the guide on the den's flat screen.

"Amazingly, yes." Allison lowered herself to the sofa next to her husband. "The promise of a story from *The Children's Book of Virtues* works magic every time." Allison explained, referring to the collection of classic stories William Bennett had published after his stint as Secretary of Education.

"Which one was it tonight?"

"Charlotte's favorite - The Song of Roland. I'm sure Charlotte wishes her own rocking horse would come to life." Allison chuckled. "I had to promise Mack he could pick the story tomorrow night. Otherwise there *would* have been a crisis."

Laying aside the tv remote, Jim reached for Allison's hand. "I'm glad to hear you laugh. You've been a thousand miles away tonight. Want to talk about it?"

"I couldn't talk about this in front of the children." The smile faded from Allison's face. "Rice is in trouble. Bad trouble."

Interrupting, Jim replied dismissively "Rice is always in trouble. What's new about that?"

"This is serious, Jim. I met with the inspector from Nationwide this afternoon. The brakes on the Lexus were disabled. The insurance company thinks Rice did this."

"That's the most ludicrous thing I've ever heard" Jim shook his head. "Even if he were smart enough to pull off a stunt like that, why in the world would Rice hurt his own children?"

"That's just it, Jim." Allison leaned towards her husband. "I thought about this the entire way back from Sumner today. I know Rice would never hurt his children. I don't think they were the target."

"Because?"

"Rice has a five million dollar life insurance policy on Mary Louise." Allison's words hung in the air. "And we both know Rice is broke."

Silence permeated the room. The potential truth was both painful and difficult to accept. "I haven't called Rice." Allison told her husband. "I wanted to talk to you first. Will you walk out to the guest house with me? I need to tell Daddy about this before I talk to Rice."

═╪═ ═╪═

Matthew sat unmoving for a long time after Allison and Jim returned to the big house. This was God's punishment, Matthew knew, no doubt about it. The consequences of his sins had finally come to rest. Yes, he knew that as surely as he knew the sun would rise in the morning. *The Lord is a vengeful Lord.* Matthew shivered as the memory took voice. A traveling preacher had pitched his tent outside Sumner's city limits the summer Matthew turned sixteen.

"Let's go" Matthew's friend Ricky Snodgrass had urged. "Chuck's mother went last night. She said the preacher took up serpents. Maybe he'll do it again tonight."

Matthew had readily agreed. The Bible said snakes wouldn't hurt a true believer, but he knew some preachers had been bitten and died. Maybe that would happen tonight.

By the time Matthew and Ricky arrived darkness was settling on the crowd gathered outside the preacher's tent. "We need to get us a good spot to watch the goings on" Ricky whispered to Matthew.

"Near the front, where we can hear what the preacher man is saying". Motioning for Matthew to follow, Ricky lifted a tent flap and the two boys crept underneath.

Whether by luck or fate Matthew would never know, but he found himself on the far left of the front row, no more than fifteen feet from the itinerant preacher.

"The Lord is a vengeful Lord! Full of anger at his children who have sinned. Woe to those who have failed to follow the Lord! Those who have chosen to follow Mammon, who have turned their backs on the Lord!" Sweat poured down the preacher's red face. "And you" the preacher pointed his fat finger in Matthew's direction, "you will feel the fires of Hell." Lifting a worn black Bible above his head, the preacher turned towards his audience. "The Good Book says, the sins of the fathers shall be visited on their sons! Beware! Beware!"

The revival had lasted another two hours. To Matthew and Ricky's disappointment, the preacher had not taken up any serpents that evening, although he had performed a couple of healings and several people had fallen out after spouting the gibberish known as speaking in tongues. Repentant attendees, eager to show their rejection of Mammon, had filled an old wooden bucket with coin and dollar bills. "The Lord will bless you" the preacher had intoned. "Remember, it is more blessed to give than to receive."

Matthew had been quiet on the walk home. "You know that's all bullshit, don't you?" Ricky asked. "Those people weren't sick, and you ain't going to Hell."

"Yeh, I know" Matthew had replied. "But that guy just creeped me out, pointing at me and all."

"He wasn't pointing at you, man." Ricky had laughed, poking Matthew in the ribs.

"I guess" Matthew had shrugged. "I just wish we had never come."

Matthew groaned as he struggled to stand. That preacher had been right. *I killed my son's spirit, and now he's killed his own children.* Leaning on the ivory tipped cane that had become his constant companion Matthew hobbled towards the bedroom where he had left his cell phone. He might be on his way to Hell, but just not yet.

"Hello, son?" Matthew asked.

"Dad, it's late. Why are you calling?"

"We need to talk, Rice."

"Talk about what, Dad?" Matthew could hear the fear in his son's question.

"About you, Rice" Matthew sighed. "About you, son, and keeping you out of prison for the rest of your life."

CHAPTER TWENTY-THREE

"Glad that's over" Allison remarked to her secretary Donna. "Next time I think about defending an unemployment case remind me how much I hate those rinky dink hearings at the Commission." Releasing her feet from the torturous high heels that complemented her charcoal pinstriped suit, Allison sank gratefully into her desk chair. Hearings before the state unemployment commission were, in her opinion, a farce. Non-lawyer hearing officers conducted administrative hearings where neither procedural or evidentiary rules applied, resulting in barely contained mayhem slanted grossly in favor of the discharged employee. "I swear, Donna, the way the Commission interprets the law, I don't think an employer can win short of firing an employee for murdering a co-worker. Stealing doesn't qualify as "gross misconduct" anymore." Exasperated, Allison added "What has happened to personal consequences for bad behavior?" As usual, Allison would file an appeal to the state trial court where, more than likely, a judge would reverse the Commission's findings and rule in favor of Allison's employer client. Many employers never appealed to the next level figuring it was more cost effective to pay unemployment for a few weeks rather than additional attorney's fees. Fortunately for Allison, at least from the firm's perspective, Allison's larger corporate clients always contested unemployment claims even through several appellate levels. "Sends a message" one of Allison's clients had once explained. "Makes 'em think twice about filing for unemployment." Allison wasn't sure she agreed with that sentiment, but she understood her client's frustration.

The McNair case, however, had caused Allison to rethink her attitude about employee claims. True, McNair wasn't an unemployment case. Sexual harassment was despicable and should never be tolerated. On more than one occasion Allison had advised her corporate clients to terminate an employee for sexually harassing a co-worker. But listening to Sherry McNair tell her story, Allison realized the courage it had taken for Sherry to stand up to her employer.

Allison strongly believed that businesses should be able to fire employees for legitimate reasons without having to pay unemployment, but the McNair case reminded her that not all employers were honest. Employers who abused employees should be held accountable in the same way as employees who had stolen, lied or abused other employees.

Accountability and consequences. Isn't that what the scales of justice represent? For every action, whether good or bad, there is a corresponding consequence? Allison pondered the question, popped a thumb drive into her computer, then retrieved a yellow legal pad and pen from her desk drawer.

Frank Martin's reports filled the screen. Quickly skimming the information, Allison began a bullet point listing:

- Steve Miller and Jeff Bishop were arrested for conspiracy to commit murder;

- Miller and Bishop both served time on lesser charges, Miller in juvie, Bishop at a penal farm;

- Ben Johnson lied about his past;

- Ben Johnson had a homosexual relationship as a teen? Still in the closet?

- Ben's phone records show numerous calls from a man named Jeff Bishop.

Allison shook her head in frustration. *So, there's a common denominator in Jeff Bishop. What is the connection to the McNair case? Why did Ben pull me off?* Deciding she needed a different perspective, Allison punched her secretary's extension into the desk phone.

"Donna, I need your opinion on something."

Walking into Allison's office Donna asked "Is this another closed door discussion?"

Allison smiled at her secretary. "No wonder we work so well together. Devious minds think alike."

After ensuring their privacy, Donna listened intently as Allison summarized the information Frank Martin had reported, then exclaimed. "Oh my Lord!"

"I know. There is some very damning information in Frank Martin's reports. Looks like both Ben Johnson and Steve Miller have reasons to keep their past lives secret."

"And you're right about that Jeff Bishop character. Whoever he is, Jeff Bishop has to be the common tie between Steve Miller and Mr. Johnson."

"Agreed" Allison nodded in reply, "but what does that connection have to do with Ben pulling me from the McNair case? Am I looking at this the wrong way. What do you think?"

"Well, what would you maybe have uncovered if you had stayed on the McNair case?"

"I've been thinking about that. I would have asked Steve Miller about any arrests or convictions when I deposed him" Allison replied, referring to questions asked under oath in front of a court reporter in the early stages of trial preparations. "That's a standard deposition question that I always ask. Even if he lied, maybe Miller was afraid I would uncover his criminal past and investigate further. Miller Industries is supposed to be going public soon. That kind of information about a company's chief executive officer might have a chilling effect on stock sales."

"So, if you were off the McNair case, and Ben gave it to his son-in-law, Ben could make the case go away." Donna offered "And that's exactly what happened when Mr. Jackson settled the claim."

"That's what it looks like to me, but Ben wouldn't have done that without a very good reason." Allison moved the cursor down the computer screen, searching for a clue.   "Frank Martin's report shows three calls to Ben Johnson's private line from a number registered to Jeff Bishop. One of those calls came in the day before Ben pulled me from the McNair case. The other two came about the time David settled the case." Allison spun her desk chair from left to right several times. "Think, Allison, think" she commanded out loud.

"Frank has uncovered a lot of bad stuff about Mr. Johnson" Donna observed dryly. "Is it possible that Steve Miller knew about Mr. Johnson's past and got this Bishop guy to threaten him?"

"I've gone round and round with the information Frank uncovered, looked at it front and back, upside down and rightside up - and I've reached the same conclusion that you just suggested.   I just don't know how Miller would have known about Ben's past."

"Maybe he didn't. Know about Mr. Johnson's past, I mean." Donna clarified. "Maybe Bishop knew something and Miller just got lucky, used that information to his advantage."

"Stranger coincidences have happened" Allison shook her head. "We're close. But my gut tells me I'm missing an important piece of this puzzle. As bad as the information in Frank's report is about Ben's family and upbringing, I don't think the threat of disclosure would have made Ben react as he did."

"What about being gay?" Donna frowned. "I'm not sure that would sit too well around here."

"I've thought about that, too, but all Frank discovered was a *he said-she said*. An alleged gay encounter from over forty years ago is pretty weak. Besides, who is more credible? Some flaming queen running a gay nightclub or an upstanding and long-married member of the community?"

"True enough" Donna laughed "but if I found out my husband had done another man he'd be lucky to be alive long enough to be served with divorce papers."

"Well shit fire and damn" Allison slapped her hand on her desk. "Maybe it wasn't just a one-time encounter forty years ago. Maybe it's never stopped."

"What? With that queen in Little Rock?"

"No. With other men. And probably not in Ft. Charles." Allison massaged her forehead, concentrating. "I need his travel records. Donna, can you get your hands on Ben's travel records for the past, say three years? No, better make it five. They are probably in off-site storage."

"Not a problem. What are you thinking?"

"That I've been focusing too much on the distant past. Maybe we're overlooking something more recent. And more damning."

"I'll ask Jenny to pull Mr. Johnson's travel file" Donna replied. "She owes me a favor and won't ask any questions."

"Good. I want Frank Martin to make one more road trip." Allison removed the thumb drive from her computer. "How many people in this firm owe you favors, Donna? Nevermind, don't answer that. I'm just glad they do." Picking up the phone, Allison placed a call to Frank Martin.

That evening Allison smiled as she relayed the conversation she had with Frank Martin to her husband.

"Frank was so funny" Allison remarked. "He told me I was in the wrong profession. When I asked him why he thought that he said because I have a sneaky mind."

"I'd say Frank is a pretty perceptive guy, although I believe I would have used a different adjective."

"And exactly what word would you have used rather than 'sneaky'?" Allison questioned, her arched eyebrows telegraphing a warning to her husband.

"Babe, I can't describe you or your mind in one word" Jim judiciously replied. Leaning across the dinner table to give Allison a quick kiss, he added "Determined, maybe for starters. Truth seeker fits too, although it makes you sound like some sort of action hero."

Allison laughed "We both know I'm no hero. But finding the truth is important to me."

"I know it is. And I know that's earned you a few enemies over the years." Jim handed his wife a cup of decaf. "Let's move to the den. You can bring me up to speed on the rest of the Ben Johnson investigation."

One cup of coffee became two while Allison relayed her findings, thoughts, suspicions and ideas to her husband. As often happened when Allison was dealing with a difficult case or issue, Jim played devil's advocate, quizzing her on her theories and questioning her reasoning until Allison had worked the thorny problem from all angles. This evening was no different, and Allison was relieved to find that her husband agreed with the conclusions she had reached in her investigation.

"I think you are spot on." Jim acknowledged. "This Bishop guy is the key. Maybe Frank will uncover something from Ben's out-of-town trips that will give you an answer."

"I sure hope so. I'll know more in a few days." Allison rose from the sofa and headed towards the kitchen door. "I'm going to visit with Daddy before I hit the sack. I need to talk to him before tomorrow. We have a meeting with Rice and Jason Brownlow here at the house at 9:00."

"Jason Brownlow is expensive" Jim replied. "Matthew paying the freight on that?"

"Yes. Daddy wanted the best criminal lawyer he could find, and Jason fits that description."

A few minutes later Allison pulled up a chair to the small table in the guest house kitchen. Matthew settled in opposite his daughter, the ever present pot of strong black coffee stationed nearby.

"Daddy, I wish you would cut back on that coffee. It can't be good for you."

"Too late now, Allison." her father replied. "Besides, coffee is one of the few pleasures I have left."

"Are you drinking that supplement Dr. James recommended?" Allison knew the answer before she asked the question.

"Hell, no." Matthew frowned. "What's the point? It's not going to cure what I've got, and I doubt it will make me live any longer."

Allison stared at her father. *He's so damn obstinate.* Taking a calming breath Allison reached for her father's hand. "Daddy, we may not always have gotten along, but I need your help right now. Rice is in serious trouble, and I can't do this by myself."

"Do what, Allison?" Matthew pulled his hand from Allison's grasp. "Do what by yourself."

"Figure out how to keep my brother from the electric chair. I think a murder charge is coming." Allison again reached for her father's hand, this time clasping the frail one between her two strong ones. "You know I don't like Rice. Can't stand him, in fact. But I don't want to see him convicted of murdering his children. And not for the reason you think." A sad smile crossed Allison's face. "When you asked Jim and me to manage Rice's inheritance we agreed for one reason, and one reason alone - so Rice wouldn't run through every dime and leave Clarke, Lucia and Matt penniless." Allison reached for a cookie from the platter next to the coffee pot. "Those darling children are gone. I can't even imagine what their last moments must have been like. I want Rice to live a long life remembering his children and what happened to them. Lethal injection is the easy way out for him."

What little color tinted Matthew's pale complexion disappeared. "What has Rice told you?" he whispered.

"Do you mean has he confessed?" Allison asked harshly. "Of course not. He didn't have to. I know what the State's case is going to be - that either Rice himself cut the brake lines on Mary Louise's car or he paid someone else to do it so he could collect the eleven million in life insurance he had on his family. When the prosecutor gets finished putting all of Rice's money and substance abuse problems in front of the jury they'll nail him to the wall."

Chair legs scraped jarringly against the old pine floors as Matthew pushed away from the table. Allison watched as her father shuffled to the kitchen sink to pour the thick black liquid from his cup. "I'm not giving up coffee in the mornings" Matthew addressed his remarks to the kitchen window. "Have Janice bring in a case of that shit Bill James wants me to drink." Matthew turned to face his daughter. "You won't have to deal with this alone."

"Just so we're on the same page." Allison looked at Matthew. "I'll give Rice the benefit of the doubt going into this. He claims some drug dealer has been threatening him, says that must be who messed with Mary Louise's car." Allison headed towards the cottage door. "I don't buy that story, and I don't think a jury will either. We'll see what Jason Brownlow has to say tomorrow. He's the criminal law expert." Allison hesitated in the doorway, shaking her head. *What in the world was Rice thinking?*

"I would never do anything to hurt my children. Never. Why won't you believe me?" Rice's whining was beginning to get on Allison's last nerve. Sitting quietly in the corner of the cottage's living room, Allison watched the interplay between her brother and his attorney. If attire was an accurate indicator of how each man valued the reason for the meeting, Allison thought, either Rice didn't have a clue about the problems he was facing or he had already given up. Wearing faded jeans that belonged in the Goodwill donation box, a soiled grey t-shirt and scuffed moccasins, Rice would not have been out of place panhandling on a street corner in downtown Ft. Charles, his appearance a sharp contrast to Brownlow's crisp business suit.

"What I believe doesn't matter." Jason Brownlow slammed his yellow legal pad on the coffee table. "I won't be sitting on the jury." Pointing a long, narrow finger at his client, Brownlow continued. "That story about a drug dealer after your ass is horse-shit. What's his name? Where'd you meet him? How many times did you buy from him? How did he know who you were, where you live?"

"Uh, uh, he must have followed me home." Rice struggled to find an explanation.

"How bad is your drug habit? Tell me the truth." Brownlow ground a half smoked cigarette into saucer turned ashtray where it joined several other menthol butts. Sensing Rice's hesitation, he added "If you insist on using this crap defense, then you better be prepared to answer all those questions and more. The prosecutor wants to hang murder one on you, Rice. Convicting a rich white boy of premeditated murder would be a feather in his cap."

Rice glanced at his father. Matthew had not uttered a word for the past two hours. Now he spoke. "Don't look at me, son. Any chance you have of staying out of the big house, or worse, lies with you being honest with your lawyer."

"You don't think I did this, do you dad?" Rice asked nervously.

An uncomfortable silence filled the cottage. Allison noticed a small muscle pulse in her father's face. *This is going to be bad.*

"Actually, son, I'm pretty sure you did." Matthew raised his hand to silence Rice's outcry. "I think you meant to kill your wife, Rice, not your children. The children were an accident. But just like everything else you've done in your life, you messed it up." Allison watched as tears began to roll down Matthew's face. Pulling a wrinkled handkerchief from his pants pocket, Matthew wiped his face. "I can't bail you out this time, Rice. I've hired the best criminal lawyer I could find," Matthew nodded towards Brownlow "and I'll pay his legal fees, but you're on your own."

"Let's try this another way." Brownlow looked at Rice. "Who is the dealer?"

Pulling a name from his past, Rice whispered "Zack Bacon. I owed him money from a long time ago. I don't know how he found me." *Why didn't I think of Zack when I wrote those letters?* Rice mentally kicked himself. "He sent me some letters - threatened me. I have them back at the house."

The disbelieving glare from Brownlow's dark eyes pierced Rice's begging ones. "You actually expect me to believe this shit?" Turning towards Matthew the criminal lawyer continued "Mr. Parker, your son is either the dumbest son-of-a-bitch I have ever met, which I seriously doubt, or he is rapidly digging himself a hole that even I probably can't pull him out of."

"But I have letters" Rice exclaimed. "They must have come from Zack."

"Do I understand you to imply that those allegedly threatening letters aren't even signed?" Shaking his head, Brownlow addressed his client. "Bring the letters to my office today and the envelopes they came in. We'll run the lot for fingerprints. My forensic team will be able to track down the make of paper, which may or may not help us figure out where it was purchased. I'll have my investigator start a search for Zack Bacon." Brownlow inclined his head towards Matthew. "I'll represent your son so long as I think he has a legitimate legal defense to the charges against him. But I need to be completely honest with you. The minute I discover he is lying to me is the minute I withdraw from this case. Is that clear?"

Matthew nodded in agreement. "Rice, you heard the man. No lying. Now or later."

Wiping his brow, Rice replied "No lies. I promise."

Leaving Rice alone with Matthew, Allison walked her brother's defense attorney to his car. "Let me know if you need anything else" she offered.

"I'd like for you to drop by the office sometime in the next few days and give a statement regarding your meeting with the insurance investigator. Make sure nothing is lost to memory."

"Be glad to" Allison replied. "I'll have my secretary call your office and set up a convenient time."

The criminal lawyer eased his lanky body into the sleek Porsche Cayenne. Reaching for the car door, Brownlow paused. "You know this case is a long shot. A plea bargain is Rice's best hope, assuming the State will agree."

"The State won't be your only problem." Allison replied. "Rice is terrified of going to prison. I'm not sure he will agree to a plea that includes jail time."

"Well, someone better give that boy a dose of reality. Absent a miracle, he's probably looking at a conviction of either murder or man one." The Porsche's engine purred as Brownlow engaged the car's ignition. "I don't believe his story, and I don't think a jury will either."

CHAPTER TWENTY-FOUR

Frank Martin retrieved the typed agenda from the brown accordion folder resting on the passenger seat of his car. Crumpled McDonald's bags littered the floor, an odorous accompaniment to the pile of dried out coffee cups bearing the same logo. Over the past two weeks he had traveled to Birmingham, Miami, Houston and Charlotte retracing Ben Johnson's travel log that Allison had procured. Operating on the assumption that Ben Johnson had used out-of-town trips for homosexual encounters, Frank and Allison had agreed that larger cities would have offered Ben both more anonymity and a larger hunting ground. Discarding the smaller towns where Ben had conducted business in the last five years, Frank had focused his time on cities with a population of two hundred thousand or more. Frank had started with the four cities he had already visited primarily because the travel records indicated that Ben had frequented those cities more often than any of the others on the list.

Now, reviewing the list before him, Frank was frustrated with the results, or lack thereof, that he had obtained. Utilizing old information was difficult, especially when the information consisted solely of hotel bookings and reimbursed travel expenses. Ben Johnson would never have expensed drinks at a gay nightclub, and talking to hotel staff had proved futile so far. Employee turnover in the hotel industry was high, and the more exclusive the hotel, Frank knew from experience, the less likely he would be to find an employee who would actually carry tales about a regular customer like Ben Johnson.

I'm not done with you yet. Frank remarked, flipping through the computer printout. People made mistakes and Ben Johnson would be no exception. All Frank needed was to find what that mistake happened to be. Frank closed his eyes, resting his head against the car's leather headrest. *The clue is in the travel log. Has to be.* As was his habit, Frank ordered his mind to review the larger cities Ben Johnson had frequented. Birmingham, Miami, Houston, Charlotte, New Orleans, Atlanta, Charleston. A question formed at the edge of Frank's thoughts.

Shuffling the paperwork now littering the car's dashboard, Frank grabbed a slim notebook. In short order Frank had created a diagram of hotels, dates and cities. Why hadn't he seen this before now? For the past five years, the only hotel Ben Johnson had stayed in was a Ritz Carleton. Except for Atlanta. According to the travel log, Ben had stayed in the Atlanta Ritz until late 2009. Although Ben had continued to frequent Ritz hotels elsewhere, on the five trips to Atlanta post 2009 Ben had stayed at the Atlanta Hilton in midtown. *Something happened there, didn't it, Ben old boy?* Frank smiled. Time to book a stay at the Atlanta Ritz. Getting someone to talk might take a few days.

"I think I may be onto something" Frank rested the phone between his shoulder and head, freeing his hands to multitask on his MAC Air. "I'm in Atlanta. Been staying on the club floor at the Atlanta Ritz Carlton since day before yesterday."

"Expensive" Allison remarked. "And not your usual resting place. What have you found?"

"An anomaly."

Allison heard faint clicking from Frank's end of the conversation. "What are you doing?" she asked. "Are you on the computer?"

"Checking Atlanta police reports for the dates Ben stayed at this hotel in October 2009."

"Wait, wait, wait." Exasperation tinted Allison's reply. "You've completely lost me, Frank. Start from the beginning."

"You know I've been checking the hotels in the cities where Ben has conducted business over the past few years. Ben always stays at Ritz Carleton hotels."

"Yes, I know." Allison replied. "So?"

"That's just it. In late 2009 Ben quit staying at the Atlanta Ritz. His last visit was in October of that year. Every time he's returned to Atlanta for business since then he's stayed at the Hilton in midtown."

"And this is significant why?" Allison was perplexed.

"If I've learned anything about Ben Johnson, it's that he is both a creature of habit and he's addicted to luxury. He always stays on the club floor at a Ritz Carleton hotel. It's an exclusive, kiss ass venue - larger rooms, catered breakfast and cocktail hours for club floor guests. Staying at the Hilton isn't slumming it, but it's a big step down from staying on the club floor at the Ritz."

"You think something happened the last time Ben stayed there, don't you?" Allison asked. "That's why you're looking at the police reports. By the way, how are you accessing that data? Do I even want to know?"

"Just bending the rules a bit." Frank explained. "I want to see if Ben Johnson reported a robbery."

"Why would Ben report a robbery?"

"Let me back up. I've been here for two days. That's given me a chance to talk to club floor employees on several shifts." Frank continued. "In casual conversation I mentioned that a business associate, Ben Johnson, had recommended the hotel to me, tried to bait the hook, so to speak. Well, last night, I got a bite. The Concierge on the club floor replied that he was sorry to lose Mr. Johnson as a customer, but he could understand why Mr. Johnson had taken his business elsewhere."

"Did he tell you why?" Allison interrupted.

"Yes, he did." Frank replied. "Ben was robbed in his suite. The thief took Ben's clothes and wallet. The hotel had to send out for new clothes so Ben could actually get home. Management wanted to call the police, but Ben refused, said he'd make a report on his way out of town."

"Have you found the report?" Allison asked.

"Ben never filed a report with the Atlanta police." Frank replied. "And I think I know why. The Concierge would lose his job if management knew he had shared this next bit of info with me, but he told me Ben had not been alone in his suite."

"Have we found the smoking gun, Frank?"

"If not the gun, then some of the bullets. Ben had a man with him that night. All night. When Ben alerted management about the theft the hotel's security chief ran the tapes from the cameras on the club floor. Ben and another man entered Ben's suite around eleven p.m. The man left the next morning carrying a suitcase. Fifteen minutes later Ben called to report all his clothes and his money had been taken."

"Who was he? Can we identify him?"

"No such luck. Neither Ben nor the hotel management mentioned the overnight visitor. When Ben insisted he would handle the police himself, hotel management figured discretion was the way to go."

"What about the surveillance tapes?" Allison asked. "Can we get a copy of those tapes somehow?"

"Even if we could get them, they no longer exist. But I do have a description. The Concierge said the guy was fairly young, slim build, dark blond hair. Not much to go on, but better than nothing."

"We've got to be able to use this somehow" Allison mused. "I can't believe Ben would have been stupid enough to bring a one night stand to his hotel room."

"I agree. Totally out of character. But, if the Concierge is right, that's exactly what Ben did." Frank replied, typing a new command into his computer. "Ben wouldn't take a chance with a street prostitute. Our mystery guy must have appeared safe, at least to Ben."

"I can hear you on the keyboard, Frank. What are you looking for now?" Allison inquired.

"Maybe Ben wasn't the guy's first target." Frank explained. "I'm looking for reports of any unusual thefts at high end Atlanta hotels in 2009."

"I don't know, Frank. If the victims are similar to Ben, they will be successful business men who are hiding their homosexuality. Why would any of them report a theft?" Allison countered. "Too much to lose, just like Ben."

"Only if they were trying to hide that lifestyle." Frank replied. "There's nothing in 2009, so I'm going to go back a year and narrow the search to the downtown Atlanta zip code."

"It's a long shot.." Allison began.

"And persistence pays off" Frank interrupted. "Bingo! February 12, 2008. St. Regis Hotel. Theft of clothing, jewelry, credit cards and cash from one Mr. Thomas Crittenden. Vic's home address is in Perdido Key, Florida. The report indicates a guest in the Vic's suite absconded with all of the Vic's belongings while Vic was in the shower." Frank pumped the air with his fist. "I'll bet you a dime to a dollar this is our guy."

"You up for a detour on the way back to Ft. Charles?"

"Absolutely. If Mr. Crittenden is still in Perdido Key I'll be talking to him by suppertime tomorrow." Hanging up the phone, Frank enjoyed in the endorphin rush that always accompanied the knowledge that he was close to the end of a difficult investigation.

Frank's work the past few years had become much too routine. Smiling, Frank reminded himself to thank Allison for hiring on him the Johnson case. He hadn't had this much fun in a long, long time.

CHAPTER TWENTY-FIVE

A heavy staccato pounding jarred Allison from a deep sleep. "Jim, wakeup" Allison shook her husband's shoulder. "Someone's at the back door." Wrapping her bathrobe securely as she ran, Allison hurried through the home's living room towards the french doors which opened onto the home's large back porch.

"Come quick." Matthew's night nurse urged as Allison unlocked and opened the screen door. "Something's happened to Mr. Matthew."

Allison felt her husband's presence behind her as she ran through the open cottage door. Matthew Parker lay sprawled on the kitchen floor, his left arm pinned underneath his body, fingers slowly twitching.

"Lorraine, call Dr. James" Allison commanded. "Not 911. Daddy said he wasn't going to a hospital, no matter what." Kneeling, Allison grasped her father's fingers to quiet them. "Daddy. Daddy, can you hear me?" she whispered, her lips barely brushing Matthew's ear. "It's Allison." Eyes closed, Matthew moaned softly, then squeezed Allison's hand as a grimace crossed over his face.

"He's in pain." Jim observed. Locating the morphine patches Dr. James had ordered, Jim looked at his wife. "Turn him to his back. Let me put a new patch on his stomach."

"Let's try to get him in the bed first." Allison replied. "We can't leave him on the floor."

"Dr. James is on his way." Lorraine hurried to help Jim and Allison move Matthew to the bedroom. "He said the main goal now was to control Mr. Matthew's pain."

He's skin and bones Allison realized as they lifted the Matthew's frail body. *There's nothing left.* Allison fought against the tears forming in her eyes. *Not now* she silently ordered her father. *Not now. You promised.*

Another moan filled the small room. Allison watched helplessly as Matthew began to clinch his teeth, grinding them so harshly that blood seeped from the side of his mouth.

"Where is Dr. James? What's taking him so long?" Allison wiped her father's face with a damp cloth. "It's okay, Daddy. It's okay." she crooned, trying to will away her father's pain. "Jim, put another morphine patch on Daddy. Maybe that will help."

"I've only got one more left after this one." Jim told his wife. "These patches don't work quickly enough to make any real difference, either. Bill James needs to get his ass here right now." Placing his hand on Allison's shoulder, he added "I'm going to call Rice. Good thing he stayed in town overnight. He needs to be here."

Thirty minutes later a disheveled Bill James stood by Matthew's bed. "Sorry it took so long. I was finishing up an emergency at the hospital." Using a stethoscope he pulled from a black doctor bag, James listened intently to Matthew's breathing. "Shallow and slow." he commented, then lifting Matthew's eyelids and shining a small light at that pupils, James observed "I think he's had a stroke. Given Matthew's wishes, all we can do now is keep him comfortable."

"I've called Rice." Jim told the doctor. "He's on his way."

"Good. Matthew won't last long in his condition. A few hours to a few days, but it won't be long." James filled a syringe, squeezed a drop to clear any air, then injected his patient. "Morphine. A significant dose. Either my nurse or I will be by every 4 hours today to give him another injection. If he's still with us tonight

I'll arrange for an R.N. to stay over so we can keep him pain free."

"There's no coming back from this, is there?" Allison whispered.

"No, there's not." Dr. James replied gently. "But hearing is the last thing to go, Allison. If there's anything you or Rice want to say to Matthew…..." Dr. James hesitated, "Tell Rice what I said."

"He's a tough old bird" Rice remarked. Almost thirty-six hours had passed and Matthew was still among the living. For most of that time Allison and Rice had remained at Matthew's side, leaving briefly only in response to nature's call or to grab a quick bite to eat. The morphine Dr. James and his nurse had regularly administered had quieted Matthew's body, but Allison knew at some subconscious level her father was refusing to acquiesce to Death's call. Matthew had lived life on his terms, and Allison knew he would fight to experience Death in the same manner.

"He's not ready to go." Allison sought a more comfortable position in the straight backed chair. "Something's undone."

"You don't believe in that mystical crap, do you?" Rice scoffed. "He's just too damn mean to die."

"Actually, Rice, I do believe in that, quote, mystical crap. I think Shakespeare got it right when he said there were more things in heaven and earth than we can understand." Giving her brother a tight smile, Allison added "And I believe in karma, too."

"You self-righteous bitch" Rice snapped. "Take the damn stick out of your eye."

Unmoved, Allison retorted "If anyone has a stick in the eye it's you, Rice. You may eventually fool a jury, but you haven't fooled me, and you sure as shit didn't fool Daddy. All the money in the world won't keep karma from biting you in the ass for what you did to your children."

"You think you're so smart. You and your ass-wipe husband." Rice's face reddened with rage. "You're a whore just like Mary Louise. I bet you fucked your way into that partnership at Johnson & Merritt. Your husband's too stupid to figure it out."

"You're an ass." Steel coated Jim Kaufman's words. Neither Allison nor Rice had heard him enter the room. Moving swiftly, Jim slammed Rice against the bedroom wall. "You will apologize to my wife. Now."

"Fuck you" Rice yelled, flinging Jim's arm away. "You can't tell me what to do."

"I can, and I will." Jim's words sliced the air. "Apologize to my wife and I'll allow you to stay here with Matthew until he passes." Observing Rice's hesitation, Jim added "Or leave now. It's your choice."

"Ughhhhhh…" An unintelligible command accosted the three adults.

"Daddy." Allison spoke softly, leaning over her father's body, her attention now focused solely on the dying man. "Can you hear me?"

"Ughhhh…" The sound whispered on Matthew's breath, accompanied by an almost imperceptible movement of his head. "Ughhhh…"

"It's alright, Daddy." Allison consoled Matthew. "It doesn't matter now, whatever it is. It's okay to let go." A calm passed over Matthew's features, the agitation of a few minutes earlier seemingly forgotten. "He heard us." Allison looked first at her husband, and then her brother. "Can we all agree to be civil until after the funeral?"

"Call me when it's over." Rice spit out his reply. "I'm going back to Sumner."

"Rice, stay. Please." Allison forced herself to issue the invitation. "Don't let your feelings about me convince you to do something you will regret."

"I know all about regret." her brother replied heading towards the cottage door. "This is nothing."

The sound of screeching tires filled the cottage, announcing Rice's hasty departure. Wrapping his arms around his wife, Jim murmured "He's a lost soul, Allison. You're not to blame for any of this."

Turning to face her husband, Allison kissed him gently. "Actually, hon, I am to blame for tonight." Seeing Jim's questioning look she explained "I baited him about the accident. I knew better and did it anyway."

Pushing Allison to arm's length, Jim lectured "Nevertheless, Rice's problems are all of his own making."

"Yes, that's true, to a degree." Allison replied as she resumed her bedside watch, moving a small pillow behind her back to soften the hardness of the chair. "I have to wonder, though, what sort of man Rice would have been if Daddy had just left him be." Gazing at her father, Allison remarked "This entire situation - the children's deaths, Mary Louise a vegetable, Rice going on trial for murder - it's beyond sadness. Rice may have been the actor, but we both know he didn't write the play."

The Sumner News Sentinel devoted a quarter of its front page to the life and death of Matthew Whitaker Parker. *"Matthew Whitaker Parker of Sumner, Tennessee passed this mortal coil to be with his Lord and Savior on January 10, 2013. A prominent son of Sumner, Mr. Parker will be remembered for his numerous charitable works and community leadership."* She couldn't read any further. Laying the paper aside, Allison walked to her closet.

Allison had plenty of black suits - sartorial battle gear as she liked to describe her courtroom attire.

Allison had always believed a woman's ability to use fashion as a discrete weapon was a great advantage over male lawyers in their standard gray pinstripes. Appearance was almost as important in the courtroom as being well prepared. Plus, juries loved seeing a woman attorney who looked like she had just stepped out of the pages of Vogue. *Must be the result of watching too many lawyer shows on television* Allison reflected as she eyed her wardrobe.

Maybe one of her little black dresses instead? *No, too fancy.* More appropriate for a cocktail party rather than a funeral. Reaching past the tailored black suits and cocktail dresses, Allison pulled out the simplest of mourning clothes. She would wear a plain black dress, knee length, with an old fashioned jewel neckline. A single strand of pearls, inherited from her mother, would add the only color.

Turning to leave the house, Allison caught a glimpse of herself in the foyer mirror. Allison Parker, smart, self-assured trial lawyer, was nowhere to be seen. In her place stood a woman barely hiding her grief, a woman who had based every decision in her entire life on the hope that, this time, whatever she had done, or whomever she had married, or whatever honor she had attained would have finally been enough to win love and approval from the man she was now getting ready to bury.

Tears rolled unbidden from Allison's dark eyes, threatening to mar her carefully applied makeup. As strange as it seemed, she was grateful for Matthew's last illness. He could have dropped dead from a heart attack or been hit by a car. *We were lucky. We had three months together after Bill James issued Daddy's death sentence.* Three months in which to repair years of pain and sorrow, to confront the demons which had afflicted their relationship, to take back the hateful words flung at each other, to try to find reconciliation before Death silenced their communion. It hadn't been much time, but it was more than a lot of people got.

Allison climbed into the limousine where her husband and children waited. "I was about to come after you." Jim remarked. Seeing the strain on his wife's face, Jim added "It's almost over, Babe. Just a few more hours."

"I haven't been able to reach Rice." Allison fretted. "I asked Sheriff Biden to check Rice's house. He said, best he could tell, no one had been there for several days. Said there were three or four newspapers in the driveway. Surely Rice won't miss Daddy's funeral?"

"Don't worry about Rice. He'll either get there or he won't." Jim replied. "I still can't believe he walked out the other night. Maybe missing Matthew's funeral is Rice's postscript to missing Matthew's last hours."

If only her husband had been right, Allison reflected. Scheduled to start at two in the afternoon, the sanctuary of Sumner First Presbyterian Church had been filled to capacity by a quarter to the hour. Sprays of flowers covered the front of the church, their fragrance surrounding the dark mahogany coffin that contained the mortal remains of Matthew Whitaker Parker. Most, if not all, of Sumner's business community sat crowded in the cushionless pews - an ascetic nod to the denomination's Calvinist roots - along with numerous local, state and regional dignitaries with whom Matthew had conducted business of one kind or another over a long and successful banking career.

At five before the hour Rev. Haseldon had asked "Where's Rice? I'd like to have the family seated now." To Allison's dismay, no one, including local law enforcement, had been able to locate her errant brother. Rice was not at his house, nor at the nursing home with Mary Louise, nor at the homes of any of his friends who were now seated in the church's sanctuary.

"I don't know where he is" Allison replied. "I haven't seen him since a few hours before Daddy died." Adding a confession, Allison explained "We had a pretty ugly argument. Rice was very angry when he left our house. I don't know whether he'll be here or not."

Rev. Haseldon glanced at an ancient appearing pocket watch he pulled from beneath his vestments. "I'll give him five more minutes. After that, I'm starting this service."

Rev. Haseldon had been true to his word. At five after two he led Allison, Jim and their children to the pew reserved by a white bow at the front of the church. Ascending the steps to the pulpit, the preacher instructed the congregants to bow their heads, and then commenced with an opening prayer. Matthew's funeral service had began like any other - a couple of songs and a few prayers preparing the mourners for what they expected would be a succinct and Biblically based homily. A typical Presbyterian service where the only difference from one funeral to the next was the name of the deceased. Or so they thought.

"We gather here today to honor Matthew Parker, a friend to many, a man who unselfishly committed himself to this community, a man who loved and cared for his family..." Rev. Haseldon began.

"What a load of horseshit." A slurred retort echoed throughout the sanctuary. "What a complete and total pile of crap."

Horrified, Allison and the rest of the congregation had turned towards the sound to see a dirty and disheveled Rice Parker lurching down the aisle. Taking a swig of dark liquid from a bottle clutched in his right hand, Rice stumbled against the end of a pew.

"Sanctimonious fuckers" Rice pointed the liquor bottle at the stunned observers. "Every fucking one of you. Sanctimonious fuckers at the funeral of the most sanctimonious fucker of them all."

Shocked into action, Allison and Jim had exited the pew to restrain Rice while Rev. Haseldon exhorted everyone to stay in their seats. Fortunately for Jim and Allison, Sheriff Biden had ignored the Reverend's instruction, and had been able to deflect Rice's attempted attack on his sister by grabbing Rice's arm before he could strike Allison with the almost empty liquor bottle.

Shackling Rice's wrists with handcuffs which had appeared from under his suit coat, Sheriff Biden had informed Rice "You're under arrest." Acknowledging Jim's status, the Sheriff reported "I'll book him on disorderly conduct and public drunkenness, Your Honor. It's a 24 hour hold. He'll be sober by the time he's released." Pushing Rice ahead of him, Sheriff Biden had exited the church without further comment from his prisoner, who now appeared slack jawed and glassy eyed, his internal demon momentarily quieted.

One had to give Rev. Haseldon credit, Allison thought, as she relived the debacle. Holding his hands as in a blessing, Rev. Haseldon had calmed the congregants, and then led them in prayer asking for God's mercy on Rice Parker, who had clearly become unhinged from grief over his father's death. *Good comeback, Rev.* Allison marveled at the memory of how smoothly Rev. Haseldon had turned the horrendous spectacle into part of his homily, encouraging the listeners to show forgiveness and understanding. *You're definitely in the right profession.*

The next day Allison had contacted Jason Brownlow and Rice had been released into his lawyer's custody. This afternoon Rice was scheduled to check into a rehab facility in Jackson, Mississippi for a thirty day stay. "Because he will be a voluntary admit, he can check himself out at any time." Brownlow had explained. "We'll just have to see how it goes." Allison had decided not to visit Rice before his departure. She wasn't sure either one of them was ready for a face-to-face. Maybe they never would be.

CHAPTER TWENTY-SIX

I could live here. Frank Martin admired the white sand beach and the crystal clear aqua water as he drove along Gulf Beach Highway on his way to Perdido Key and his meeting with Tom Crittenden. *Who am I kidding?* he laughed. *This is way beyond my pay grade.*

"Turn left". The Bitch-in-the-Box, as Frank affectionately referred to his GPS, instructed tersely. "Turn left." According to the Bitch, Frank would arrive at his destination in ten minutes. Locating Tom Crittenden had not been difficult. Still residing at the same address as when he was robbed in Atlanta at the St. Regis, Crittenden had been quick to agree to a meeting with Frank. "Be glad to talk to you." Crittenden had responded when Frank asked if he would entertain a short visit. Matthew Parker's death and subsequent funeral had delayed Frank's meeting, but a week after his initial conversation with Crittenden Frank had rescheduled the face-to-face with his most promising lead.

"Arriving at destination" Frank's electronic companion announced. "On right."

An impressive two story stucco house covered the better part of a fully landscaped yard, adorned with towering palmettos, mature Oleander, and fragrant Camellias. Although partially obscured by thick shrubbery at the side of the home, Frank caught a glimpse of a sailboat tethered at the end of a long boardwalk. *Money, no doubt about it.*

Frank's ring of the doorbell was quickly answered by a young woman of apparent Latin descent.

"My name is Frank Martin. I have an appointment with Mr. Crittenden."

"Si, Senor" the young woman replied. "Senor Crittenden is expecting you."

Following his guide down a long hall, Frank took note of the home's furnishings. Thick rugs, large, presumably original paintings, and exquisitely upholstered pieces of furniture adorned every room he passed. Not just money, Frank surmised. This is old money. How had he never heard of this guy?

The hallway opened into a light filled conservatory. All sorts of tropical plants were scattered about the room, from small specimens in delicate containers to a large ficus which took up the better part of one corner of the room. A cool breeze kissed Frank's cheek. Looking upward Frank saw an enormous ceiling fan lazily rotating carved blades. Beyond the large windows which comprised the entire back wall of the room, the sailboat Frank had earlier glimpsed rocked gently on the inland waterway.

"You must be Mr. Martin." A tall man wearing khaki slacks, a navy blazer and soft leather loafers waved a manicured hand in Frank's direction. Tan, trim and well dressed, Tom Crittenden reminded Frank of the character George Hamilton had played in *Where the Boys Are*, a 1960's coming of age film about teenagers on Easter break in Ft. Lauderdale. *No way this guy is seventy years old,* Frank thought. Had he not known Crittenden's age from the Atlanta police report, Frank would have pegged the man standing in front of him no older than his early fifties. *He must have a hell of a plastic surgeon* Frank mused.

"Thank you, Rosita. You may leave us now." Motioning to a table which displayed an assortment of fruits and pastries, Crittenden continued "I had Cook prepare us a small repast. I'm sure you would enjoy some refreshments after your long drive."

Frank wondered if he had stumbled into a 1920's movie set. Surely people did not live like this anymore. At least, Frank thought, no one that he knew. "Thank you, Mr. Crittenden" Frank answered. "I appreciate you taking the time to talk to me - in fact, being willing to talk to me about what must have been a very disturbing event."

"Not at all, young man. Not at all." Crittenden indicated Frank should sit. "But, first, let's enjoy what Cook has prepared. There's plenty of time to discuss unpleasant topics."

After two cups of coffee, several delectable croissants, and assorted fresh berries, Frank had suffered enough of Crittenden's enforced tea time. "Mr. Crittenden, I appreciate your hospitality, but I need to head back to Ft. Charles pretty soon. Can we talk about Atlanta?"

Tom Crittenden removed the linen napkin from his lap, folded it carefully, then placed it on the table. Examining his polished fingernails, Crittenden pushed back from the table, crossed his legs and opened the conversation with a frank statement. "I'm homosexual."

"Ugh, is that relevant?" Frank stammered. "I mean, I don't care what your sexual preference is."

Crittenden laughed. "Oh, it's relevant alright. That's how I was robbed at the St. Regis." Reaching for the silver tea pot, Crittenden poured hot water into a delicate china coffee cup, then added a tea bag to seep. "More?" he inquired.

"No, thanks." Frank shook his head. "What do you mean? Did someone target you because you're gay?"

"Someone targeted me because I was stupid and careless. Being gay just gave him a lever."

"What happened? As much as you can remember would be helpful."

"I was in Atlanta for a gallery opening in Buckhead." Crittenden began. "Always stayed at the St. Regis - that hotel has a lovely lounge, you know. Anyway, at the opening I met a handsome young man who seemed very interested in me. We talked for an hour or more while we enjoyed the gala, and then I invited him back to the hotel for a nightcap."

"The police report stated the robbery occurred in your hotel suite." Frank looked at the report. "Is that correct?"

"Yes." Crittenden nodded. "About midnight we headed to my suite. The next morning, when I awoke, my guest was gone and so were my clothes and money."

"My client had a similar encounter" Frank fibbed. "He didn't file a police report for personal reasons. May I ask why you did?"

Crittenden arched his eyebrows, a tight smile causing two small dimples to appear. "Your client must not be 'out'. I've never hidden my sexuality. There was no reason for me not to report the crime."

"Did you ever hear from the man after that night?" Frank was anxious to hear Crittenden's reply.

"As a matter of fact I did. That sorry son-of-a-bitch tried to blackmail me. Threatened to expose me as a fag - his words, not mine." Crittenden took a final sip of tea, then added "He certainly was surprised when I told him to go right ahead. Never did hear another word from him after that."

"That was it?" Frank asked incredulously. "He just went away?"

"He was only in it for easy money. He didn't have the leverage on me he thought he had, so I became work for him. Given that we're having this conversation, I imagine he had some leverage on your man?"

"Unfortunately, yes." Frank wondered if this answer was actually truthful rather than another lie. "Did this man ever tell you his name? There's nothing about that on the police report."

"I didn't see any reason to give the police his name. I'm sure it wasn't his real one. He told me to call him 'Chris'. No last name." Crittenden reached for a silver cigarette case lying on the credenza behind him. "I do so admire lovely things, don't you Mr. Martin?" he asked, closing the lid after retrieving one of its contents. "That's what got me in trouble in Atlanta that time. Scoundrel or not, my thief was a lovely specimen. Anyway..." Crittenden paused to tap the tobacco to the end of his cigarette, "he got what was coming to him."

"What do you mean?" Frank wondered where the conversation was heading. "I thought you never had further contact with the guy?"

"I did not. But a year or so ago there was a news story in the Pensacola paper. The body of an un-identified man had been found in some outlying county - can't remember now exactly where - but he'd been shot execution style. The story had a picture of the victim drawn by a police artist and a number to call if the man looked familiar."

"Did he?" Frank could barely contain his excitement.

Crittenden took a deep drag on his cigarette. "If it wasn't the same guy it was his clone. Guess he finally blackmailed the wrong guy."

Frank called Allison as he pulled out of Crittenden's driveway. "I'd like to stop by your house tonight. This case has taken a disturbing turn."

"What's going on?" Allison was surprised by the ur-gency in Frank's voice.

"I think we may be dealing with more than we thought." Frank replied. "I want Jim to hear this too. I should be back by eight tonight."

"Alright. I'll let Jim know. See you when you get here." Allison severed the connection. *What has Frank discovered?*

Jim let out a low whistle. "Holy shit" he exclaimed. Turning to his wife, he added "If this is what I think it is, both you and Frank could be in danger."

"That's my read on this, too" Frank added before Allison could reply. "We don't have a complete picture yet, but the pieces we do have look a whole lot like murder."

"Let's say you're right." Allison looked at Jim and Frank. "Some guy was targeting affluent gay men for blackmail. What we know about Ben's robbery and Tom Crittenden's robbery could point to a pattern. Especially if there are other Atlanta robberies that follow the same M.O. But all we have now is a description of Ben's alleged thief which seems to match the newspaper picture Tom Crittenden showed Frank of the man he thinks robbed him - the guy who was found murdered outside Pensacola. We don't know if this is the same person, we don't know who murdered the guy, we don't have anything to connect Ben to this alleged murder, and assuming we could prove everything we suspicion, do you really think the local D.A. would even take the case?"

"We're a long way from taking our findings to the D.A." Jim interjected. "My concern, and I think yours, too, Frank" Jim nodded towards the investigator "is whether we proceed with our investigation to find those pieces, or whether we walk away."

"Yes. It is" Frank continued, a look of concern etching his features. "I think the murder victim in Pensacola was, in fact, Tom Crittenden's failed blackmailer. Someone like Crittenden would remember the man who tried to victimize him. If it's the same guy who robbed Ben, we have to ask ourselves, did he blackmail Ben as well?"

"I know what you are suggesting, Frank" Allison acknowledged, "but I can't see Ben killing someone. That's where you're going with this, isn't it?"

"I don't think Ben could actually kill someone, either." Jim agreed with his wife's assessment. "However, Ben Johnson had a lot to lose if he was being blackmailed for being gay. Desperation makes men, and women, do despicable acts - I've seen it over and over in my courtroom."

"Both of you are correct, in my opinion" Frank replied. "And that is why I am worried. Take a minute to review what we do know.   Allison hired me to investigate Ben Johnson, Steve Miller and Miller Industries after Ben removed her from the McNair case. What's the common denominator between Ben Johnson and Steve Miller?"

"Jeff Bishop." Allison quickly answered. "Donna and I noticed the connection a while back, but with Daddy passing and Rice going crazy I hadn't followed up on this Bishop character." Allison glanced at the men. "What do we know about Jeff Bishop? Anything other than his childhood association with Steve Miller?"

"Being arrested for conspiracy to commit murder is more than a childhood association, Allison" Jim admonished his wife.

"No convictions, Your Honor" Allison retorted.

"Pleas to lesser offenses. You know that doesn't mean they didn't commit the crime for which they were originally charged." Jim responded. "There just wasn't enough evidence to convict."

"I called in some favors on the way back today, had a friend take a deeper look at Jeff Bishop." Frank interjected. "What I discovered gives me real pause about going further - at least without being aware of the risks."

"And?" Allison asked.

"Jeff Bishop owns several auto body shops in Alabama. On the surface, he looks harmless. A guy from the wrong side of the tracks who put his past behind him, worked hard, and built a successful blue collar business. Wife, a couple of kids, nice ranch house outside Huntsville." Frank skimmed the information that had been emailed to his phone. "He's got a sheet, though. An assault about fifteen years ago, an arrest for receiving and concealing in 2000 but no conviction. He did eighteen months in the mid nineties for insurance fraud."

"Receiving and concealing is a long way from murder" Allison observed, repeating the shorthand legal expression for receiving and hiding stolen property. But, thanks to my brother, we know what insurance fraud can encompass."

"I want to take a closer look at Jeff Bishop" Frank replied. "I've followed every other lead to its conclusion, and we still don't have a satisfactory answer. I think Bishop is the key - and it may be dangerous, especially if the murder in Pensacola is somehow related to Ben."

"I don't know" Allison fretted. "Maybe it's time to let this go. Sherry McNair was my main concern when I first contacted Frank. As it turned out, and for whatever reason, she got a decent settlement." Allison picked up a gold framed picture from the table beside the sofa where she was sitting. The photograph had been taken last summer in Gulf Shores during the family's annual beach trip. Smiling and happy, the suntanned faces of her children had been captured in a pure moment of childhood pleasure. Allison loved her children, more than she could ever adequately express. Part of that love, she knew, was modeling for her children the courage to make the right, and often very hard, decisions. Returning the picture to its spot, Allison addressed Jim and Frank. "But, the fact remains that Ben Johnson abused his position and likely manipulated the judicial process for personal reasons. I took an oath as an officer of the court to uphold justice, the law and the legal system. I'm not letting this go until we have our answer." Reaching for her husband's hand, Allison asked "You understand, don't you?"

Jim raised Allison's hand to his lips. "Do you even need to ask?"

CHAPTER TWENTY-SEVEN

The call from Mike Williams, the attorney handling Matthew's matters, reminded Allison that she needed to face the sad and unpleasant task of clearing her father's clothing and other possessions from the guest house. With Rice still at COPAC, the residential alcohol and drug rehab facility in Jackson, Mississippi, there had been no rush for the family to meet with Williams for a reading of Matthew's Will and accompanying Trust. Likewise, with the recent events of the Ben Johnson investigation coupled with Allison's regular caseload and family obligations, Allison had pushed the chore of cleaning out the guest house to the bottom of her to-do list.

The cottage had a musty, sick smell, reminiscent of nursing homes and hospitals. Wrinkling her nose at the sour odor, Allison moved quickly through the few rooms to open the windows. No way she could spend the next few hours breathing that smell. A thin layer of dust coated the kitchen table, and two coffee cups - last used the night Matthew died - sat unwashed in the kitchen sink, their bottoms permanently stained a deep brown. *Gross* Allison thought. *I should have cleaned this place weeks ago.*

Most of Matthew's wardrobe had gone to the Goodwill when he moved from his home in Sumner to the guest cottage. Tailor made suits, Italian leather shoes, custom dress shirts. Allison appreciated the irony of life as she imagined who might now be sporting her father's expensive attire. At one time appearances had mattered to Matthew Parker. Allison had been surprised at how easily her father had relinquished most of his clothing and all of the furnishings in his home after Dr. James had rendered his diagnosis. *Facing death tends to do that to a person* Allison reflected.

Time passed swiftly as Allison folded and bagged the meager wardrobe that had accompanied her father to his last abode. She would drop the clothes at one of the thrift stores on her way to work on Monday. Wiping her hands on her jeans, Allison turned her attention to the bedside table. Matthew's reading glasses, a half empty box of kleenex, and a bag of Hall's cough drops crowded the table's top, covering a worn, black notebook. During the last three months of his life Allison had observed her father hunched over the notebook, writing furiously. When she asked what he was writing Matthew always answered the same way. "Some things are easier to write than to say" he would reply, closing the notebook and returning it to its spot by his bed. "You'll read it soon enough."

Feeling the smooth worness of the notebook's cover, Allison hesitated. Would she regret reading what her father had written? No, she told herself, she would not. If the past three months had taught her anything, Allison knew holding onto regret was a losing proposition. The past was the past. No changing it, no matter how hard one tried or wished.

After Matthew had moved into the guest house, Allison had vented her frustration and anger about having to take her father into into her home. "I don't have a single happy memory about him" Allison had complained to a close friend. "Not one. How pitiful is that?"

Instead of sympathizing with Allison, her friend had asked "What are you afraid of Allison? That you'll have to forgive him for being a crappy father?"

"Maybe" Allison had admitted. "That's pretty damn pitiful too."

"I think you're confusing forgiveness with reconciliation." her friend replied.

"What do you mean?" Allison was curious.

"Just because you forgive someone for what he's done to you, it doesn't mean you have to have a relationship with him going forward " her friend offered. "You know that slogan about not shutting the door on the past or having any regrets about it, don't you?" Hugging Allison, her friend had added "Your dad is probably as worried about all of this as you are. Ya'll just need to cut each other some slack."

Allison had taken her friend's advice to heart, and before Matthew died Allison and her father had made peace with one another. No pleas for forgiveness from Matthew - that wasn't his style - and no flowery expressions of love from Allison - too many unloving years between them made such an overture an impossible step for her to take. But, they had accepted one another, and Allison knew at least as far as she was concerned there were no regrets.

Recalling Matthew's words that she would read what he was writing in the notebook "soon enough", Allison returned to the cottage's main room, settled herself on the sofa, and opened the black notebook.

Why can't I tell her how I feel? She's my daughter, for God's sake. Does it make me weak to admit my failings? Ha!- failings - that's a word I never applied to myself. Funny how one's perspective changes when the shit hits the fan. For all the power I once had, for all the ways I manipulated the people around me - God I hate to write those words - there's not a fucking thing I can do about this disease. It's killing me, literally and figuratively, and I can't do a damn thing to change the outcome. Allison would say it's karma. Rev. Haseldon would quote the Scriptures, telling me I'm reaping what I sowed. Whether it's punishment or fate, it's a pile of unremitting crap, a living nightmare from which there is no escape...

I've done a lot of thinking these past weeks and I have to admit I don't like what I've uncovered about myself. It's not like I didn't know what I was doing all those years. I just didn't give a shit about anything or anyone but myself. That's a terrible truth to accept. A terrible, terrible truth. And something I can't admit to anyone. Fucking pride. Even now it rules me. Is pride what keeps me from my daughter? I know she hates me, even though she's letting me die in this cottage. What happened between us? ...... Come on, Old Man. You know exactly what happened. You put all your chips on Rice. Allison was just an afterthought. That's not it either, is it? Don't lie all the way to the grave Old Man..... Jesus! I'm talking to myself ..... writing to myself....

Am I losing my mind...

I abused my wife. And I made my best friend cover for me. I beat my daughter. And punished her mother for trying to protect her child. I should have let Helene leave, let her take Allison. Maybe Helene would still be alive and Allison wouldn't hate me. Maybe time and distance would have made a difference. Maybe, maybe, maybe….mother-fucking maybe…

I'm getting weaker. Can't sleep. Nothing tastes good. Can't get comfortable. I'm dying but not fast enough now…. the struggle to stay alive is exhausting. I promised Allison she wouldn't have to deal with Rice's trial by herself. Please, Jesus, let me be able to keep that promise. I know I don't deserve any favors, but how about just this one? Hell, who am I kidding. The Almighty isn't going to answer any prayer from me. He's too eager to let me trade the pain of this living Hell for the eternal pain of the real thing…

Allison. I know you'll read this journal. When I began it, I intended to purge myself of my sins and then burn the book. But the more I wrote, the more I uncovered about myself, I knew you had been my intended reader all along. I wish I had the courage to tell you these things in person, but after all is said and done, I've come to realize that I'm a coward. An arrogant, prideful coward who is deeply afraid that you will always hate me. Afraid to risk your rejection if my apology is insufficient. At least if I am dead I won't know. Or at least that is my hope. … I know that no apology can change the past. So whatever I say, or write, will always be weighed against the harm that resulted from my actions all those years ago. … I don't know why I reacted to you the way I did, why I got so angry with you. Maybe because even as a child I saw an iron will in you that made me both afraid and angry.

Afraid of who you might become, and angry because I could not control you. ... I don't even know how to be honest with myself - am I still making excuses? Does it matter? .....

It's dark outside. Well past midnight. Lorraine is asleep in the living room and all the lights are off in the main house. I imagine you, Jim, Charlotte and Mack asleep in your beds, untroubled by the demons I carry, hopefully never tormented by demons of your own. You did well, Allison. All on your own and in spite of me, you did so well. And then I think of Rice - did I make him into the demon that he became? A murderer of his own progeny? In the middle of this night I fear the answer is yes. ... I won't be here to help you with your brother. I can hear Death's call, feel his cold breath, and I am reconciled to the inevitable end. It won't be long. ... I love you, Allison. If you believe nothing else I have written, please believe that.

Time passed silently, a mute accompaniment to the tears that wet Allison's cheeks. The emotional warfare that had raged within Allison while she read Matthew's journal had taken its toll. Whatever emotions had fought within her during the last few hours were totally depleted. Weary beyond belief, Allison closed the black notebook and reflected on what she had read. She knew she would never show the journal to Rice. She wasn't even sure she would show it to Jim. Reading her father's most private and anguished thoughts had made Allison feel almost like a voyeur. The writing was too naked, too personal.

A cardboard banker's box, the kind Johnson & Merritt used to store legal files, stood half filled on the kitchen counter. In it Allison had earlier placed the few personal items Matthew had brought with him to the cottage - a picture of Allison's mother, a hand-made birthday card Rice's children had made for their grandfather one year, her great-grandfather's pocket watch. Allison had been surprised at the eclectic selection. The bottom of the box would be a secure place for Matthew's journal until she decided what to do with it. Allison needed time to process what she had read.

CHAPTER TWENTY-EIGHT

Skimming the daytimer on her office computer, Allison breathed a sigh of relief. Judge Lee had just granted her Motion for Summary Judgment in the age discrimination case she was handling for one of her larger corporate clients. Removing that particular case from the trial calendar had freed up a large chunk of Allison's time. The weeks she had blocked for witness prep, categorizing trial exhibits, writing direct and cross examination questions, and all the other assorted necessary minituae that accompanied trial preparation had been erased with a click of her computer mouse. *Thank you, Judge Lee.* Allison enjoyed the modern version of hand to hand combat that actual trial entailed, but the physical and mental energy required in the months and weeks leading up to the days in the courtroom was sometimes overwhelming.

The past months had taken a toll on Allison. Losing her father had been hard, and Rice's problems were far from over. But most of Allison's added stress and anxiety was due in large part to the secret investigation she had commissioned. An investigation that had gotten stranger and stranger as Frank Martin continued to follow leads. Now, with a clear calendar for the next few weeks, Allison was determined to bring the investigation to a close.

Retrieving a folder from her bottom desk drawer Allison withdrew a copy of the newspaper article and picture of the man Tom Crittenden claimed had robbed and tried to blackmail him. After she, Jim and Frank met the last time, Frank had called Tom Crittenden asking if he would make a copy of the article he had shown Frank during his recent visit. "Certainly. I'll post it in the morning" Crittenden had replied. "Let me know if I may be of further assistance." Allison had smiled listening to Frank repeat Crittenden's remarks. Tom Crittenden sounded like a character from a novel. Allison hoped she'd have a chance to meet him one day.

True to his word, Crittenden had completed the requested task in a timely fashion, allowing Allison the opportunity to read the crime beat article that had been published in the Pensacola News Journal in July

2011. The headlines gave almost as much information as the article itself - the body of an unidentified male had been found by a couple of teenagers. The police had no leads, no witnesses had come forward, yada, yada. The article concluded by listing the number for a tip line and the assurance that all calls would be confidential.

Execution style murder in the Florida panhandle was not as unusual as one would think. Allison knew the coast's reputation. The so-called Mississippi Mafia had its fingers in a lot of pies between New Orleans and Pensacola, including murder-for-hire or just plain murder. If this had been a "hit" anyone with information who wanted to remain alive would also want to remain anonymous. The accompanying photograph, fortunately an artist's rendering rather than an actual bloody photograph of the deceased, depicted a handsome man, probably in his mid to late thirties, with blondish hair stylishly cut. *Clean cut* thought Allison. *A few years younger and he'd fit right in at the Sigma Chi house at Bama. What I need* Allison concluded, *is a way to show this picture to Ben, to see if it causes a reaction.* After reviewing several possible scenarios, Allison placed the photo in a manila envelope and headed towards David Jackson's office. She would bring Frank and Jim up to speed later.

David's office door was open, a sign that an inter-ruption would not be unwelcome. Stepping just inside the threshold, Allison asked "Are you busy?"

"I'm always busy" Jackson pointed at a mess of pa-pers covering his desk. "At least I'm supposed to be." Motioning for Allison to take a seat, he added "The correct question is 'do you need a break?'"

"Do you?" Allison smiled in response and hoped the 'break' she was about to offer would not be reject-ed. Or she betrayed.

"I've missed working with you" Jackson answered, his statement replacing a direct answer to Allison's question. "After that business with the McNair case I wasn't sure you'd want to anymore."

"The McNair 'business', aptly put I might add, was not your fault, David. I think Ben used you because he could - took advantage of being your father-in-law - to get rid of that case."

Jackson put a finger to his lips, then rose to shut his office door. "Never know who's listening" he ex-plained. Returning to his desk he continued "I think so too. What Ben did has been a real eye opener for me. If I hadn't been able to get a good settlement for our client I don't know what I would have done, and I've asked myself that question more times that you can imagine, but when Miller folded on that hundred and fifty thousand settlement demand I convinced my-self 'no harm no foul' and pushed the question to the back of my mind." Jackson pursed his lips, a resigned expression taking up residence on his face. "It's not over, is it? That's why you're here."

"No, it's not." Allison removed her glasses and absentmindedly wiped them on her skirt. Concern replaced Jackson's resignation as he recognized Allison's tell for anxiety.

"You remember a couple of months ago I told you I had hired Frank Martin to investigate Ben and Steve Miller?"

"Yes, and I told you I thought you had lost your mind, or words to that effect."

David's response evoked a grin from Allison. "I do remember your warning. You were pretty adamant about it, too."

"I assume by your presence today in my office that you ignored my advice to leave well enough alone?"

"Yep, you would be right" Allison replied, a serious expression replacing her smile. "Before we go any further in this discussion, David, I need to know whether I can trust you not to disclose what I am about to tell you, what I am about to ask you to do, even if you decide you don't believe what I say, or can't do what I ask."

David had a comfortable life, a family he loved, a secure position in one of the state's most successful law firms. David knew without asking that if he listened to what Allison was getting ready to share with him there would be no going back. After the McNair case he had spent too many sleepless nights asking himself what sort of man he was, too many nights where the answer he found was not the one he wanted. When David faced the naked truth, he knew he had allowed his ethics to be compromised the minute he bowed to Ben's demands. He would not allow it to happen again, no matter what the consequences.

"You have my word. And my assistance."

"Are you sure David?" Allison questioned. "You haven't heard me out yet."

"I'm sure." David replied, knowing with certainty that he was.

Withdrawing the picture of the man Tom Crittenden had provided from the manila envelope she had brought with her, Allison placed it in front of David. "I think everything started with this man."

"Who is he?" David asked, examining the picture. "I don't recognize him. Should I?"

"He's a blackmailer. His body was discovered near Pensacola about eighteen months ago. One shot to the head, no wallet or other identifiers with the body. He came to our attention through a third party a few days ago."

"What does this have to do with Ben?" David asked.

"Best case scenario, the dead guy blackmailed Ben." Allison hesitated. Taking a deep breath she added "Worst case scenario, the dead guy blackmailed Ben and Ben had the guy killed."

"Are you kidding me?" David hissed. "No way Ben Johnson would have someone killed. You have lost your mind, Allison, no doubt about it. And what in the world would this guy or anyone else have on Ben?"

"Before you dismiss my proposition, listen to the facts." Allison retorted. "Frank Martin is nothing if not thorough. The information he has uncovered, the people he has interviewed - it's all been checked, cross checked and checked again." Taking the picture from David, Allison kicked off her shoes, pulled her feet underneath her on the cushioned chair, and asked "Are you ready to hear why I think Ben pulled me off the McNair case?"

David nodded, unable to trust himself to reply in the affirmative.

Two hours passed before Allison stopped talking. Trained to present a succinct and detailed argument to judges and juries, Allison presented facts and theories to David Jackson, closing loopholes as they appeared, ultimately carrying David to the same conclusion she, Frank and Jim had reached. "We believe the same man who attempted to blackmail Tom Crittenden more than likely made the same attempt with Ben. Unlike Crittenden, Ben would have lost everything important to him if his sexuality became public knowledge. We're still not sure how this Jeff Bishop guy is involved, but we do know that both Ben and Steve Miller were in contact with Bishop around the time Ben pulled me from the McNair case as well as around the time he forced you to make the settlement overture to Jack Striker. And, we know that Jeff Bishop did time following an arrest on a murder for hire charge that was eventually pled down to a lesser offense. The working theory that the three of us came up with is the only one that makes sense to us: Somehow, eighteen months ago, Ben Johnson hired Jeff Bishop to get rid of the blackmailer. When we sued Steve Miller and his company on the McNair case, we think Miller was afraid we'd uncover his criminal connection to Jeff Bishop, and he used his connection to Bishop to pressure Ben to get me off the case and have you, or someone else in the firm, settle the claim."

"That's a lot of ifs, Allison, and a bunch of undotted i's and uncrossed t's," David replied. "although I do tend to agree it's a workable theory. But that's all it is - a theory. There's not a shred of solid evidence linking Ben to murder.

"I know" Allison replied. "That's where you come in."

"How so?" David was curious.

"I want you to show this picture to Ben."

The clock on his computer glowed 5:55. Johnson & Merritt strictly enforced eight-thirty to five as working hours for its hourly staff. No need to waste money on overtime. Even the few secretaries assigned to attorneys who pushed the envelope by keeping staff past the golden hour would be gone by now. That morning David had sent an interoffice email to Ben, asking if Ben could spare time to meet with him at six, apologizing for the afterhours request, but claiming client business prohibited an earlier meeting. The plan David and Allison had settled upon the preceding afternoon required privacy. They had decided the fewer people around when David showed Ben the picture the more likely David would be to get an honest reaction from Ben.

Ben's corner office was located on the floor above David's. David had initially found it weird to see his father-in-law as the man Allison had described, but critically examining the facts uncovered by Frank Martin had convinced him of Ben's probable culpability. Now, as he made his way to the third floor, the tapping of David's shoes on the concrete stairwell echoed the pounding of his heart. Could he pull off this charade? The next fifteen minutes would tell the tale.

David had tried unsuccessfully to persuade Allison of the plan's inherent danger. Ben was a powerful opponent, well established, and - if Allison's theory was correct - an opponent who would use every weapon at his disposal to ensure his own survival. And therein lay the danger of Allison's plan. Arguing with Allison had been to no avail. "We have to flush him out" Allison had insisted. "It's the only way". As he pushed open the heavy stairwell door David wondered if Jim Kaufman had agreed to this scheme? Knowing Kaufman, David was surprised the judge would agree to anything that might put his wife's life in danger. *I should have called him myself* David thought exiting the stairwell. *Maybe he could have talked his wife into taking a different tact.*

The quiet hallway, its thick carpet muffling David's steps, seemed almost sinister. *Get a grip* David ordered his imagination. Moving quietly David passed by empty secretarial stations where pens, message pads and other clerical paraphernalia, neatly stacked on their owners' desks, evidenced the absence of their work day inhabitants. Most of the attorney office doors he passed were open, but no sounds came from the interiors. As David and Allison had hoped, the third floor's regular inhabitants were gone for the evening.

"Good evening, Ben" A glance around the large office assured David that he and his father-in-law were alone. "Thanks for staying late to see me."

"Sure, son" Ben replied jovially, pushing aside a stack of folders. "What's on your mind."

"I'm not sure where to start" David selected one of the tooled leather chairs grouped in front of Ben's desk. Resting a cowboy booted foot on his knee, David continued "I had the strangest conversation with Allison Parker yesterday."

"Oh?" Ben asked, indicating with a nod for David to proceed.

"You know she didn't take being removed from the McNair case very well." Start with the truth David figured.

"I'm sure she did not" Ben's acknowledged "However, the firm's interests were more important than Allison Parker's feelings."

"You never did tell me why you took that case away from Allison." David looked directly at Ben. "All she would tell me at the time was that a complaint had been lodged against her."

"That's right." Ben nodded. "Ms. McNair called me. She didn't think Allison was handling her case correctly."

David struggled to keep disbelief from showing. Sherry McNair never made any such call. He knew that for a fact.

"Well, anyway," David continued, "when Allison came to me yesterday with this crazy story about black-mail and murder I figured this was her way of getting back at you for handing me the case." David watched Ben's face closely.

A slight narrowing of the eyes preceded Ben's response. "Did I hear you correctly? Blackmail and murder?"

"I know, I know." David made reassuring sounds. "I just laughed at her when she started talking all this crazy nonsense. But then she showed me this." David withdrew the newspaper picture from his jacket and handed it to Ben.

David had always thought the expression 'white as a sheet' to be an overused hack expression. The spectacle standing before him instantly disabused him of that notion, for Ben Johnson could have passed for a corpse. What little color Ben's normal milky complexion displayed had vanished as soon as David had spoke the words 'blackmail and murder'. *My God* thought David. *He's going to have a heart attack.*

Ben wiped his forehead with a handkerchief. "I don't know why this has been such a shock to me. I should have seen it coming."

Ben's reply was not what David had expected. "What do you mean, Ben?"

Years of leading a double life had honed beyond perfection Ben's ability to lie convincingly. "It's just so sad. All that talent, wasted." Assuming a conspiratorial expression, Ben continued "You know mental illness runs in the Parker line. Just look at her brother. Now there's a murderer for you." Wiping a non-existent tear from his eye, Ben offered his hand to David. "Thank you for bringing this to my attention, David. I know it couldn't have been easy for you." Ushering David from his office Ben advised "Don't you worry about any of this. I'll take care of it."

Closing the door of his office, Ben waited. He could see the exit of the firm's parking garage from his window. Ten minutes later, Ben watched as David Jackson's red Miata exited the garage and headed west on Broad Street. Ben wasn't sure what he was going to do about his son-in-law. Wasn't sure where that boy's loyalties would lie, especially after Allison Parker was removed from the picture. Ben would hate to make his daughter a widow. Maybe he wouldn't have to.

Anger mounting, Ben dialed Jeff Bishop's number. This was Bishop's fault.

"You have a problem" Ben announced coldly after Bishop answered. "And you're going to fix it."

"Is that you, Johnson?" irritation coated Bishop's question. "What the fuck are you talking about?"

"I paid you a shit pile of money to make sure Chris Cannon would disappear forever." Ben's voice began to rise. "You guaranteed me no one would ever make the connection between him and me."

"Quit yelling" Bishop demanded. "There's no way anyone's made that connection."

"Then tell my why I was justed handed a picture of Chris Cannon by my son-in-law, and why Allison Parker thinks I murdered him?" Ben's voice was icey. "This is your problem, Bishop. Fix it."

"What is it with that bitch?" Bishop asked. "First Steve and now you. She's a fucking pain in everyone's ass."

"And she's your problem now, Jeff." Ben assured him. "Get rid of her."

"I don't think that's very smart, Ben." Bishop interjected. "Not until you know who else she's shared her suspicions with."

Ben hesitated. Bishop had a point. He knew Allison had talked to David Jackson. Surely she had talked to her husband too. Killing a judge made Ben nervous, but what choice did he have?

"You'll have to add two others to your list" Ben told Bishop, handing over the names of his son-in-law and Allison's husband. "Get rid of all of them."

"I'll do the woman at no charge." Bishop agreed. "You want the two men taken care of, you'll have to pay for it."

Ben stifled the urge to curse. "How much?" was his only response.

CHAPTER TWENTY-NINE

J eff Bishop didn't like sloppy endings. Sloppy endings were dangerous, and this business with Allison Parker had all the makings of a sloppy ending. Allison Parker - he wished he'd never heard her name. If Steve hadn't freaked out about the woman discovering his juvie record during that damn court case - something Jeff doubted would have happened anyway - all of this could have been avoided. Well, Steve owed him on this one, and Jeff would make sure Steve paid up. Killing three people, all of whom were related to each other in some form or fashion, was risky business. Jeff wasn't doing this alone.

First, though, Jeff would need a plan. Should he take the Parker woman by herself? Maybe it would be better to get her and her husband at the same time, make it look like a home invasion. That had definite possibilities. Somehow related to the Judge's work, a red herring to distract the authorities. The more Jeff thought about the home invasion angle the better he liked his idea. *Piece of cake.* Jeff smiled at his ingenuity.

The Jackson guy might be more difficult. Ben Johnson had been adamant about how that hit would go down. "He's married to my daughter. Make it quick and clean. I don't want Sarah to have to identify a bloody mess." Jeff laughed at the memory of Ben's directive. *Who does Ben Johnson think he is, telling me how to do a job?* Rich clients who wanted to keep their hands clean, clients like Ben Johnson, were a pain in the ass made tolerable only by the outrageous amount of money Jeff was able to charge for his services. Not once in the twenty years he had been in this business had a single client told him to take care of the matter however he felt best. No, the client always wanted something extra, always had some demand or need, and then wanted an assurance that the deed would never be traced back to them. *Idiots. All of them.*

Jeff didn't give a shit who David Jackson was married to, but he did care about unnecessary collateral damage. How much did Jackson really know? Even if Jackson got suspicious when the other two were killed, would he connect it to Ben? Or to him? Was David Jackson a problem that needed to be removed for Jeff's ultimate protection, or was Ben using the Parker business to rid himself of a personal family problem? In the end, Jeff decided it didn't matter. There was no way to be sure how Jackson would react if Parker and Kaufman were killed. Another potential messy ending that Jeff could not risk. Jackson would have to be removed.

Now the only question for Jeff was one of logistics. Should he kill Jackson first, or go after the other two? Ben was a smart man. An angry and frightened smart man. There was no doubt in Jeff's mind that Ben would toss Jeff to the authorities if doing so would save Ben's own skin. Hell, the Parker woman could go to the District Attorney at any time. Someone in the D.A's office would call Ben, give him a head's up, and the rest would be history. Jeff would be spit and roasted. No one would believe his word against that of someone like Ben Johnson. The movie played in Jeff's head. Arrest, trial, death penalty, years on death row, escaping execution only if illness claimed him first. Before the credits had ceased to roll Jeff had made up his mind. The hits would have to be simultaneous.

A single unshaded light bulb illuminated the side door of Becker's Pawn and Gun. A battered pickup, its color indeterminate in the weak light, perched on four cinder blocks a few feet away, a stark contrast to the sleek Corvette parked in front of the wooden door. Steve Miller cut the engine of his Mercedes, braking to a stop beside and to the back of the pickup. Hopefully, his car would not be noticed by anyone still out at this late hour.

Music escaped from the crack between the pawn shop's side door and the concrete slab which supported the decrepit building. 'Under the boardwalk, down by the sea, on a blanket with my baby is where I'll be ….'. the Drifters crooned, their harmony disturbed by loud voices. Worried, Steve pushed open the door. "Jeff? It's me, Steve." Steve hoped his announcement would forestall any itchy fingers that might be holding a firearm. "You in here?"

Jeff Bishop was seated at a card table near the back of the small room. Across from Bishop, attired in jeans and a t-shirt, sat a man who looked familiar to Steve.

"Do I know you?" Steve asked, looking at the stranger.

"Doubtful" the man replied. "Unless you've done time at Angola" he added, referring to the hellhole Louisiana used for its state prison.

"Fortunately for me, that's a place I've never been." Steve replied. Pulling a chair up to the table, Steve examined the man more closely. Gray hair and wrinkled face seemed out of place on the man's trim and obviously fit body, an incongruity that made guessing the man's age impossible. The appearance of worn jeans and t-shirt were no help. Steve had paid way too much money at Abercrombie & Fitch for the same look. This guy could be anybody and any age. Dismissing the sensation of deja vu, Steve shrugged. "Guess you just remind me of someone else."

"What took you so long?" Jeff Bishop cast an irritated look in Steve's direction. "I haven't got all night and neither does Jake."

"Jake Cleveland." The named stranger added "Nice to meet 'cha."

"Jake showed up at the shop this afternoon. Referred by a lawyer I know in south Mississippi." Jeff explained to Steve. "Perfect timing, too. Jake needs work, and I've got a job that needs doing. Several jobs in fact."

"So why am I here?" Steve asked. The meeting was beginning to make Steve uncomfortable.

"You're here, Stevie boy, because all of this started with you. Favors go both ways, and I'm calling one in now."

"What?" Steve stammered. "What are you talking about?"

"That damn Parker woman." Bishop spat. "You shouldn't have panicked, and I shouldn't have listened to you." Bishop was visibly agitated. "Getting her kicked off that stupid employment case was the wrong move. Apparently she's spent the last several months trying to figure out why, and now she's tied Ben Johnson to that hit I did for him a couple of years ago."

"Mother of God" was Steve's only reply.

"The damn Virgin isn't going to clean up this mess." Bishop pointed at Steve. "You and Jake are going to clean it up. Permanently."

Steve was aware of a slight movement to his left. Jake Cleveland had moved his chair away from the table. Was he reaching for something inside his jacket? A gun? No, Steve realized with relief, as Jake pulled a pack of Marlboros from this jacket pocket and lit up a smoke.

"Dickie didn't mention anything about a cleanup" Jake commented, exhaling a perfect smoke ring. "Not that I care, mind you. I thought I was going to be carrying some merchandise for you, is all. That's what Dickie said."

"You will be once this problem is handled." Bishop assured Jake, a slight smile creasing his lips. "Look at this as your audition."

"Suits me" Jake replied laconically.

"Well, it sure as hell doesn't suit me" Steve Miller found his voice. "I don't kill people. If anyone should know that it would be you, Jeff."

"You're not sixteen anymore." Bishop reminded Steve. "You're a big boy now. And big boys clean up their own messes." Turning to address Jake Cleveland,

Bishop instructed "You'll be taking out the Parker woman and her husband. Make it look like a home invasion. They've got two kids. Don't harm them unless it's unavoidable." Bishop leaned across the table and looked directly at Steve. "Ben's son-in-law David Jackson knows something, too. Not sure how much and can't take a chance leaving him alive. He's your target, Stevie boy."

Jake Cleveland stretched his arms and yawned. "Time table?"

"The sooner the better. My only requirement is that the hits go down at the same time. You and Steve figure out the details. Let me know when you're ready to move on this."

CHAPTER THIRTY

J ake Cleveland tucked the G32 into the back of his
pants. Glock made a nice gun he mused, adjusting
his jacket to cover any bulge the compact piece might
show. Studying the assortment of handguns he had
spread out on the bed in his motel room, Jake selected
a .22 snubnose for his backup piece. The small caliber weapon didn't have much punch, but being able to
easily conceal the gun in his boot made it the logical
choice. Lastly, out of habit rather than necessity, Jake
tucked a switchblade into the side pocket of his jacket.
Jake didn't like using a blade, but he'd be a fool not to
have it with him.

The success of tonight's mission was far from guaranteed. Jake had spent all afternoon with Steve Miller

going over their plans, coordinating schedules, and tying down loose ends. According to the information Ben Johnson had provided Jeff Bishop, Tuesday was David Jackson's poker night. Jackson would have supper with his family and then leave around 7:30 to head to the Knights of Columbus clubhouse on the west side of Ft. Charles.

"You'll need to park close to the clubhouse, close enough for you to get to your car quickly after you've done Jackson" Jake had advised Steve Miller. Wait 'til he's finished playing. He'll have had a few beers and be distracted. Come at him from behind, and give him two taps here." Jake demonstrated the technique, his finger an imaginary .45 pressed to the back of Miller's head. "Drop the weapon and walk away as fast as you can. Don't run. You'll draw attention to yourself if you run. The gun's silenced. No one will hear a thing."

"I've never killed anybody" Miller had fretted, his forehead sprouting small beads of sweat. "I'm not sure I can do this."

Picking up a black backpack, Jake tossed in a couple of extra magazines for the G32. Reflecting on the afternoon's events, Jake figured there was a 50-50 chance Miller would back out of the assignment. While Miller's involvement wasn't critical, if they could catch him making the assassination attempt on Jackson his boss would get two criminals instead of the one they had originally targeted. Funny how things happened sometimes Jake thought. Instead of infiltrating a smuggling ring Jake had walked straight into a triple murder plot. With the new intel about Jeff Bishop's activities, Jake was pretty certain the Bureau would take a deeper look at Dickie Lott. The deal Lott had cut with the Feds on the money laundering charge only went so far. Accessory to murder was another matter altogether. Well, that wasn't Jake's concern. His orders were to take down Jeff Bishop. By the end of the night Jake intended to have accomplished his mission.

David Jackson's willingness to put himself at risk had impressed Jake. Several agents would be hidden in and near the Knights of Columbus parking lot, and Jackson would be wearing a Kevlar vest, but the risk of being shot could not be eliminated. Jake knew from yesterday's briefing that Jackson's father-in-law was a suspect in an earlier murder believed to have been committed by Bishop. Jackson had a set of balls, no doubt about it.

"Do you understand the risk you are taking Mr. Jackson?" Wilson Mackey, the FBI Agent in charge of the field operation had asked. "Mr. Miller is an attractive bonus for the Bureau, but catching him is not crucial to the operation as a whole. We'll have agents in place, and we anticipate taking out Miller before he can hurt you, but there's no guarantee in the field. No matter how well we plan - and we plan better than anyone else - bad shit can happen."

"I know that" Jackson had replied grimly. "You can't guarantee my safety, and I accept that. But this has become personal."

"Just keep your personal feelings under control Mr. Jackson" Mackey had warned. "Personal feelings can get people killed."

Jake threw the backpack in the passenger seat and started the engine of the rental car. Wilson Mackey was an experienced agent. He'd have plenty of cover on David Jackson. As long as Jackson didn't decide to be a cowboy the Bureau should have Steve Miller under wraps by midnight. The trickier task in Jake's mind would be the one awaiting him once Miller was under arrest. The proof of death that Bishop had required on the Parker woman would take a great deal of finesse and even more luck.

Turning into Allison's driveway Jake admired the view as he approached the white farm house. Maybe one day, after he retired from the Bureau, he'd find a place like this. Smaller, of course, but with a little land. A good place to grow old. In the meantime Jake thought, reality replacing wishful thinking, he and Allison Parker had a long evening ahead of them.

Jake's knock on the front door was answered immediately. "Come on in" Jim Kaufman beckoned. "The children are staying with friends tonight and tomorrow" he explained. Motioning for Jake to follow, Jim headed towards the rear of the house. "Allison's in the kitchen."

The aroma of freshly ground coffee hung in the air like a gentle caress. Dressed in jeans and a cream colored fisherman's sweater, Jakes's primary target was perched on a stool at the kitchen's butcher block island. "I eat when I get nervous" Allison explained, fork poised over a generous slice of caramel cake. "Want some?"

"No thanks" Jake smiled. "I like a natural buzz when I'm getting ready for serious work." Settling his six foot frame on one of the empty stools across from Allison, Jake inquired "How're you doing? You ready for this?"

"Ready Freddy" Allison replied, a weak smile conveying her true feelings.

"You'll do fine" Jake reassured her. Turning to include Jim in the conversation Jake added "Let's go over how this is going to work. Did you get the delivery this afternoon?"

"Yes." Jim replied, retrieving a medium sized box from underneath the island. "I haven't opened it."

Jake pulled his switchblade from its hiding place. "All the necessary props we'll need should be in here." Slicing through the packing tape and releasing the folded cardboard top, Jake began to retrieve the box's contents and place them on the island's countertop.

"Is that a Polaroid camera?" Allison asked. "I didn't think they made those any more."

"Never know when you may need old technology" Jake replied. "Remember I'm supposed to kill Jim too. A picture is worth a thousand words, plus I want to have something to distract Bishop from looking too closely at your body."

"I'm not comfortable with that part of this plan" Jim interrupted. "Allison, I know we agreed to play this the way the Bureau has asked, but I'm having second thoughts now." Addressing his question to Jake, Jim asked "Why can't you take pictures of both of us? I'm sure you can make us look properly dead."

"Jeff Bishop knows that, too, which is why I think he wants me to show him Allison's body." Jake explained.

"That doesn't make sense." Jim liked puzzle pieces to fit and these didn't. "Unless Bishop has reason to suspect you aren't who you say you are. Unless he's worried about a double cross. If there's even the slightest chance of that, it's too dangerous for Allison."

"No way he's made me, or this operation." Jake reassured Jim and Allison. "The intro to Bishop that I got from Dickie Lott was legit. Lott has too much on the line to double cross the Bureau."

"Then why is Bishop demanding you bring him Allison's body?" Jim pressed. "I don't like this."

"It doesn't matter why" Allison looked at both men. "And it's not important. I'll be in the trunk of Jake's car. Bishop will have to leave the pawn shop and come into the parking lot to see my body. When he does the Bureau's snipers will have him in their sights. Jake will be right there, too. Surely someone will be fast enough to take Bishop out if he decides to shoot my dead body." Giving a short laugh, Allison added "At least that's my theory."

The ring of a doorbell caught the group's attention. "That will be our makeup artist and one of the Bureau's forensic techs." Jake motioned towards the front door. "Jimmy's great at re-creating murder scenes - guess that's an unexpected talent derived from years of processing the real thing. Sandy got her start doing makeup for theater productions. Wilson enticed her away about ten years ago. By the time she's finished even you will think you're dead. She's got the touch."

By the time Jim had escorted the tech and makeup artist to the kitchen Jake had emptied the remainder of the box's contents. Several plastic bags filled with blackish red, plasma looking goo were scattered about, along with what appeared to be professional grade cosmetics, brushes, and other paraphernalia Allison could not identify.

Glancing at Allison's cream colored sweater, the makeup tech posed a question. "You got anything else you can wear? That pretty sweater's going to be ruined if you keep it on."

"Won't the blood show up better on something like this?" Allison asked in reply. Seeing the tech's nod, Allison continued "Then it's worth being ruined. We've got one shot at this and I want to look as bloody and dead as possible."

After a brief discussion of where best to set the murder scene, Jake and the forensic tech decided to stage the kill in the small den off the kitchen. That location would be a reasonable place for Jake to have surprised the couple, and would explain an easy entrance to the home should Bishop inquire about particulars.

Pulling a straight backed chair from the kitchen, the forensic tech placed it in front of the stone fireplace. "I'll need to tie you to the chair Ms. Parker and then cut the ropes while you are sitting there to make sure I get the placement right. Let me know when Sandy's finished with you." Moving towards the corduroy sofa, the tech knocked over a lamp, and brushed a framed family photo onto the floor. "After we position Judge Kaufman I'll see if there's anything else I need to add." Seeing the looks of dismay on Jim's and Allison's faces, the tech apologized "I guess no one told you - you'll want to recover that sofa, and probably replace the rug in here. It's going to get messy, and that stuff Sandy uses doesn't come out of fabrics."

Squeezing her husband's hand Allison tried for a light reply. "Well, I've been wanting an excuse to redecorate. Guess I've got one now."

"It's not too late to say 'no', Babe." Jim looked at his wife.

"I know" Allison replied. "But I've made my decision." Relinquishing her husband's hand with a final squeeze Allison headed towards the kitchen. "Here I come, Sandy. I'm all yours."

After Sandy completed her living masterpieces, Jake and Jimmy had positioned Jim and Allison for a macabre photo shoot. Looking at the polaroids Jake had laid on the kitchen island to dry, Allison shuddered. Jim's body lay sprawled on the sofa, his right arm flung across the neighboring side table, his left arm limp in his lap, head thrown back against the top of the sofa, sightless eyes staring towards the ceiling. A dark trail of blood formed a forked path around Jim's nose, its origin a small hole in the center of Jim's forehead. The corduroy sofa where Charlotte and Mack had watched cartoons just that afternoon now showed a deep red stain across the top and down the back of the soft fabric. Fake blood splatter covered the sofa table behind, including a pewter sculpture Allison had given Jim for his birthday one year. A bloody Rorschach patterned the back wall. "Even a small caliber round will have enough velocity to cause a spray five or six feet away from the target" Jimmy had explained.

Pushing the pictures of her husband to the side, Allison felt a wave of nausea as she relived her own staged death. Even knowing everything was for show, being tied to the chair had upset Allison. She couldn't imagine the terror the real thing would instill in a victim. Picking up one of the photos Jake had taken of her, Allison shuddered. Head hanging down, her body straining at the ropes tying her arms, hands and feet to the kitchen chair, blood covering the front of her sweater - Allison's hands moved involuntarily to her throat.

"Don't touch that." Sandy batted Allison's hands. "You're gonna mess up my work."

"What is this stuff you've glued to my neck?" Allison asked reaching for a nearby hand mirror. "I know it's not real, but looking at it makes me wonder if I'm having an out-of-body experience and I'm really dead afterall."

"Thanks for the compliment." The makeup tech laughed as she returned the remains of her product to the cardboard box on the island countertop. "We aim to please."

The taps on Jake Cleveland's boots clicked on the kitchen's tile floor. "You ready?" he asked Allison. "We need to be on the road within the next thirty minutes. I've got to position you in the trunk of my car so Jimmy can set that scene too. Guess it's a little late to ask if you're claustrophobic."

"I'm too scared to be claustrophobic." Allison replied, laying aside the mirror. "I just need for this to be over."

"Allison, just say the word" Jim Kaufman looked directly at his wife. "You don't have to do this. Jake can use the pictures."

"No." Allison replied. "I didn't start this, but I'm sure as hell going to finish it."

CHAPTER THIRTY-ONE

The Ft. Charles Knights of Columbus was a popular place on Tuesday nights. Founded in 1882 by a parish priest in Connecticut as a means of assisting low income Catholic immigrants, by the mid 1900's the Knights had grown into the largest Catholic service organization in the world. While still involved in doing good deeds and raising money for worthy causes, local KC clubs also offered a place for members to drink, play card games, and hold other social functions. Raised a Cradle Catholic, David Jackson couldn't remember a time when going to the local KC club hadn't been a part of his life - Easter Egg hunts and picnics when he was young, dances and youth group as a teen, and now Tuesday poker nights as an adult. David was pretty sure tonight's soon-to-be, and hopefully for his sake, 'attempted' shooting in the KC parking lot would be a first.

Wilson Mackey had phoned David around five that afternoon. "Jake told Steve to wait until you leave the club tonight, so let most of the members leave before you head out. Less chance of collateral damage that way."

"What if Miller decides to take me on the way in?" David's nerves caused a slight tremor in his voice. "He told Jake that Ben gave him my usual routine for poker nights at the clubhouse."

"I don't think that will happen. Jake told Miller his best chance of getting away with the hit would be to wait until most of the members had left." Mackay explained. "But don't worry. My snipers will be in place by six. You'll be covered going in and coming out."

Most of the regulars at the weekly poker game still punched a time clock, so by ten or ten-thirty hands would be folding and losers paying up with good natured grumbling. David had bowed out of the game early. Putting up a jovial front had been hard enough. Keeping his mind on the cards had proved an impossibility.

Preoccupied with his thoughts, David jumped when a hand touched his shoulder. "I thought that was you" a familiar voice commented. "Took me a while to find you."

"Frank, what are you doing here?" David was surprised to see the investigator. "I didn't know you were a member."

"I'm not" Frank replied. "A little bird told me there might be closure this evening to an investigation I've been working on for a while."

Motioning for Frank to sit, David whispered "A little bird? A female bird?"

"Actually, no" Frank smiled. "The little bird's husband. He asked me to watch out for you. He's tailing Allison and Jake."

David stared at Frank Martin. "Has Jim lost his mind? Tailing Allison and Jake?"

"You forget Jim's background." Frank shifted his bulk on the metal folding chair. "Four years in the Marines between high school and college. Jim won't compromise the mission."

"Does Cleveland know about this? About you and Jim?"

"Nah" Frank winked. "Need to know only."

"I'm supposed to wait until most of the guys are gone" David explained, sharing the plan with Frank. "Looks like it's about that time."

"Give me ten minutes. I want to get outside ahead of you." Frank heaved himself to a standing position. "The minute you feel someone close to your back, hit the ground. Miller won't be prepared for that."

Frank moved quickly for a man his size. In less than a minute Martin was gone, pushing through a door at the back of the main room. David hoped one of the Bureau's snipers didn't take a shot at Frank. Maybe he ought to let Mackey know about Frank's unexpected presence. Pulling the burn phone the FBI agent had given him from his pocket, David quickly texted "Frank Martin outside. He knows. Don't shoot him."

There were less than a dozen men remaining inside the clubhouse. David recognized most of them as the diehards who would play until the lights were extinguished at 11:00. He had given Martin more than a ten minute lead. Time to go. Reaching inside his shirt, David activated the wire Wilson Mackey had insisted he wear. "Miller may not say a word, but if he does we'll have him recorded." Giving his wife and children a mental kiss, David opened the front door of the clubhouse and stepped into the parking lot.

The members who had purchased the land for the KC clubhouse in the late '50's had been men of vision - and men who eventually made a lot of money as Ft. Charles crept westward annexing land the men had bought years before. The five acres purchased in 1952 for $2500 were now worth one hundred times that amount had the Knights been willing to sell. The rambling clubhouse was set midway back on the property, leaving a large expanse of land for members' parking. Originally a dirt lot, the clubhouse parking area had sported a coat of blacktop for many years. Tonight a yellowish gleam emanating from spotlights on two tall wooden poles softly illuminated the asphalt lot, most of the evening's four wheeled inhabitants having already departed for garages and carports closer to town. As instructed, David had parked his car as close to the center of the lot as possible. "Don't look around" Mackey had instructed. "Just walk towards your car. Miller will either show or he won't."

David noticed a white pickup parked a few feet away from his car. It hadn't been there when he parked earlier that evening, and David didn't recognize the vehicle as belonging to any of the men playing a last round of cards inside the clubhouse. Trying to watch for movement from the white pickup without being obvious was easier said than done David realized with some chagrin. *Don't scare him off* David cautioned himself. *Let this play out.*

Walking the fifty or so yards from the clubhouse to his car seemed to take forever. The sound of crickets and tree frogs, sounds David associated with spring and summer evenings, belied the terrible finality of what might occur. *It isn't going to happen* David thought as he reached his car. The words had barely formed in David's consciousness when a hooded figure rolled from underneath the pickup, and springing to his feet, pointed a chrome colored pistol at David's face.

"Not a sound" a man's voice commanded. Using the pistol for emphasis, the figure motioned towards David's car. "Get in, put your hands on the steering wheel and look straight ahead."

"What do you want?" David asked. This wasn't how it was supposed to happen. Was this a robbery? Where was Steve Miller? "I've got two hundred bucks in my wallet. Just take it" David pleaded.

"I don't want your money." the man replied, moving the gun towards David. "Just your silence."

A deafening 'crack' pierced David's eardrum, followed almost simultaneously by an exploding pain. As from a great distance David heard what seemed to be human voices, but he couldn't understand what they were saying. Touching his hand to the side of his face, David felt a warm, wet mush. Where was his ear?

"Call for an ambulance." David heard Wilson Mackey demand. "And get me something to staunch this bleeding." Mackey's fat fingers probed the left side of David's face.

"Shit, that hurts" David moaned. The buzzing sound in David's head was diminishing in about the same proportion that his awareness and pain level were increasing.

"It's just a flesh wound, David." Mackey observed, removing sticky fingers from his patient's ear. "You'll be fine."

"What about Miller?" David heard another voice ask.

"Stabilize him best you can. There's a chopper coming for him." Mackey replied. "I'd like to keep him alive, if possible. Got a lot of questions for him."

Frank Martin appeared at David's side. "You alright, man?"

"Good shooting, Martin" Wilson Mackey clapped his hand on Frank's back. Turning to David, Mackey explained. "Mr. Martin here took the shot that saved your life. He had a better angle than my snipers, and he didn't hesitate once he saw Miller raise his gun to your head."

"Looks like you made the right call." David's huge smile acknowledged Frank's role. "Saying 'thank you' doesn't come close to expressing my gratitude to you right now."

"Speaking of the right call" Mackey interrupted "What were you doing here tonight?" Mackey cast raised eyebrows in Frank's direction. "Did you know what was set to go down with Miller?"

A moment's hesitation allowed Frank to quickly process the pros and cons of being honest with the FBI man. While Frank often bent the truth, he had never outright lied to the authorities. Weighing the possible outcomes of a less than truthful response, including a possible obstruction of justice charge, Frank decided complete honesty dictated full disclosure. Besides,

Mackey couldn't interfere with Jim at this point without compromising the sting on Bishop. "Yes. Judge Kaufman called me late this afternoon. Told me what was going to happen. Asked me to keep on eye on David."

Mackey's eyebrows capped an incredulous expression. "You expect me to believe Judge Kaufman asked you to watch this guy and not his wife? What else did the judge tell you?"

Hoping Jim had planned for such a contingency, Frank replied "Jim's tailing Cleveland to the meet."

Mackey's explosive reply was drowned out by the sound of the approaching medevac helicopter, but the agent's bulging eyes and red face more than adequately expressed the man's feelings about what Frank had just shared. David and Frank watched with concern as Mackey walked quickly towards the clubhouse, cell phone pressed to his ear, mouthing what they feared were orders to the other team to intercept Jim before he reached the meet site.

"Shit" Martin muttered. "I hope I haven't screwed the pooch."

CHAPTER THIRTY-TWO

A small black box was mounted inside the trunk of Jake Cleveland's car. Positioned in the upper left corner close to the car's interior, the unobtrusive device allowed communication between Jake and Allison on the drive to Becker's Pawn and would hopefully record any conversations with Jeff Bishop as he stood over Allison's body.

"You doing alright back there?" Jake inquired.

"I wish you had sedated me" Allison replied. "I feel like the victim in Poe's *The Premature Burial*."

"Couldn't risk it" Jake explained. "I need you in full control of your faculties."

"How much further?" Allison's legs were beginning to cramp. The forensic tech had arranged Allison's

body to appear lifeless, including an awkward po-
sitioning of her legs and arms. "Don't move" Jimmy
had cautioned before shutting Allison into darkness.
"You'll smear the blood." It wouldn't matter if she was
in full control of her faculties or not, Allison thought.
Her legs would be paralyzed by the time she needed
to move.

"We're here" came a terse reply. "No more talking."

Allison tried to remain limp, allowing her body
to be jostled by the car's rocking movements as Jake
manoeuvered the rocky parking lot. Lying immobile
once Jake opened the car's trunk would take all of
Allison's concentration. Thankfully, Jimmy and Jake
had agreed they could position Allison's body facing
towards the inside of the trunk. Even though Allison
knew having her back to a man who wanted her dead
would be disconcerting, Allison was more afraid that
an inadvertent facial expression would give away the
ruse. Sandy had glued a prosthetic mimicking a gunshot exit wound to the back of Allison's head, then
matted 'brain matter' and 'blood' into Allison's hair.
Allison prayed that Sandy's work would be sufficient
and Jeff Bishop wouldn't look too closely.

"I'm going inside" Jake whispered, slamming the
door to announce his arrival. Waiting was the worst
Allison thought, her mind playing out multiple tragic
endings to her current situation ranging from Jake

being murdered inside the pawn shop to Bishop raping and torturing her after discovering the double cross. *No* Allison ordered her mind. *Don't go there.*

The sound of crunching gravel interrupted Allison's foreboding. Someone was coming. Click. Allison recognized the sound. One of the car doors was being opened. Was it Bishop? Allison's senses went to high alert as she felt the car springs slightly shift with the weight of the intruder. Why would Bishop be inside the car? Where was Jake? A pinprick of light appeared in the upper back corner of the trunk near where Jake had planted the transmitter. Allison watched fearfully as the opening increased to the size of a quarter. What was happening?

"Allison" came a whisper.

"Jim" The sound of her husband's voice caused Allison's startled reply. "What are you doing? Why are you here?"

"Making sure nothing happens to you" Jim replied.

"You can't hide in the backseat of the car" Allison told her husband. "Bishop will see you and we'll all be killed."

"My feelings are hurt" Jim replied with a soft laugh. "Don't worry. This afternoon I spent some time with Jake's car while he and Mackey were plotting inside the house."

Allison heard a noise behind the trunk's rear panel. "What's that noise?"

"That, my dear, is the sound of me crawling inside the backseat." Jim explained. "I did a bit of retrofitting, the better to see you with."

Allison smiled. Only her husband would think of a nursery rhyme at a time like this. "Are you the big bad wolf?"

"I am Jeff Bishop's worst nightmare" Jim replied, then added quietly. "Shussh. I hear voices."

"Yeah, I got her body in the trunk, just like you wanted." Jake Cleveland's voice had assumed the country twang his disguise demanded. "Can't understand why I had to bring her all the way out here, though. Ain't gonna look like a home invasion with one of the victims missing."

"It'll look like a home invasion and kidnapping" Bishop replied. "Anyway, what business is it of yours?"

"I'm the one that done the work" Jake replied. "Makes it my business, much as yours." Jake leaned against the back of his car. "What are you going to do with the woman's body?"

"Haven't decided" Bishop gave an ugly laugh. "That bitch caused me a lot of trouble. Maybe I'll use her body for target practice." Motioning for Jake to open the trunk Bishop ordered "Let me see her."

"There isn't gonna be any shootin' up the inside of my car" Jake raised his voice a decibel. "This is a rental. You want to shoot a corpse just tell me where to put it."

"Open the fucking trunk" came Bishop's angry reply.

Pulling the car key from his pants pocket and turning to unlock the trunk Jake asked "What'd this woman do to make you so mad?"

"She figured out a contract hit I did for her boss." Bishop spat a reply. "Nosy bitch."

"What?" Jake turned to face Bishop. "Is she a cop? I don't kill cops."

"No, she's not a cop. She's a damn attorney. She spooked a friend of mine who called in a favor." Bishop motioned towards the car trunk again. "Details don't matter. She looked where she shouldn't have and got herself killed. Now open that trunk."

Allison heard the lock cylinder turn and metal rods squeak as the trunk slowly opened. *Please God* she prayed, *let me get home to my children.*

"Wish we could do more business together, Cleveland" Allison heard Bishop lament. "But I can't afford any witnesses."

Pulling a .38 from his jacket, Bishop pointed the revolver at Cleveland and fired. "Uh" the sound escaped Cleveland's lips as he fell backwards to the ground, his shirt torn where the bullet had entered the center of his chest. Allison cringed, her body unable to prevent the autonomic reaction the sound of the gun's discharge had caused.

"Stay down" Jim's command was barely audible over the explosion of sound coming from his .45 as he opened a large hole in the car's interior. Bishop returned fire and Allison felt a sharp sting across her hip. Foam, upholstery and wire showered Allison's body as Jim fought his way into the trunk. Report from the .45 assaulted her ears as Jim shielded Allison's body with his own. Then, Allison felt Jim's body jerk as a bullet found its mark. "No" Allison screamed, and then the shooting stopped.

"Jim" Allison heard Jake Cleveland call her husband's name. "Jim, stay with us."

Rolling from underneath her husband's limp body, Allison cupped her husband's face in her hands. "Jim Kaufman, don't you dare die on me" Allison cried. "Don't you dare."

Jim's eyes slowly opened. "Not gonna" he whispered reaching for Allison's hand.

The sharp shrill of sirens sounded in the distance. "Mackey" Jake explained. "He insisted that the communication device in the trunk transmit our conversations to tech support in real time."

"Bishop?" Allison and Jake heard the question in Jim's voice.

"Dead" Jake replied. "His shot knocked the wind out of me, even with the vest. Took me a few minutes to be able to move."

"Good" Jim replied, a slight smile briefly replacing the pain etched on his face.

Two ambulances roared into the parking lot, red flashing lights engulfing the wounded trio. Several black SUVs followed close behind, disgorging Mackey and other FBI agents before their drivers had rolled to a complete stop.

"Cleveland" Mackey shouted running towards Jake and Allison. "Where's the judge?"

"Here" Jake replied pointing inside the trunk. "Alive but slipping in and out of consciousness."

After a quick triage Jim was loaded into one of the ambulances. "We're headed to UAB Birmingham." a paramedic informed Allison, referring to the nationally ranked teaching hospital. "Closest trauma center. You and that guy" he added nodding towards Jake "will be taken to the hospital in Ft. Charles. You can follow on to Birmingham after they clear you."

"You've swabbed me with disinfectant and I'm not bleeding anymore" she told the paramedic. Then turning to Mackey she informed the FBI agent "I'm going where my husband is. One of your men can take me."

"You've got everything you need on tape and you'll have my report on your desk by morning." Jake interjected before Mackey could respond. "We owe her, and her husband."

Mackey scowled. He really hated it when civilians messed in Bureau business. But Cleveland was right. Calling to one of the younger agents, Mackey ordered his underling to take Allison to the Birmingham hospital. "Stay with Ms. Parker as long as she needs you" he instructed the agent. "She's your assignment until you hear otherwise."

Jake and Mackey watched the taillights belonging to the SUV carrying Allison fade from sight. "It's been a hell of a night" Mackey observed shaking his head. "First that jack-legged private investigator, and then a judge who thinks he's still in the Marines. It's a miracle Bishop's the only corpse."

"From what the guys told me" Jake replied, motioning to a couple of the other field agents "it's a damn good thing Frank Martin ended up where he did."

"Yeh" Mackey grudgingly acknowledged "he saved Jackson's life."

"And you can't blame the judge for wanting to protect his wife" Jake pointed out. "Plus, had his shooting not distracted Bishop, Allison would likely be dead right now. I'd never have gotten off a shot in time.

The two men headed towards Jake's car. The driver from Franklin Towing had just about finished loading it onto the truck's flatbed. "That thing reminds me of the aftermath of a Bonnie and Clyde shootout" Jake laughed. "Maybe that's what I ought to put on my expense voucher when I file my incident report on tonight's activities."

Examining the riddled Chevy Mackey asked "That's not your own car, is it?"

"No, but I wish it were" Jake replied. "I could use a new ride. Particularly one paid for by Uncle Sam."

"Just be glad Uncle Sugar will cover the damage to the rental." Mackey wryly observed before changing the subject. "You want to be in on Johnson's arrest? We've got enough to pick him up."

"Tonight?" Jake asked.

"Tomorrow should be soon enough" Mackey replied. "Besides, arresting him at his office seems appropriate given his profession."

The call that ended Ben Johnson's life came at two in the morning.

"Ben? Toby Trowbridge here." Ben was instantly awake. A call from the Calhoun County Sheriff was not a good sign. "Sorry to wake you, but I've got a situation down here…"

"What kind of situation?" Ben asked warily, slipping out of his bedroom and down the hall to the home's study. He didn't want to wake Linda.

"FBI just brought in a prisoner. Guy named Steve Miller. We've got him in isolation - he was treated at

General for a gunshot wound and then booked over here by the District Attorney on attempted murder charges." Ben heard the hesitation in the Sheriff's voice. "Uh, this guy is talking his head off, crazy stuff. Says you're involved. Thought you'd want to know."

Ben could barely frame a response. "Thanks, Toby. I have no idea who Steve Miller is, much less how he knows my name. I'll get someone to look into this first thing in the morning."

"Sure thing, Ben" Sheriff Trowbridge replied.

"By the way" Ben added before the Sheriff could terminate the call. "What's the FBI saying about all this?"

"You know the Feds" Trowbridge snorted. "Zipped lips. But there's a big wig here - top dog out of the Birmingham office. Something's gone down, I just don't know what and no one's talking. Well, no one other than that Miller guy."

Thanking the Sheriff once more, Ben ended the call.

Ben sat unmoving, his eyes perusing the meaningless accumulations of a lifetime which were displayed about the room. An award from the Chamber of Commerce, the trophy from a golf tournament he had won when he had a decent handicap, a framed picture of Ben with John McCain when McCain was campaigning for president. And for what? Life as he knew it would soon be over, Ben was sure of that.

A library table Linda used as a desk for paying bills filled one corner of the study. Pulling open the middle drawer Ben retrieved a pen and several sheets of paper. Ben was a coward, and he was taking the coward's way out, but he owed Linda an explanation.

A tear slipped down Ben's cheek as he folded the letter to his wife and placed it in an envelope. He needed to hurry. They could be coming for him at any minute. The keys to his Mercedes hung on a brass rack by the kitchen door. Palming the silver keys Ben eased open the door and slipped out of the house. Linda had always complained about the unattached garage and Ben had promised to add an enclosed walkway to the house later this summer. Now, he was glad the garage stood separate. No need to harm anyone but himself.

The inside of the garage was pitch black. Just like his probable destination Ben thought with remorse. Locking the door he had just entered, Ben disarmed the power to the garage door. The car's soft leather cushioned Ben's body. He hoped when death released his bowels the leather wouldn't stain too badly. Ben couldn't imagine Linda keeping the car after he killed himself in it, and at this point what was the point in worrying? Starting the ignition, Ben rolled down all four car windows and inserted a Chopin concerto into the car's stereo player. Resting his head against the cushioned headrest, Ben closed his eyes. *Soon*, Ben thought as the soothing strains of the concerto caressed his tortured soul. *Soon.* He only coughed a few times.

CHAPTER THIRTY-THREE

Three Months Later

"How many more boxes are you expecting?" Donna Pevey asked her boss. "The reception area is full and the furniture for that room is being delivered later today."

"David said he had one more car load, I think" Allison replied pulling a dustrag from her jean pocket to wipe her forehead. "This thing is nasty" she exclaimed staring at the dirty fabric in her hand. "Who knew books were so filthy?"

The new office space was small, and it wasn't really new. The building which now housed the law offices of Parker & Jackson was located in the same block of buildings as Frank Martin's private investigative firm.

In another year Allison and David hoped to add a third attorney to their firm and so had taken an option on additional space once the lease on the property next door expired. When and if the firm expanded they would need to hire another legal secretary, and maybe a runner for courthouse errands, deliveries and other more mundane tasks associated with running a law office. In the meantime, a small reception area, a space for Donna halfway between Allison's and David's offices, a compact kitchen and the necessary water closet rounded out the office space.

The office where Allison was unpacking law books would be hers. Not as large as her office at Johnson & Merritt and with no view to speak of, the office nevertheless exuded a comfortable warmth that Allison had found lacking at her previous firm.

"The rug is perfect" Donna announced, sticking her head in Allison's office.

"Yes, it is." Allison agreed admiring the beautiful rug that covered a large portion of the office's pine floor. "It was my mother's favorite. I'm so glad the auction house in Atlanta tracked me down when they saw the article in the Atlanta Constitution. Daddy and the Constitution's Editor were friends. I guess that's how the accident and Rice's arrest made the paper there." Allison added two heavy law books to those already displayed in the glass fronted cherry cabinet standing against the back wall of her office. "I know it's just stuff, but I hate to think that everything would have gone to strangers. Thank goodness we were able to recover most of the pieces before they were sold."

"Speaking of Rice" Donna replied changing the subject "isn't his trial coming up soon?"

"Yes" Thinking of her brother and his problems made Allison sad. "Jason Brownlow has been trying to convince Rice to take the plea deal the D.A. offered, but Rice won't listen."

"What's wrong with that boy?" Donna exclaimed. "He knows Alabama has the death penalty doesn't he?"

"That's part of the problem. Rice says he has nothing to live for. Jason told me he's not even sure Rice will agree to put on a defense when the case gets to trial."

"Sounds like your brother has lost his mind for sure." Donna observed. "Maybe the best thing for him would be to put him out of his misery."

Allison put the last book on the cabinet shelf and closed the glass door. "When the children were killed all I wanted was for Rice to suffer" she told Donna. "But not anymore. Maybe almost losing Jim caused a change of heart" Allison shrugged. "Maybe just a gift of unexpected grace. I really don't know. Whatever happened, all I feel for Rice now is pity and unbearable sadness."

"Y'all back there?" David Jackson's soft drawl sounded from the reception area.

"In here" Allison called, grateful for an interruption to a conversation that had become rather depressing.

Pushing a cart loaded with boxes and topped by a poorly balanced lamp, David ambled past Allison's office. When he and Allison had first examined the potential office space David had immediately gravitated to an office at the far end of hallway. "Perfect" he had proclaimed. "Private, quiet, close to the back door and away from you two women." Allison smiled remembering that day.

"Is this everything?" Allison asked seeing the overloaded cart.

"Everything except a bookcase I'm bringing from the house. Linda gave Sarah the oak bookcase from Ben's office. Sarah wants to use it at home, so I'm bringing the old one here."

"How's Sarah doing?" Allison asked following David to his office. "She's been on my mind a lot recently."

"Some days are better than others" David replied grimly. "Linda showed her the letter Ben left. I don't know what has hurt Sarah more - learning about her father's double life or knowing he had a man murdered. Healing is going to take a long time for her and for her mother, too." Rescuing the lamp from its precarious perch David placed it on a side table and began removing boxes from the hand cart. "I asked her to help me decorate this office, but she wasn't interested. You know Sarah. When she's not interested in decorating there's something wrong."

"I can recommend an excellent therapist if Sarah wants to talk to a professional." Allison offered. "Nothing wrong with getting help for the big issues. Believe me. I know."

"Thanks" David replied. "Not sure she'll listen though."

"Tell Sarah we're only as sick as our secrets" Allison added. "And in this instance, all the secrets are already in the public domain, so to speak. I doubt there's a person in Ft. Charles who hasn't heard about Ben's past. In another month or so it will all be old news and people will be gossiping about someone else." Reflecting on Ben's suicide Allison added "We're never as important as we think we are. If only Ben had realized that, maybe he wouldn't have taken his life."

"No" David replied. "Ben couldn't face prison, and that's where he was headed. Suicide was his only option."

"Shit" Donna interjected confronting the two lawyers. "Suicide is never an option. I didn't like the man a damn bit, but I feel sorry for him if he thought suicide was the only way out. That's just plain sad." Clapping her hands for effect, Donna gave her bosses a stern look. "Enough of this depressing chit chat. We've got an office to set up. Get your legal eagle butts moving - clients will be here tomorrow and this place needs to look sharp."

"Lord, Donna" Allison laughed. "What would I do without you to keep me on the straight and narrow?"

"Just remember that when it's time for my raise" Donna smiled in reply.

The next several hours passed quickly. While Donna supervised the arrangement of furniture for the firm's reception area Allison and David unboxed, put away, straightened up and generally coerced order out of mayhem in their respective offices. By 6:00 all that remained was the placement of a few paintings in the firm's common areas.

"Looks like a law office" Jim Kaufman remarked walking through the front door.

"What else would it look like?" Donna asked grumpily. Then, reconsidering her snippy retort she added "Sorry, Judge. It's been a long day." Donna reached for the three large flat boxes Jim was carrying. "How's your shoulder?"

"Probably as good as it's going to get. I've got about ninety percent range of motion back. And I'm not complaining. Doc said a few millimeters the other way and that shot would've killed me."

"What is that heavenly smell?" Allison asked walking into the reception area. "Is that pizza?"

"A large Greek, a large meat lovers, and a large plain cheese. Frank Martin's right behind me with the beer and sodas." Jim explained. "I figured you'd want to include Frank. He's as much a part of this 'family' as anyone now."

"I'll wait for Frank" she told the others as they headed towards the kitchen to attack the pizzas. *What would the future hold?* The question rose unbidden in Allison's thoughts. A year ago when she had accepted Sherry McNair's sexual harassment case the only worry Allison had was whether or not she could win a plaintiff's case after so many years on the other side. Never in her wildest dreams - to use a worn cliche' - would she have imagined the path that opened in front of her. Murder, blackmail, the demise of Johnson & Merritt, the birth of her own firm - all the makings of a good movie she mused, just one she would have preferred to watch rather than have a starring role.

Her reverie reminded Allison of advice her mother had given during Allison's tumultuous teen years. "Life happens" Helene would remark "when you least expect it. You can't predict it, and you can't control it. All you can do is decide how you will respond to it. Make the best decision you can, and don't look back."

Good advice, Allison realized, and it was exactly what she had done. The close brush with death that she and Jim had faced had caused them to reassess their lives. Having her own law firm would give Allison much needed flexibility in her personal and family life. When Allison had shared her plan with David Jackson he had asked to join her. Having a partner had been another right decision, and Allison was excited about the firm's future. True, there were still difficult matters to address outside of work - Rice's trial, continued care for Mary Louise - but she and Jim would work through the details one day at a time.

The office door swung open to reveal Frank Martin's large frame. "My favorite giant" Allison laughed, ribbing Frank with the nickname she had created for him. "Ready for some pizza?"

"Hell yes. I'm starving." Frank ambled inside, a six-pack of beer in one hand, a six-pack of Coca-Cola in the other. "Listen, we need to talk. I've got a client to refer to you. You'll never believe this......".

END